ALL THE NICE GIRLS

ALSO BY BARBARA ANDERSON

I think we should go into the jungle

Girls High

Portrait of the Artist's Wife

ALL THE NICE GIRLS

BARBARA ANDERSON

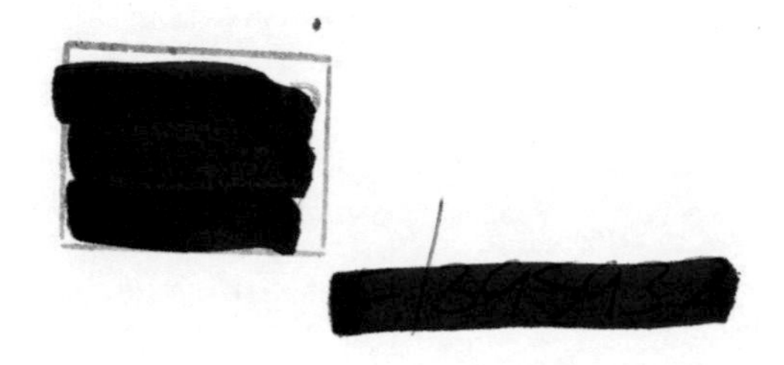

JONATHAN CAPE
LONDON

First published in the United Kingdom in 1994

1 3 5 7 9 10 8 6 4 2

The author gratefully acknowledges the assistance of a
project grant from the QEII Arts Council of
New Zealand

First published in the United Kingdom in 1994 by
Jonathan Cape
Random House, 20 Vauxhall Bridge Road, London
SW1V 2SA

Random House Australia (Pty) Limited
20 Alfred Street, Milsons Point, Sydney,
New South Wales 2061, Australia

Random House New Zealand Limited
18 Poland Road, Glenfield,
Auckland 10, New Zealand

Random House South Africa (Pty) Limited
PO Box 337, Bergvlei, South Africa

Random House UK Limited Reg. No. 954009

A CIP catalogue record for this book is available from
the British Library

ISBN 0–224–03976–8

Printed in Great Britain by Mackays of Chatham PLC,
Chatham, Kent

A Sailor's Prayer

Lord,
Now we're on board
Look after all sailors at sea,
And me.
And remember once more
Our folk ashore.

Keep me out of the Ditch
In the middle watch,
And back from sea
I promise I'll be
At Sunday church
With a clean white front
And polished shoes
And no booze.

Denis Glover

ONE

The clouds parted above Devonport Naval Base. The sun was fitful, that was the word, fitful. Pale shafts of light poured through the rose window at the east end of the Memorial Chapel of St Christopher, illuminating the head of the Commodore in the front pew.

Sophie Flynn, a child on either side, watched with interest from the pew behind. She sat very still—large, calm and confused in the house of God.

She crossed her legs, straightened her shoulders. Buck up fatso. Confusion is out. Yes.

Commodore Edward Sand, Royal New Zealand Navy, sat by himself because his wife was dead. Leading Steward Tollerton, clothes brush in hand, normally checked his dark winter uniform for hairs each morning, leaping at him with quick 'Excuse-me-sir' civility. But not on Sundays. On Sundays the Commodore was on his own, twisting and turning before the mirror in the dark bedroom where he slept alone. Two missed hairs lay centre back below his collar. Sophie's fingers twitched to remove them. It was neither the time, the place nor the gesture. Acquaintances, especially naval wives, do not remove hairs. It is the privilege of an intimate, an equal. A friend. The small bare patch on the back of the head in front gleamed round and brown, surrounded by silky grey hair. He was a well-set-up man the Commodore; a man of parts hoping for promotion next year in '63.

The Intake shuffled and stirred at the back of the chapel. They were all young men, boys really, aged about sixteen. They were bored, bored to distraction, bored to sobbing bitter tears. It was hard to see how they would learn faith in Christ Jesus from Church Parade. It was not what they joined for. But what could you do.

'I am come that ye may have life and that ye may have it more abundantly,' Sophie's Sunday School attendance card had said. 'What does "abundantly" mean?' she asked her father as he kicked off his work boots at the back door. 'Lots,' he replied. 'Packed down tight and running over. Why do you ask?' She told him. 'Ah,' he said.

Seven-year-old Kit was practising knots, his knees spread wide to hide his hands, his shoulders hunched in rejection of a navigator's gaze from the pew behind. The navigator leaned forward, his facial tic working. He had forgotten that one.

Kit gave up, stowed the string in his pocket, the back of his neck naked and vulnerable as a sailor's.

Rebecca's clear hazel eyes stared straight ahead. Rebecca was an all-rounder. She came top of the class and was in teams. She had escorted the Lady Mayoress to her seat at the dais at the Stanley Bay Prize-Giving last year with friendly ease, whipped back to her seat and returned almost immediately to receive *Swallows and Amazons* for Good Work in Standard Four. Sophie was proud of Rebecca but puzzled by her. She seemed unfamiliar. This used to worry Sophie but not now. She has got used to it.

The Memorial Chapel of St Christopher at HMNZS Philomel is beautiful and hallowed by memories of men who died too young. The curved pulpit originally adorned the quarterdeck of HMS New Zealand, a battle cruiser donated to the mother country in

1912/3 by the loyal subjects of the Dominion. Heraldic dead sheep in each quarter represent the pastoral background of the donor nation, the supporters are a helmetless Britannia and an upright moa. Battle honours and memorial plaques line the walls. Ancient flags hang high, their fabric changing and decaying throughout the years. Behind the pews and the stackable chairs of the Intake are vaulting horses, wall bars, ropes from the ceiling and large coir mats.

Kit dragged his diagram of the life cycle of a frog from his pocket. He stabbed a finger at the tadpole. 'When?' he whispered.

'Spring,' murmured Sophie. Tadpoles were a fact of life, part of the matrix of Devonport boyhood along with mud and mangroves, sea and sand. It was not the tadpoles she objected to but their limited shelf life. One minute they wriggled blimp-like and obscene in jars, bulging in places indicative of future legs, the next they floated belly-up enmeshed in scum. Generations had been brought home in buckets from the swamp. All had succumbed. Once the cat ate them, scooping with quick dripping paw from the Agee jar on the window sill. At least she assumed he had. There was no sign of them and Ginger lay torpid and sated in the sun. Kit was bereft, Sophie appalled, though she realised it was not Ginger's fault and worse things had happened at sea—an expression used often by her absent husband William.

Everyone was now standing, Sophie a little later than most as she had not been paying attention. Tadpoles, illicit love, swollen cats swarmed in her mind as she leaped to her feet. 'Hymn 370,' cried Padre Bell, glad and happy at the thought. 'Eternal Father, strong to save, / Whose arm hath bound the restless wave.' The officers and men present sang with enthusiasm. They had sung this hymn since they joined and knew it by heart. The words had not changed nor ever would. They knew this. It is a comforting hymn, especially when sung with the strong tidal surge of deep male voices like the navigator's in the pew behind. Kit glanced at his mother who smiled. Sophie's heart lifted with conviction. 'Oh Trinity of love and power, / Our brethren shield in danger's hour; / From rock and tempest, fire and foe, / Protect them wheresoe'er they go,' she sang and thought of William.

Padre Bell held up one hand. 'Whoa,' he said. The congregation lurched to a halt. The organist (Leading Sick Bay Attendant Butterworth), taken by surprise, looked blank. The organ ran down wailing. The congregation stared. Padre Bell—large, hirsute, a good pair of hands in a line-out—smiled back. 'This is a wonderful hymn,' he said. Sophie nodded. Nobody else did anything.

'But we're dragging!' continued the Padre who was musical. Silence.

Followed by sniggers from the Intake.

'Watch the beat. My hand. Watch my hand.'

Sophie watched intently. As always she felt responsible. When she and William gave a party which was seldom, she was torn between providing food and keeping an eye on things. She felt if she were not present at all times ensuring happiness her guests would lapse behind her back, would stand eating and drinking with tears of sorrow leaking from their eyes.

Padre Bell's hand was still poised. 'Now!' Leading Sick Bay Attendant Butterworth's attack had returned, the congregation roared through 'Eternal Father' with hearts high; or the Commodore and the navigator and LSBA Butterworth and Padre Bell did. Sophie was not sure about those behind and the Intake behind them but Rebecca and Kit entered into the spirit of the thing. Men's singing is stirring. You want to be part.

'Much better,' said the Padre. LSBA Butterworth also smiled. He was well respected, a loyal man. In Suva during the last Island Cruise his Captain had appeared on board at five a.m. with one hand to his neck. 'Boils,' he snapped at William who had the morning watch. 'Send the LSBA to my cabin.' Later photographs show the Captain's neck bandaged. Neither William nor LSBA Butterworth has ever mentioned the incident.

The Commodore moved to the lectern. The Captain of Philomel, Harold Pickett, closed his eyes. His wife poked him. He frowned briefly, screwed his eyes tighter.

Sophie's eyes were on the Commodore. She was able to observe the bone structure, the ears, the way the hair grew. The fingers on the bookmark interested her, the firm voice. 'The Lesson is taken from the Gospel According to St Matthew, Chapter 11, Verses 25-30.' Strong words of comfort rolled over them.

'Come unto me all ye that labour and are heavy laden, and I will give you rest.'

The Commodore lifted his eyes.

'For my yoke is easy,' he said, 'and my lurden is bight.'

Sophie's yelping snort was echoed by the Intake, grateful for this momentary release from torpor. Tears of hopeless joy, of God-given anticlimax, ran down her face. What was she *fussing* about. Her shoulders shook. 'Mum,' whispered Rebecca, 'Heh Mum.'

'You'd better mop up,' said Kit kindly.

She did so. The Commodore's face was calm. The service continued.

The congregation rose to their feet after the Padre's peremptory blessing. It was only a matter of asking for it in his opinion. The Padre knew that his Redeemer lived.

The sun had disappeared, the air was crisp as the congregation left the chapel to its folding doors, its East/West polarity of body and soul, its weekly metamorphosis into a gymnasium.

The Intake marched off.

The Commodore's hand scrubbed Kit's crew cut. 'Hullo, Sophie,' he said.

There had been a song in her youth, 'The sailor with the navy blue eyes'. Her sister Mary had sung it, roaring the 'Yo ho ho ho ho, *ho*' when she first sighted her sister's minuscule engagement ring. Girls, Sophie remembered, had lined up.

'Hullo,' she said.

William's eyes are brown.

'Coming up to Wardroom, lad? It's a bun fight for the new Padre,' said the Commodore. 'Tea and stickies.'

Kit laughed. He was an odd-looking child, Kit: toothy grin, skinny legs, impossible hair. He had a delight in the workings of things, an enthusiasm, a tendency to yarn. Sophie couldn't think where Kit came from either. He delighted her.

Rebecca was kicking the scoria rocks surrounding the beds of pansies beside the figurehead from Ocean Ranger, a bearded Ralph Rackstraw in a straw hat of wood. Ships' figureheads, however different in form, are all equally unimpressed by the turbulent seas through which they pass. Sophie had never seen a smiling one. The Royal New Zealand Navy was lucky to have Ocean Ranger, shaky though he was. His contemporaries had rotted to pieces.

'Stop kicking those stupid rocks, Rebecca,' she said.

Rebecca gave another quick testing-the-water kick. The few pansies already in flower lifted their faces to the non-existent sun.

'Stop that, Becca,' said Liz Kelson. Rebecca stopped.

Liz Kelson strode through life as though through a newly opened Self Help, the plan of which she had sussed out in an instant. She never fumbled. She tossed what she needed or desired into her basket with a clear eye and a sure hand. She knew the price of everything, what it was worth to her and what she was prepared to pay for it. Sophie admired her quick certainty, her attack.

She had been an actress originally. 'I was useless, but you do get the chance to ponce around a bit. It was fun.' About her days as an air hostess she was less enthusiastic. 'Dead low water. I was either rushed off my feet or terrified.' Her fingers stroked her throat in remembrance. 'Still, it was better when we landed. There were opportunities. And I liked the different men. It was fun. Though of course those days are over.'

Sophie nodded. Her own past seemed unabundant. Not much of it.

Liz's mid-winter legs were still brown. Her thick straight hair was held back by plastic tortoiseshell and swung free. Her husband, Paul Kelson (Commander, Royal Navy, on exchange to New Zealand) loved his New Zealand wife and the country itself. He would willingly have stayed for ever, but Paul is a submariner, the

RNZN don't have any, and they are his life. Apart from Liz.

'Ready, darling?' he said, handing her into a station wagon with a vast yellow dog panting behind bars in the back. Sophie watched Paul's archaic gesture. He really *handed* her in. He opened her door, put his hand beneath hers and gave a slight heave as though assisting a frail form into a carriage. Like in *Agnes Grey* when the curate handed Agnes in after church rather than the rich lady and Sophie, hidden behind the apple grader in Greytown, knew it would end up all right.

Celia Pickett, the Captain's wife, stumped around the pansies in her boat-like suedes to greet them which was kind of her. Husbands at sea tend to make wives invisible.

'Any disasters yet?' she asked.

'No.'

'There will be,' said Celia.

She propped her left suede on a rock to retie it. 'Never believe, darlink,' she said, 'that the navy is not a man's world.' Sophie, who was watching the Commodore who was talking to Harold Pickett who was watching the Kelsons' car disappear up the hill to the Wardroom, nodded. What did Celia expect.

'Come on,' called Harold Pickett. His hand tapped a leg to indicate impatience. Celia looked at him in silence and moved to their car. There was no handing up.

'Want a lift?' called Celia. The speed of the tapping hand increased.

Rebecca ran to the Snipe, the toe plates of her scuffed white shoes clicking. She was pleased to avoid the hill and liked the smell of real leather.

'Where would we be without our friends?' naval wives say to one another. They tell one another how lucky they are which they already know. Think of unmarried mothers, they say.

They help one another when the men are at sea. They are competent. 'We have to be,' wives say, touching their marcasite naval crowns as they answer themselves. 'We certainly do!' However some are better at coping than others. Sophie's neighbour

Nancy Ogilvie is one of the former and thus admired by all. Great emphasis is put on coping. Some wives don't cope at all. Some run amuck completely.

Celia does not have to cope. Her daughters are at boarding school, she has private means and HMNZS Philomel is a shore establishment. The Captain does not go to sea..

He shoved the car into low gear and headed up the hill. A few midshipmen from Church Parade strode manfully up the steep curve. The Commodore was ahead of them all.

'Shouldn't we offer him a lift?' said Celia.

Harold's eyes flicked from the road ahead. 'Why on earth?'

Celia shrugged. Sophie watched the Commodore's back view. The Snipe was on his heels. The Commodore, forced to walk even more manfully, lengthened his stride. Rebecca giggled. 'Pass him,' said Celia.

'It won't kill him.'

After a few moments he relented, pulled out and gave the man a wide berth.

The Commodore, his face scarlet, lifted a hand.

The Wardroom was cool, high ceilinged, a large room with a dining area down one end. The carpet was heavy-duty ultramarine. Rebecca gave a quick decisive sniff. 'Curry,' she said.

A table covered with a stiff white cloth bore plates of white plasterwork meringues, chocolate eclairs and club sandwiches in honour of the new Padre. Kit stood in front of the polished teapot hoping to see himself upside down. 'That's spoons dummy,' said Rebecca.

She ran to get first go at a pair of outsized spoils-of-war binoculars mounted at the window overlooking the harbour. She stood tiptoe, her face anxious. Last week Kit had seen a man land a fish across the harbour. Rebecca needed two. There were occasional jokes in the Wardroom about the Japanese binoculars. Half-dressed maidens on cruise ships, things of that nature. Mild jokes suitable for the restraints of mixed company. The presence of women changed things.

Last year on board an RN destroyer Sophie had retreated to the lavatory in boredom. Followed by the astonishing roar of the ship's flushing mechanism, she edged past the dining space to rejoin the other women in the Captain's day cabin. The atmosphere behind the curtain was convivial. She heard the lack of enthusiasm in the languid query, 'Shall we join the ladies?'

Thérèse, a visitor from Tahiti, couldn't understand it. 'Why are they in there,' she demanded, 'while we are here? We could talk with them in there, why not?'

'It is the custom,' explained the Captain's wife.

'Why?'

Celia lifted a hand in defeat. A diamond as big as a pea blinked on her finger.

'Let us go. Leave. To a nightclub why not?' Thérèse was excited, scrabbling for her black satin bag, leaping to her feet as the men entered to dispose themselves in hopeful gaps between seated females.

'It is too late,' cried Thérèse, her face pink, her bag clutched to her décolletage. 'We are going to a nightclub. All the ladies. Now.'

The men laughed. They knew she was joking.

There were more people in the Wardroom than was usual after church. People wished to show willing, to welcome the new Padre who stood benign and happy beside his wife Carol. Carol's auburn hair was plaited, her smile shy. She hoped life would be better now Peter was in the navy. The parish had been a killer. She smiled at the navigator. 'You have a beautiful voice,' she told him. His tic worked harder, winking and leering at her in pleased confusion. 'I used to belong to a choral group in Torbay but my wife Lorraine . . . Well, it's different isn't it, when you own your own house.'

'I don't know,' said Carol gently.

The Commodore had still not arrived. The spread for the new Padre lay untouched. Steward Benson stood relaxed and at ease in his high-necked white uniform, his arms hanging. During the visit of Admiral Mountbatten, Sophie had wondered if his collar was too tight but it must have been awe.

Three midshipmen arrived, their faces pinker than ever, their air of half-baked exuberance enhanced by exercise. Two of them were round-eyed and eager as Hewey and Dewey Duck. The third was tougher, his eyes already guarded.

The Commodore entered on their heels, shiny about the face, his eyes bright. 'Good heavens, you haven't waited for me, have you. Benson?' Steward Benson began pouring the tea which was cold as it had been ready for some time on the standby to standby principle.

The Commodore shook the Padre's wife by the hand and told her how delighted he was to have her on board if she would excuse the expression. Carol Bell's hand lay in his. He shook it again and held his other hand over it as if reassuring a small frightened bird.

He congratulated Padre Bell on his entry into the Royal New Zealand Navy. They discussed the Memorial Chapel of St Christopher and the good work done by naval padres both at sea and ashore. 'No offence,' said the navigator, whose name Sophie could never remember, 'but I always found the Catholic padres more use at sea and I'm not a mick. Pragmatic lot, by and large. Condoms at the gangplank, that sort of thing.'

'Have a meringue,' said Sophie, shoving them at Kit who was standing beside her.

'My teeth wouldn't go in.'

Sophie took one. He was right.

Harold Pickett disinterred the story, ancient as a songline, about the upper set of false teeth trapped in a Royal Garden Party meringue. 'The Queen was ropeable!'

'I don't believe that story,' said Sophie.

His eyebrows leaped at her. 'Why not?'

'It's the sort of thing people say. And I don't think the Queen . . . I mean, who would *tell* her.'

'Well, I can't give you chapter and verse.' Harold Pickett glanced angrily at his watch as if it was withholding the information.

'You remember the chap, Celia? At New Zealand House.'

'No,' said his wife.

The meringues were inspected once more. Victims of a design fault, they sat rocklike and uneaten.

'We'll have to send the cook back to requalify,' said the Commodore. 'I liked that business with "Eternal Father", Padre. If it's not good enough do it again.'

The Padre was pleased. He had done the right thing. He had taken charge.

The Commodore watched Sophie's pink face as she attempted to dispose of the remains of her meringue. She hid the plate behind Steward Benson's hot water jug. Steward Benson, his face expressionless, moved the jug to reveal it again.

'Christ,' said Harold, 'I've broken a tooth.' Everyone, beaten to the ground by the topic, laughed once more.

'Sun's over the yardarm,' said the Commodore. 'Bar open, Benson?'

'Yes, sir.'

There was a sense of wellbeing, a lifting. Things were going to improve.

'Sophie,' said the Commodore, his hair shining, his eyes kind, 'what would you like to drink?'

Her gin was refreshing and redemptive; the clink of ice therapeutic. The Commodore lifted his glass to hers.

Conversation became general but no more interesting. Ladies were present. Shop talk, the thing which drove them, the passion of their commitment to their job, like smut, was not a subject for mixed company. Royal visits were. The Queen and the Duke of Edinburgh were due early next year. There was also a buzz that the Duke planned a swing around the Pacific later for Wildlife. 'Animals,' said Harold Pickett. And the head of a friendly Asian power and his consort were coming soon. August wasn't it. Yes, August.

'Come, come, Sophie,' said the Commodore taking her empty glass, 'You can't fly on one wing.'

Sophie was firm. They left, smiling and waving. 'Goodbye,' they said. 'Bye.'

The winter sun sat on their heads as they walked home. Rebecca and Kit ran down Calliope Road, skipping and jumping as though they had invented this levitating release.

Sophie joined them. Kit and Rebecca leaped higher.

Someone was running behind her. A hand touched her shoulder in mid-leap. 'Higher. You can do it, Soph. Higher, higher,' exhorted her sister.

They stared at each other laughing. Poles apart, oil to water, chalk to cheese and loving withal, Mary and Sophie were pleased to see each other.

Sophie was breathing deeply. 'Where've you been?'

Mary flicked back the hair which hung loose beneath a small peaked cap, a gesture which irritated William. 'Down the Coromandel. Ben's still there.'

'Oh. Why?'

Mary was a good mimic, always had been, she caught the essence. The wide-apart legs, the flat-footed stance, the faint worry in the tone evoked her older more troubled sister. 'Oh. Why?' She flung her hands wide. 'He likes it there, that's why.'

Mary's lover Ben had appeared from nowhere last Christmas and moved in. He was American, a long lean lazy American. A combination which also irritated William. Americans were efficient, busy, on the ball, not elongated layabouts with eyelashes. 'What does he do?' he asked Sophie.

'He's an artist.'

'Does he sell stuff?'

'I don't think so.'

'Then how does he live?'

'I'm not sure. He likes the Coromandel.'

'What's that got to do with it? He's a bum, you know that. He's just going to bum on Mary till her money's gone and then he's going to bum on the taxpayer.' William slapped his chest. 'Me. And look what's happened to Mary. Why's she given up her job?'

'Ask her yourself.'

'And they're not going to get married, you know that.'

'He's got too many wives already. He told me.'

'Total shit. Total. And who's this Kerouac he's on about?'

'He's written a book.'

'Huh. And why the Coromandel? Plenty of good beaches on the North Shore.'

Everything about the man was suspect. To William, Ben was licence, fornication, and not doing a stroke.

Sophie found Ben interesting. Different but interesting.

Mary, Ben and occasional visiting friends lived on the lower floor of an old house further down the road notable for the octagonal tower sprouting from an upstairs bedroom. Mary and Sophie were nieces of the owner. Aunty Bertha had ignored the advice of her *own* sister (as their mother reminded them frequently) in buying it. Mary and Ben paid a modest rent and appeared to enjoy life.

Mary put an arm around her sister. 'Dear old Soph.'

'Goodness,' said Sophie. 'There's the Commodore.'

'Goodness,' said Mary. 'So it is.'

The Commodore strode towards them along the sparkling road. 'Ah, Sophie,' he said.

'Have you met my sister Mary, Commodore?'

They shook hands, their eyes wary as sniffing dogs.

'How nice to meet you.'

Mary's head lifted. 'Hullo.'

'I didn't know Sophie had a sister.'

'She has. Me.'

He stopped smiling, nodded. 'I didn't know. Would you excuse us a moment?'

Mary stood there, just stood there, hands hanging, face expressionless as Steward Benson's, waiting for him to get on with it. To get on with it and shove off.

Sophie, now smiling for two, leered at the man. Encouraged by one sibling, he continued, 'You know Captain and Mrs Featherston, don't you, Sophie?'

'Yes.'

'They've asked me if you'd like to join them for a meal at their house with me. On Tuesday.'

'Yes, please.' No babysitting caveats. Nothing. 'Yes, I would.'

'Great.' He touched her arm, waved, an expansive gesture indicating the harbour, the bridge, a green hill far away, touched her arm again and walked on.

'Oh Soph,' said Mary.

Sophie said nothing.

Hands in pockets, the matter dismissed for things of importance, Mary stared down the empty Sunday road. 'Have you seen Chester?'

'No.' Sophie's voice rose. 'Is he lost again?'

'God, I hope not.'

'They do wander, Burmese.'

'What help's that!'

Chester's endearing grace, the slink of his exits, his entrances, the sheen of his black copper coat hung before them.

'He'll turn up,' said Sophie. 'He always has.'

TWO

The grocer's shop was closed. Arnold McNally's eyes closed in brief despair. It's Sunday you fool. Sunday. Should've thought of that first shouldn't you. Should've thought of that before you come all the way down. You can think of it now. You can think of it every step up the bloody hill, Sunday Sunday Sunday. And she won't let you have any at the dairy. Not eggs. They can orbit the earth but you can't buy an egg on Sunday. Not in Devonport.

No use even trying with tarpaulins over anything anyone would want and only open for sweets and rubbish. 'I'm sorry dear, I wouldn't dare. Not on a Sunday. They've got snoopers everywhere. They'd see you coming out with them.'

He stood on the pavement blinking at the unexpected sunlight. His sniff was loud. They'd said it was going to rain. They weren't as good now. They used to be world class, the forecasts, second to none and now look at it. Eyebrows locked in irritation, Arnie headed up the hill.

How did you know the eggs were fresh anyhow? You didn't. Not really. So why did he treat them like treasure, carry them up the hill in their brown paper bag as if they were something precious as well as fragile. Because they were easy, that was why. Even he

could cook an egg. His irritation increased.

Arnie slogged on, puzzled by his anger, his distrust. The eggs were a case in point. Why in the name of heaven would anyone want to do a fresh egg fiddle? The logistics rolled before his eyes, faceless deceitful men in white substituting, restowing, transporting. Arnie gave a short bark of self-disgust. He would have to watch it. It wasn't a good idea, this creeping suspicion, this rage.

He sighed. Accepted the real reason for his rage. He had lost the first ones. He had bought half a dozen yesterday at the dairy and by the time he'd got home they had disappeared. Disappeared, dropped through the hole in the world. Which was impossible. He had spent the day looking for them, rage and despair increasing as he rechecked the fridge, the empty safe, the cupboards, the fernery, the verandah. He had lain awake at night, *seen* the bag, its bulging shape, the tiny saw-tooth edge. He was going mad. He'd been a cheerful cove all his life, by and large. 'He's been fun to live with. Cross-grained yes, but fun,' Win had told Cora next door when she had run in to pack Win's night things for the operation.

Which had gone wrong. An embolism, they said. Very rare nowadays.

The brown suitcase returned with his receipt from Patient's Effects remained unpacked, stowed deep in Win's wardrobe behind unsorted clothes and the card table left over from euchre evenings. They hadn't used it for years but might one day, she said. You never knew.

Head down to the wind, jaw clamped like a snapping turtle's with contempt for the whole sodding world, Arnie rounded the slow bend into Calliope Road.

It was a year since she died. Each morning told him so and the day confirmed it. He glared at the pepper tree branch dangling in front of his gate. He was ridiculous and knew it.

There were no children, no one duty bound to care, to be stuck with sharing. People had tried, but as Cora next door said to her husband, 'You can only do so much.'

Invasive as nicotine, Arnie's tight-arsed grief hung in Cora and

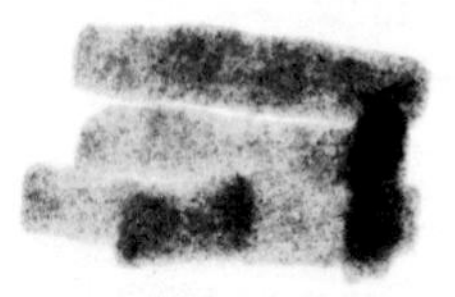

Bob's airless lounge, got into the curtains and stayed there. You could *hear* the misery, feel its damp chill. It reminded Cora of one of those old films where the candle goes out for no apparent reason and you know it's the ghostly presence, the aura of the unseen dead. And all the time the silly old bugger sat there muttering his way through her steak and kidney, moaning about Holyoake's latest rip-off and refusing to mention Win's name however hard Cora tried. 'Mad,' she said as Arnie left at nine o'clock on the dot. 'You can only do so much,' she said.

Bob nodded. He had never done anything except attend the funeral and he didn't mind those. Quite liked them in fact; the ritual, the tidiness, the well-organised finality of the process. The coming in and the sitting down, the standing up and the following out. All were pleasing to Bob. It was the least you could do, attend funerals. And be seen to be doing. Occasionally too, there was a bonus in the drama, the tragedy of loss. Not at Win's though. They could have been burying the cat. No wake afterwards. Nothing.

Arnie knew Bob's reaction and was pleased by it. He carried it in his heart. Occasionally he took it out, inspected it, blew on the spark of bitterness required to keep it bright and restowed it.

Arnie leaned on his gatepost gasping for breath. There was something wrong with him. It had happened a few times lately, this lurching thump of his heart as it flung itself about his chest like a beached trout. He clung onto his ancient tin letterbox and concentrated on the gate he had made years ago at metalwork. Arnie had taught upholstery at night classes at Takapuna Grammar for a thousand years, till just before Win died. He and the metalwork teacher had an unspoken arrangement—a swappage of skills, a usage of tools and equipment, a blind eye. A wrought-iron galleon tossed motionless, trapped for ever in the centre of Arnie's gate, imprisoned in a circle of iron from which spokes radiated to each corner of the square. The centring had not been easy. Three smaller galleons beat across the top frieze. The whole thing was painted Aztec Gold. Win had been proud of it.

'When I wake up,' she told him, her hands reaching for her early morning cup, 'I think something good's happened. Then I remember the gate.' Her thin pale hair trailed across the pillow. She put it up during the day.

Arnie kicked the gate hard. It swung back grating. He groped in the letterbox before remembering. Sunday for Christ's sake, Sunday. His hand felt something. It was his bag of eggs. He looked at them in horror. When had he put them there? He must've put them in there for safe keeping while he, while he . . . While he what? He couldn't remember. He couldn't bloody remember.

Granny bonnet seed heads were banging the bottom of the tin. She wouldn't have liked that either. He stood trying to work out what to do. Cut them? They would grow again. Holding his bag of eggs to his chest like a begging dog, his eyes clouded with impossible decisions, Arnie slogged up the concrete path.

At the verandah he swayed. Still careful, still remembering the fragility of his burden, he unlocked the door, felt his way down the wide corridor out through the fernery and onto the back porch. Sparrows racketed about in the sun, rose in a cloud from his scattered bread damped to defeat marauding dogs. Arnie placed his bag on the shining boards and sank down onto the old brown armchair. It was prickly and damp. He closed his eyes. It was not physical, this sudden weakness. It was despair at his egg-engendered panic. 'I'm going mad, Jesus Christ, I'm going insane. I used to be all right I used to be . . .' He thought back to that other country when he was all right, a seaman originally, a young thruster, a man on his way. He wanted to dash out, to leap onto the street (as if he could), to grab someone, anyone, make them tell him he had been all right. 'I was all right, remember?' Win had always told him he was an able man, a fixer, one who could turn his hand to anything. Look how he'd picked up upholstery and made a living from scratch when they first arrived.

He didn't believe it. Numb with despair, Arnie lifted a foot and kicked the eggs. Viscous yellow and pale slime oozed from the sodden bag. Breathing heavily, he watched as the brown paper disintegrated, became furry at the edges and yellowed, changed to a new substance entirely. Separate rivulets of yolk and white flowed across the painted boards. Arnie was shivering.

'What did you do that for?' said a voice behind him.

He swung around, recognised her instantly. She lived in the house with the tower three doors up. People sat around on the steps, drinking beer in the sun, not laughing, not talking, usually more men than women. The young women were ratty-looking little scraps of things. Too young. Too scrappy looking. Except for this one.

Arnie was on his feet. 'What are you doing here? Out. Out.'

'I'll get a cloth.' She came back with a bucket of water, a cloth and newspaper, dropped to her heels beside him. 'Yuck, what a daft thing to do.'

Arnie heard his own voice. In the midst of outrage, deep inside his head he heard his voice, the snivelling whine of a daft old man. 'That's the wrong cloth,' he said.

She took no notice. Her long brown hair swung forward beneath a cheap copy of a French fisherman's peaked cap. Her dungarees were men's.

'Shut up,' she said. 'You'll explode.'

Breathless, his heart thudding, Arnie clutched the chair arms, felt the prickles. She was right. His heart was exploding. It couldn't go on like this. He would die. Stop breathing and die.

His shoulders sagged as the thought sank into his mind, seeped into the hollows of his brain. He could cease to be. Rage could get him dead. Could end this endless shoving through of days. Cunning, acceptance, joy almost at this solution flowed through him, pumped in the purple ropes of his hands, drummed in his ears.

She was still at his feet, her hands in slimy water. 'You're smiling,' she said, shaking them and rinsing them under the tap at the end of the porch.

'I just thought of something.'

She did not smile back. He stared at her eyes, her skin, the neat nose, moved his head against the unshaved roughness of the chair.

He would have to get angry. He couldn't go on sitting there drenched in calm, gazing benignly at the intruder.

Rage was essential. But there was plenty of time. Even if she went now, even if she'd nicked something as she probably had, he could go up the road and demand to see her. He could stoke up his rage, keep it going like his spark of contempt for Bob next door.

She was sniffing her hands. 'I'll go and wash them properly.'

He was going to have to get it right. It was no use frittering his anger away in spurts. Her proprietorial attitude to his pink tongue-and-groove bathroom was irritating but nothing like the initial death-inducing violation of his house, the tearing of the silence in his fernery.

She now sat cross-legged beside him, supple as a child gymnast.

'How did you get in?'

'The back door was open.'

His eyes swam. He and Win had always been so *careful.* They had checked and double-checked, laughed at themselves, assured each other they were better to be sure than sorry. He mopped his face. 'It's still trespass.'

'I had to go somewhere.'

Arnie felt the sag of tiredness in his legs, the back of his neck. It was all going to take too long. He should have stoked his rage, kept his head of steam at the start. He began the long grind back to self-induced outrage, apoplexy and oblivion.

'Why did you have to go anywhere?'

'I had to get out. It's one of my flatmates. A shocker,' she touched her upper arms, her chest. 'Quite violent.'

Arnie looked at her with suspicion. He'd seen by the paper that violence in the home was on the increase. But she looked too relaxed, her eyes too calm beneath the jaunty cap. If it had been one of those other poor little things who sat about on the steps he would have been more concerned. The one with the mad hair, or the one seen in the dairy with a bandage on her arm. But he was a daft old man. He didn't want to know about it. He didn't believe her.

'You can't stay here,' he said.

The instantaneousness of youth, the sheer wanton waste of energy. Up, down, down, up. She was now in the fernery. 'Nice,' she said. 'Or has been.'

Dragging himself upright in his chair, Arnie lurched towards her.

She patted his arm. 'All right, all *right*.'

He leaned against the door jamb. There was no sound but his breathing.

The overgrown garden gleamed before them. Two sparrows were fighting, all beaks and outstretched wings. A gull swooped, stabbed and sailed upwards, the one dry crust hanging.

'I told you,' she said, turning back to the ferns. 'You'll drop dead if you go on like that.'

The fernery had been Win's idea. Arnie had built the slatted benches, arranged the rake of the shelves to her specifications, accepted her thanks and signed off. The final result, the green perfection of a place which had once been a passage to the bathroom, was her work. There had never been a brown frond in her day, let alone a dead one. Maidenhair shimmered beside hen and chicken, blechnum outgrew astelia. She borrowed books from the library, studied them, showed him the fertile fronds and was careful not to overwater. The small diamonds of black and white linoleum beneath reflected the greenness. It was now a shrine, a failed shrine. Something was killing them. In the past year the ferns had languished, faded away before his baffled eyes like a Victorian heroine in a decline. Fronds withered, were transformed to brown grasping claws. Big pinnules turned yellow, small pinnules sulked, the lino had ceased to shine. The shrine had gone wrong.

Arnie moved a shaking hand. 'Ashes,' he muttered, 'my wife's ashes.'

She was open-mouthed, staring at the serried pots. 'Whaat?'

Peace, unexpected as weather change, descended again. Why he had told her he didn't know, couldn't imagine. Arnie's eyes closed in gratitude to something, anything, whatever it was that had quietened him. He heard her voice.

'That's probably what's killing them.'

His eyes snapped open. She peered at a drooping True Maidenhead in a cracked pot, put out a hand and touched it.

He stumbled, clutched the architrave, shouting. 'No! No!'

She shrugged and moved out to the verandah. 'Have it your way.'

He sank down panting. Why had she come, let alone stayed. Why did he not hate her. Because she might be useful. Or something. He watched the sparrows. They had calmed down too. There was plenty for all.

'You can stay for an egg if you like,' he said eventually.

'There aren't any, unless you've any others.'

'No.'

She was unconcerned. 'That's it then.'

'I've got some bread. Cheese. Lots of jam.' Acres of jam going sugary on shelf after shelf.

'I like marmalade.'

'There's plenty.' He paused, watching her. She was sitting beside him again. At ease, cross-legged, attentive. He was tempted to tell her about his hiccough attacks. Resisted. Felt infinitely tired. The thought of stoking up a rage after two wasted opportunities exhausted him. He didn't believe her story but there would be time, time tomorrow when he felt better. But then she'd have to stay the night. Oh God. He looked at her bleakly.

She smiled for the first time. The slow secret smile of those who smile seldom. Who don't squander the product.

'Who owns the house where you live?'

'My Aunt Bertha.' She turned, her hair moving beneath the silly little cap.

He remembered her, a piratical figure in trousers. 'Mrs Boniface.' She nodded.

'Well then. Get the police. He has no legal right . . . this man.'

'Not legal, no.'

'There must be someone to advise you. Some man.'

'Man?' She stretched her legs in front of her and inspected the dungarees, sucked her finger and rubbed at something. Licked it again and rerubbed. 'My sister's married to a naval officer. William Flynn.'

He saw the large amiable shape outlined against the pittosporum at the back door, the hands proffering two tin containers and plastic pottles of congealed custard. She had admired the fernery. 'A Mrs Flynn brought us Meals on Wheels when my wife was sick. Sophie Flynn.' How on earth had he remembered that.

'That's her.'

It couldn't be. She was lying again.

'God, what a prick the man is,' she said.

There was no reaction.

'Go to your sister. Your brother-in-law,' he said finally. Authority would get him out of this. Navy blue arm-swinging authority, fixed bayonets and gaiters would solve this mess.

'He's at sea.'

Arnie sighed. Everything was impossible. His decision to use her as a catalyst for self-slaughter was ridiculous. He could see that now. He was too tired and would be tomorrow. He'd run out of puff. Even his rage at Win's betrayal in leaving him had lessened.

'You'll have to go,' he said.

'Actually,' she said, giving the word the attention of a small child, 'I've been lying to you.'

The face was still wooden. 'Why?'

'The man I live with . . . Ben,' she bent forward laughing, 'is a genuine ex-Californian no-hoper. Well, sort of. He's a good painter but he's too tired to move over, let alone hit anything. William loathes him,' she added smugly.

'Why did you lie to me?'

'My cat's disappeared. I haven't seen him since this morning.'

He waited.

'I've been searching all the backyards in the road. The door was open, like I said. I thought he might have slipped in, you know how cats do. He's . . . I'm very fond of Chester. And then you came home and I thought he'll think I've pinched something and he'll never believe I'm looking for Chester, so I lied. I made it up.'

'Do you always lie?' As if it mattered. Arnie wanted her to keep talking, to tell him more things, to continue.

'Only to irritate William.'

'You're different to your sister.'

The slow smile reappeared. 'Yes,' she said. 'I am.'

Sophie and Mary sat with their feet up after lunch, their behinds deep in deckchairs, their legs propped on the balustrade of the verandah. Their eyes followed the Kestrel as, predestined as a tram, she left Devonport ferry wharf and shoved across the harbour. There was no sign of Chester. Sophie offered advice. 'Contact the SPCA, put notices in shops, the papers.'

'It's Sunday, dumb-bum.'

'Oh yes.'

'An old man thought I'd pinched something. This morning, when I was looking for Ches. Well, the door was open . . .' She was silent. Not the ashes, not now. And anyhow Sophie was half asleep.

Chester-loving Sophie had stopped listening. She was thinking.

'Why on earth did Mum and Dad get married in the first place?' she said later, knocking aside a lone blowfly left over from summer.

Mary picked up the rubber swat which lay to hand. Caught on the wing, the fat black thing now whizzed in circles, thread legs kicking. The swat moved again. Silence. 'God knows,' she said, righting herself.

'It's odd, isn't it, how you can never be sure of anything.'

'I can.'

'Yes.' Sophie paused. 'And Mum, of course. But Dad, say.' The pause was longer. 'Remember the Portuguese generals?'

Small waves glinted below them, reassembled themselves, glinted again. It was mild for June. Mary's eyes closed. 'What?'

'That's the only definite statement I ever remember him

making. "All Portuguese generals are fat." He said that, one Sunday.'

Mary's eyes did not open.

Sophie saw the knife slicing the top off the forequarter for cold tomorrow, dividing the chined chops beneath with speed. She couldn't remember how the generals cropped up. Conversation was limited at River Bend Orchard. Usually the four of them sat in silence at meal times, the bracket clock ticking on the sideboard and the Doyenne du Comice trees lined in rows beyond the window.

'I wondered at the time how he knew,' said Sophie.

'He didn't.'

'No. But at least he said something.'

The unease of childhood returned, the silences, the tight lips up one end, the carver's fingers on the steel. And outside the pear trees and the dusty heat for miles. The slow cycle from bare branches to laden to naked once more gave their mother no comfort. Not a drop.

'He must've thought it was a safe topic,' said Sophie eventually.

'Hh.'

Sophie heaved herself upright. 'Hang on,' she said to Mary who hadn't moved. 'I'll get Mum's letter.' She was not swift footed, Sophie. Unlike Mary she did not dart, leap, appear and disappear with speed. She had her own grace however; she flowed. She was a comely woman. Vague, but comely.

She returned and flopped into the vacant deckchair, wriggled, rearranged the fullness of her skirt, attentive to its placement as a sitting hen. The letter, her busy mother's letter, hung from her hand.

'Dad told me,' she said, waving the letter slightly to indicate the connection, 'that he could tell from the tone of her voice which one of us Mum was talking to. If it was you her voice brightened. He could tell, he said, even from the packing shed.'

'Balls.'

Sophie's voice was mild. 'That's what he said. I mean, I don't mind or anything.'

The ferry had berthed, slipped alongside the city wharf, made it dead on time.

Mary realigned her moccasins on the balustrade, shifted them from side to side in quick irritation. 'It was thirty years ago! Grow up. Why on earth did he tell you? It's a dumb thing to tell anyone. Let alone a quaking bog.'

'Bog?' Sophie's smile lightened the faint heaviness of her face, brightened her eyes. Like Mary's it achieved a lot, but more often. 'He wasn't being, you know, nasty or anything. He just thought it was interesting.'

'Hopeless.' Mary snorted. 'And typical.'

A white-fronted tern dived, wings cranked back, beak poised. Surfaced again. Wheeled upwards for another go. 'And anyway you don't like him. I do.'

'Dear old Soph.'

'And don't call me Soph.'

Mary didn't bother to reply.

Sophie had always liked her name. Nana Barnsley had told her it was a nice comfortable name but even this had not put her off. But Soph is not the same; amputation has killed it.

She did not know where her mother found the name. It never occurred to her that her father could have had any part in the decision. It was considered suspect at Primary and weird at High. Now there are hundreds. The name has caught on.

'Sophie,' she used to murmur to herself as a child, as though her doppelgänger, her spirited other half, would appear from behind the speckled mirror and melt into her, whereupon both she and life itself would be a great deal better. She desired the end but disliked the process, the staring into that face, the concentration, the nothingness. The hairs on the back of her neck pricked as the unknown stared back. 'Sophie,' she insisted to its blankness. 'Your name is Sophie. Sophie Driscoll. You live with your nice kind mother and your father and your sister Mary at River Bend Road Orchard, Greytown.' The face remained doubtful.

Mary, two years younger and sensible beyond her years, thought she was mad. 'Get into *bed*, Soph!' she said, clutching her winceyette nightie with elves on it tight round her and taking a running jump at hers.

'I prefer to be called Sophie,' Sophie told the now-returning ferry.

'All right,' said Mary who never would. The letter hung from Sophie's hand. She should have insisted years ago. But it was not too late. Her feet tapped in affirmation. She will tell William when his ship comes home. She is thirty-three for heaven's sake.

The Commodore always called her Sophie.

'What does Mum say?' asked Mary.

'They're coming up.'

'Oh!' Mary scratched her nose and inspected the result. 'When?'

'After the last of the Granny Smiths are in. Before the pruning. Next month.'

Their mother, Erin, did not write often as she was busy. She was busy in the packing shed because their father was useless and she had to organise the packers and the pickers and the outdoor staff, to say nothing of the business side of things. Not only was their father useless but their mother had to do all the cooking and the house as well which was enough in all conscience let alone at her age. 'But it's the so-called slack time now the last of the Grannys are in and I'm thinking he and I might come up soon, how about that?'

'Hh.' said Mary. She paused. 'Have you noticed her bottom teeth lately?'

'No.'

Mary's eyes were on the ferry wharf again. 'They're getting more and more horselike. Leading a life of their own down there. Huge.'

'I hadn't noticed.'

Useless people should not be useless; Sophie knew this, had always known it. It was their fault. As Erin (and William) said, someone has to get the show on the road. Life is hard for the forceful. They have so much to do, their own tasks, organising the useless, and then there is all the checking up required, the gleeful pouncing on sins of omission. Life for those in charge is exhausting and never-ending and frustrating beyond words. Sophie had learnt this at her mother's knee.

She did not blame anyone for her failure to seize life and knock it into shape. After all, look at Mary. She eyed her sister, a quick sideways glance. Mary was slim, almost wiry. Yesterday in the middle of winter she'd worn Sea Island cotton. Today it was Ben's paint-stained dungarees. She lived in chaos or had since Ben moved in. She had thrown up a well-paid job and taken up beachcombing. She searched the wild black sands of west coast beaches and came back with the boot of the Morris crammed. She cleaned the pieces of driftwood and gave them names. *Kare kare, Kotuku, Spume.* Sometimes she added a spinifex. People bought them and ikebana was a help. No one could call her unenterprising and she and Sophie had had the same parents had they not, the same upbringing. There was nothing different at all. Except that right from the start Mary could make Erin laugh, sing even. She would drag her mother to the piano, the wet saucepan still dangling from her hand. 'Play "Irish Eyes" Mum. *Please.*' Later Mary took over, hamming up the old songs. 'Girls were made to love and *kees,*' she roared till the shivery grass in the mug on the upright shook and Tip the collie howled with delight or pain.

'Stop it, stop it,' cried her mother, tears rolling down her cheeks. 'I'll wet my pants!' But Mary was ruthless.

'Give me some men who are stout-hearted men / And I'll soon give you ten thousand *more,*' she bellowed as her mother begged for mercy.

Sophie and their father watched smiling and hesitant from the doorway. Sophie's fingers were stretched wide. Such moments were rare. Next day was the spraying and more incompetence on his part with smudge pots unlit and subsequent frost losses. Keith Driscoll certainly seemed ineffective to his offspring but their mother would not accept this either. It was his own fault. He had ruined himself. Gone to pot to spite her. He could have done anything! Anything. Look at his hands. He still had the hands. He could have done anything.

It is difficult to be a successful orchardist. If you survive natural disasters of drought, flood, frosts and disease, other people have too and the result is a glut. Arms folded to her chest, Erin had the answer. 'He won't help himself. Never has.'

Her heartbreaking impotent frustration went back as far as they could remember.

Sophie and Mary had played in the packing shed since they were babies. It was (and still is) a large unlined building, the roof cathedral high, the old grader clanking away at the back in the apple season. Their father lifted them up to watch the sorting process whereby each apple found its ordained slot to slip through, tripped its leather trapdoor and flopped down to lie with its own kind in segregated pens: Small, Medium, Large.

Their father smelled of apples and sweat and was patient, stepping around and over them as they played on the floor, restowing them and their Dinky toys and clapped-out dolls beneath the smoko table when they strayed too near the grader. Tip hunted for fleas beside them. Mary chose the games, marshalled her battery of cars, let Sophie be the bowser lady as she roared up for petrol and burned off again with phantom brakes squealing. Sophie read comics till her sister's return to base.

Their cot hung high above them in the rafters, cocooned in cobwebs and lit by the skylight. The Plunket wickerwork pram hung alongside. 'No more of that nonsense, thank God,' Erin told Esther, the most reliable of the pickers. Bunches of dusty oreganum dried ten years ago hung lower down. Pieces of obsolete machinery lay rusting in a heap of mangled iron at the back. Pre-cut pine slabs waiting to be made into apple boxes lay in teetering piles alongside. It was not a tidy shed. Their mother, as she said frequently, had given up on appearances. She had enough on her plate keeping her head above water. She banished the children from the shed at the height of the season. They were in the way. They retreated to the rough grass beneath the Golden Queens and watched out for wasps. 'Don't blame me if you get stung,' she told them. 'I've warned you.'

Good pickers are difficult to keep and gentle-fingered packers rare. A rough one can ruin tray after tray of quality dessert peaches with his or her bruising incompetence. Their mother was an expert packer. Immensely fast, sure fingered and gentle, she could select, wrap and stow a tray of peaches then top with a sharp-leafed spray in seconds.

She was, as their father said, pretty to watch. Sophie was hopeless, Mary not much better.

It is their legs Sophie remembers most. Her father's, tanned like hide above sockless work boots, her mother's a lighter brown, the left one mapped with a wandering knobbled vein which disappeared beneath the hem of her stained and splashed tub-frock.

Later the girls joined the workers; picked, made apple boxes when it rained, kept out of Erin's way and loved the place. Smokos stay with them; the yarners arguing around the long dusty table or slumped in silence if exhausted, the occasional bursts of laughter from the group of characters who came year after year and assured them their Mum was OK really, which they already knew. They were an odd bunch. Esther who was asthmatic and chewed her nails, tearing at them like a small fierce rodent, oblivious of them all in her concentration, lost in a world of chew and tear as she waited for her enamel mug from the vast pot-bellied teapot wielded by their mother with strength and accuracy. Peace Treadgold who was endlessly cross. Ted Butler who nodded off the moment he sat down. The lean and the portly, the frisky and the sad. The pickers were stable features of Sophie and Mary's lives. They were their extended family and the Driscolls a family in need of extension.

Their mother left the shed at five with the pickers. 'I knock off work to carry bricks,' she told them each night as they revved their ancient cars or pedalled off on upright bikes, one or two of which still had skirt guards. Erin's strong square shape strode across the gravel by the dahlia bed, ignoring Sophie's tepid offers of help because she was as useless as a piece of fixed furniture or occasionally a bandicoot. Sophie retreated with relief to read behind the apple boxes. Keith Driscoll never revealed her hiding place. He had his own cache of thrillers and *The Times* crossword puzzle books up the other end behind the grader. It would have been better if they had acknowledged their joint deceit. It would have been better if her father had said, 'Go and help your mother, Sophie. Now!'

'But Dad, I said I would and she said . . .'

'Off you go! Now.'

It would have been better but it never happened. Like secret drinkers, father and daughter ignored each other's lapses in exchange for toleration of their own. They said nothing; their silence rode shotgun for them, keeping their paths safe from the forceful and the enraged.

'Tell us the funnies, Mary,' said Erin each night and Mary would perform. She learned to save up the funny bits from Primary, Secondary and the flicks on Saturdays. Anything which would make her mother laugh. Mary walked on her hands, she stood on her head, she practised her pratfalls. She was, as her mother said, a born comic.

'What would I do without you,' cried Erin.

'Mum,' said Sophie standing at the doorway in her pink before the sixth form social, 'Do I look all right, Mum?'

Her mother stared at her, gave her daughter both time and attention. 'Turn round. Of course you look all right,' she said finally, 'you've got two arms, two legs, a nose.'

Mary was bright, very bright and a lovely little worker. 'She's going to do science down south. Mad, I know, but she insists,' Erin told Esther. 'I'll have to sell the bracket clock. He won't notice.' Esther said nothing, her pale eyes stared above torn nails as she chewed.

Erin sold it for a large sum. She was right. He didn't notice; or not till later. 'What's happened to the clock?' he said.

'There are eight carriages round the corner,' roared the loud-speaker as Mary made her break for freedom the next February, squeezing down the ferry gangway in Christchurch, cheek by cheek and jowl by jowl with the rest of the herd heading South.

'Eight carriages round the corner!'

She had made it. Encumbered by bags, clutching her suitcase, Mary surged on.

Eight, a whole eight. Tons of carriages. Plenty of room. The wonder of her life hit her, escape knocked her breathless. A man trod on her heel. 'Watch it, girlie,' he said.

Sophie married William on her nineteenth birthday.

THREE

William is now First Lieutenant of one of the frigates and loves his job; it has a lot of sea time, which is what you join the navy for after all. His ship is taking part in the Island Cruise, a training exercise in the South Pacific undertaken each winter by one of the ships of the Royal New Zealand Navy. This is a stressful time for him as promotion to full Commander is dependent on merit and might hang upon his performance in this ship. This is his promotion job. His chance. Sophie was proud of him and his job. The Royal New Zealand Navy is second to none, as has been demonstrated time after time in action and always on naval exercises with Australia and the United States and, whenever possible, the Royal Navy. The latter is now giving cause for concern. There have been persistent rumours that the Brits might pull out east of Suez in the seventies, albeit slowly.

William has always said that the Jimmy, the First Lieutenant, should be the most hated man on board because he must crack the whip. William is happy with this situation. Everyone on board, he tells Sophie, should admire the Captain and hate the Jimmy, though this varies according to the Old Man as no one can fool sailors. They have a sixth sense when it comes to spotting a phoney, especially an officer.

Some naval wives never got used to the life and worked upon their husbands to resign. This manipulation by disgruntled females was frowned upon. Especially by the other wives, which puzzled Sophie. It was regarded as letting the side down. Whose side? And why? Sophie had in the past not given much thought to her life as a naval wife. It was just what had happened. The structured enclosed life had not worried her; she liked to know where she was. And she could cope. Now she was thinking a lot about the subject, was puzzled by contrasts of total charge while William was at sea and head-patting indulgence when he returned. She was no longer at ease, though she knew she should be happy as a large white clam. There was no requirement (William) for her to feel otherwise. Sophie told herself so.

The breeze on the harbour below her kitchen freshened. Two keelers near the shore rocked in stately calm. A few smaller more skittish yachts raced about the harbour, gybing and luffing and going about as they headed up harbour towards the bridge.

Look how lucky they were renting a house in Calliope Road, for example. Naval houses in the road were usually allocated to senior officers and no one could call a Lieutenant Commander senior but there had been a temporary lack of senior applicants at the time and William had been a flipper to the front. The verandah faced south to the same view as that from the Wardroom of HMNZS Philomel. William and Sophie agreed that a cool verandah was preferable in Auckland as the butter did not melt when they ate meals there. It was one of the things they discussed quite often. Sophie was grateful to William for being a flipper to the front and enabling them to live with such a view, though she was conscious that she was a very junior wife in Calliope Road. No one said anything but she knew. How could she not.

People were friendly however, especially the Captain's wife, Celia Pickett, that large rangy Englishwoman with big feet. Celia didn't give a damn about anything, least of all the Royal New Zealand Navy to which her husband belonged.

This, Sophie suspected, was because of Celia's private means. It was a well-known fact said Liz Kelson, who also lived in the road, that the whole of Harold Pickett's pay just covered Celia's income tax. It was not the money which impressed Sophie but the fact that Celia had it. Sophie was reminded of other sports of nature, such as stick insects, where the female is much larger and more impressive than the male. Some insects eat their mates after copulation or is that only spiders?

Sophie was grateful for Celia's friendliness to a junior officer's wife but she wished the Captain's wife had more to do. Independent means plus inbuilt ineptitude had resulted in cleaning ladies and ironing ladies and a gardening man, all of whom left Celia free to drift along Calliope Road on her coffee run, as she called it, to mount her rump each morning on Sophie's kitchen table, to edge the cereal packet to the left, smile her lopsided smile and begin her day. 'Well, Soph. What's the dirt?'

Sometimes before Sophie had got the washing out.

This morning Celia draped herself over the kitchen table, cushioned her bosom on her golden arms and smiled, her face inviting as an espaliered peach from Mother's walled garden in Hampshire.

She stood a china Punch and Judy salt and pepper on their heads while she waited. Sophie righted them. They were a present from Kit, brought home in triumph from a school White Elephant. 'Any news?' asked Celia.

'They're blocked,' said Sophie. 'I must get at them with a pin.'

No one can help being vague and there is such a thing, as Celia had told Liz Kelson the other day, as being too sharp. However, vagueness does limit Sophie's value as a source of who's-fucking-whom talk. Celia swears like a Chief Stoker (William). Though no one actually stokes now. Knobs are turned.

Sophie sat thinking about authority. About men and women and duty and life. She wished to go through the rubble of her mind, to tidy the clutter and think. Blind acceptance of authority, corpse-like obedience to the views of others, she decided as Celia played with the sugar, was not enough.

Of course people must obey rules for their own good, belong to a disciplined force if any, must cross on the green and stay put on the red. But what about the leakage, the downward seep of power, the Pooh-Bah in the home. Who says? Who's Boss? Who knows? There are things Sophie must get to grips with. Including a job. Independence as every fool knows needs money. She stared at the golden hairs on Celia's arm and remembered Mary's reaction.

'I'm going to get a job nurse aiding,' she told her, 'and train later.'

'You did eighteen months sixteen years ago. Do something interesting, for God's sake.'

Mary had been a marine biologist with a special interest in molluscs until she threw it all away. The ocean floor was a whole new world she told her sister. It was time Sophie got herself educated. Why not now? It is never too late. 'No,' said Sophie flinging aside the night-class brochure. 'It's people I want, not the Ocean Floor, or Estuaries, or the Hub of Life on the Continental Shelf.' She stood, large white and serious in front of the sister who was rearranging her life for her own good.

'And what about you?' she said. 'You've dumped all that.'

'Ah, me.' Mary smiled. 'Don't you worry about me.'

'How're you getting on without William?' asked Celia, accepting a mug with a black cat washing a leg in the air.

'All right, thanks,' said Sophie turning her back. Just for a second, a micron of a mini second, she had forgotten William was at sea, that he would not come skidding up the vinyl-squared hall that evening to tell her about the air conditioning in the Ops Room and who'd won the inter-ship pulling and what about a beer. That he was in fact far away, buried inside the steel cocoon of his ship as she thrust her proud way through the coral-rich waters of the South Pacific. She knew how important the Island Cruise was, what a chance it was for William to show how good he was at the different aspects of his demanding job in the finest of Her Majesty's New Zealand Ships. Her momentary amnesia appalled her, her palms sweated.

She had tried to discuss their shaky finances before the ship sailed. William told her you couldn't get blood from a stone and they made love. They always made love the night before the ship sailed. Carnal frolics at the last moment, however tender and loving, however connubial, are traditional, indeed expected, before a ship sails. It is not only natural, it is also desirable to keep the men going while they are away. To top up, as it were, at the last moment. And the women of course.

'Anything packed up yet?' said Celia. Sophie, nervous as well as guilty, shook her head.

Celia's voice was gentle. 'How's the Commodore? Have you seen him lately?'

'No. But I'm going with him to Captain and Mrs Featherston's tomorrow night for a meal.'

Celia's lips parted. 'Ah,' she said. 'So you're his lady now.'

'What?'

'Edward always has a partner on the arm. The last was Fiona Banks. But of course Graeme's back now.' The Captain of Philomel's wife, kind to grass widows and strays of any kind, nodded. 'Last week,' she said.

'Have you seen my sister's Burmese?' said Sophie. 'Chester?'

'No.' Celia flicked a finger beneath her nose. 'But Burmese do wander.'

Oh shut up you silly old bat. 'Perhaps you could keep an eye out for him, seeing you're going along the road.'

Celia was an amiable woman. She drained her mug and left.

Sophie stretched her arms to the ceiling and let them flop. Rupert Brooke surfaced from the sixth form.

> Fish say they have their Stream and Pond
> But is there anything Beyond?
> This life cannot be All, they swear
> For how unpleasant if it were.

It was not the afterlife of fish which interested her. Sophie, troubled and confused with no requirement to be either, moved about her cleaning tasks with slow competence. 'No requirement, no requirement, no requirement,' thumped the washing machine. The shelf above shuddered, preserving jars rattled, a nail brush clanged into the empty tub. She closed the door on the lot, picked up a magazine abandoned in Celia's haste, and flicked through high-gloss pages of pouting women and smouldering men, looking for Travel. It featured a luxury resort in Bermuda. Silver bays were fringed with tropical palms. Individual cabins had a staff of two. There were photographs. A white man and woman lounged in cushioned cane chairs and were offered drinks from silver trays by two black men in white clothes who smiled broadly. The guests also smiled, but faintly. More from politeness. This way of life was no surprise to them.

Sophie checked the facilities available; the golf links, the tennis courts, the water skiing and, of course, the dancing nightly to the steel band in the main concourse. On the golf course there were little motorised buggies called Eisenhowers to carry the players and their golf clubs so they would not have to walk between hits. There were both double and single Eisenhowers available. Sophie read on as if it was imperative for her to find out how things were arranged at this place, as if she would go there. Not in a bull's roar nor would want to, so why read about it.

She read on.

The Eisenhowers, she discovered, did not have to be hired at the desk. They were freely available on request at the links. Which must mean there were a lot of Eisenhowers. Prices were given both for the air fare and the daily rate at the hotel. Astronomic. Mr McNally on her Meals on Wheels run had discussed world economics with her, his hands trembling in his insistence that Holyoake had got it wrong. That something would have to be done. That when he thought back to 1935 when politicians were committed to the good of the country and the betterment of the poor he could weep and what did Mrs Flynn think? Yes, and did Mr McNally think the Black Budget had been the burial of Labour hopes? Yes he did and what about this lot and their 'fair shares for all'. They have to get in first, don't they?

The telephone rang, echoing down the black-and-white vinyl tiles laid diagonally by William on his last leave. The pseudo-marble effect looked well but the space echoed and the skid marks showed.

'Hullo,' said Sophie, still visualising serried rows of Eisenhowers at the links. They would go rusty too. The moving parts.

'Mrs Flynn? This is Kate Calder speaking, Captain of Philomel's office. Hold the line, would you. The Captain would like to speak to you.'

Sophie sat down on the same black chest as the telephone. The voice was warm, a dark rich baritone. 'That you, Sophie?' said Harold Pickett.

'Yes.'

'There's something I'd like to ask you to do for me. A favour. Rather an intimate one perhaps. Could you pop along for a minute? By any chance?'

'Now?'

'If it suits you.'

Sophie's eyes focused on the skid marks.

'All right. I'll walk down the hill.'

'Thank you so much. Come straight to my office. We'll let the guard know. Ten minutes?'

Sophie brushed her hair, smiled briefly at herself. Women should not do this, she had read recently. Something to do with vanity and politics of the harem. She turned off the washing machine and headed down the hill.

Kate, pin trim and smiling, showed her into the Captain of Philomel's office.

The Captain leaped to his feet before subsiding again behind a large flat-topped desk. 'Sophie, my dear,' he cried. 'Please sit down. Thank you, Kate.' The door closed gently.

Sophie sat in a small navy blue chair in front of his desk with her feet together.

The Captain of Philomel's office was not far from the Memorial Chapel of St Christopher. Three copies of the Royal New Zealand

Navy List lay beside undefinable volumes in a small bookcase near the desk. Several ships' badges mounted on wooden plaques hung on the wall beside a large framed print depicting a bygone Spithead Review. A scale model of an old warship sat in a glass case.

'Would you like a cup of coffee, Sophie?' The Captain was leaning forward with his hands clasped loosely on his desk as though he was being photographed and Sophie was the camera.

She shook her head. She could think of nothing to say except why was she here.

The Captain took his time. He picked up a pencil. Put it down again and smiled once more.

Sophie smiled back. It was a beautiful day outside. Someone shouted a parade ground order. A gunnery officer? The sound echoed up the hill. Sophie sat silent.

'Sophie,' continued the Captain, 'I have a rather extraordinary request to make to you. I can't think of anyone else I could trust with it.'

'Oh.'

The hair across the front of the Captain's forehead was blue-black and shiny. Sleek, she thought. Harold Pickett is sleek as a hand-fed seal.

He laughed, flung back his head as if he was having a wonderful time. If you saw him from a bus window you would think, there is a man whose laughter is uninhibited and carefree. But the Captain has many cares, though not as many as the Commodore. What about the situation in South-East Asia. The training scheme. The new Intake. The logistics involved in moving HMNZS Tamaki to the mainland next year.

'You know we're expecting a visit soon from one of the friendly Asian powers?' He leaned forward again.

It was all tied up. South-East Asia, escalation and despair. Sophie could feel her heart.

'Yes.'

The Captain's face was grave. 'I'm worried about the toilet that we will make available for his wife.'

She gave a ridiculous yelp of relief. 'What?'

'The VIP of course, and his retinue, will use the facilities in the Captain of Philomel's flat before lunch, but it's his lady we're worried about. There's only the Ladies' on the ground floor available.'

'Oh.'

'Yes. And it's pretty basic as you know.'

He looked into her eyes. He had never noticed them before. Large brown eyes, eyes you could see into. Candid.

'You know those decorative covers for the tops of lavatories?' he continued quickly. 'They have a matching floor-mat thing that fits round the er pedestal.' He was becoming less happy. 'They're made of sort of,' his hands moved, 'towelling.'

'Yes.'

'I am right?'

'I think so.'

'In the States they have matching sets.' The Captain sighed. 'But you can't get them here.'

'Oh.'

He leaned forward, his eyes anxious. 'I wondered, Sophie. I wondered if you could make a set for me?'

Sophie said nothing. He tried again, renewed his smile. 'To cheer it up a bit for the friendly Asian lady.'

Her hands clasped the arms of her chair. She stood very straight. Never, never, never. Her voice was choking, harsh. 'Make it yourself,' she said.

The Captain was also on his feet, his face stiff with shock. He was around the desk, clasping her hands. She pulled them back. He grabbed them again.

'I would if I could,' he said sadly, 'but I can't.'

'What about Celia!'

'Celia!' gasped the Captain of Philomel. 'Oh, *Celia* couldn't do anything like that.'

The arrogant-sod assumption that some people could never be expected to know anything as insane as how to make a towelling set to tart up a lavatory, let alone do it, and that others could and would and she was one of them, enraged her further. She was sick of it. Sick to the depths of her bruised angry heart.

'I thought you'd like to help,' said the Captain of Philomel, his face puzzled, his eyes despairing.

Sophie saw the bleak cloakroom, the friendly Asian lady's sorrow, the yellowing tiles. Saw the pain in the face in front of her.

'Oh all right,' she said, filled with the self-loathing of the weak-kneed.

The Captain was delighted. He clasped her hands in his yet again.

The pattern was no problem, he explained. Someone could make a paper template.

Who? Worse beyond worse peculiar. There seemed no end to the ludicrous aspects of the task to which she had committed herself. Sophie shook her head. 'No, no. I can get a pattern. I have seen them in Takapuna. Butterick, I think. Yes, Butterick.'

His hand dropped to his doeskin pocket. 'No!' Sweaty and unclean, Sophie blundered from the spotless office out into the room where Kate and another Wren officer worked which acted as an air lock between the Captain and the rest of the world, out into the sun and the wind and the screaming gulls of Devonport.

She wished to explain. To tell someone or something of her snivelling self-disgust, to lay it with the real worries, the tragedies, the agonies and the screams of pain. She rattled the door of the Memorial Chapel of St Christopher. It was locked. She turned away with a slight gasp. What in the name of heaven was she *doing*.

The Commodore was striding back from the base tailor. 'Sophie,' he said, arms out, palms upward in welcome. 'What on earth are you doing here?'

She walked into them by the Ocean Ranger figurehead. He did not leap away. He led her around the back of the Memorial Chapel of St Christopher, flung his cap on the grass and held her. He took her face in one hand and studied it. 'What's wrong, Sophie?'

'Nothing,' she said and kissed him.

He released her eventually. 'Sophie.'

'I love you,' she said. The words echoed, thundered across the harbour, swept back. She was laughing. 'What the hell,' cried Sophie.

Edward Sand stared down at her. His face was serious. 'I'll see you tomorrow.' He picked up his cap from the grass and departed.

Sophie, filled with the illicit heady joy of the sinner, was working out how to love her lover. John Donne had not featured in the sixth form but she had found him later.

She walked out the main gate. The guard on duty looked at her with interest. It was some time since the office had telephoned to say she was on her way.

She walked past the small tidy houses on the waterfront between the main gate and Devonport; past the clock on the ferry wharf and the Esplanade Hotel where the women's lavatory was labelled 'Mermaids only' in brass. The seagulls were shrieking, tearing the air to pieces as they soared upwards to fling themselves around the gun emplacements on North Head, which was riddled with ammunition tunnels left over from the war.

She would pick up a squeegee mop refill at *Stirlings* the hardware shop. Life must go on, thought Sophie, beaming at a defecating dog squatting by a shop front.

One of the times Sophie had been aware of loneliness, had caught the whiff of rejection from the Ark of two by two, was when she saw naval men and their wives shopping together. It is a connubial activity, buying things for the home when you have both saved up. Before William left for the Island Cruise they had bought a heater. Similar ones lined the back of the cavernous shop. They were paraffin heaters but did not smell at all if you kept them well cleaned. Stuart the salesman had shown them how, removing the tube which shielded the flame when lit, dropping on his hot tan heels, his face anxious as he glanced up at them, his hands busy with the wick cleaner as he demonstrated on the virginal wick which had never been lit. William, she remembered, had nodded. 'Background warmth is what we need, isn't it, Soph?'

'Yes.'

'You'll find the heat will permeate right through your house.' Stuart, still anxious, was now upright.

'Done.' William, after inspection, rubbed his hands together. 'Sold to the lady in the paper hat.'

Stuart was pleased but not surprised. He was used to ribaldry and bonhomie at the time of purchase.

Sophie stood at the back of the shop, her eyes on the upright paraffin heaters for background warmth and permeation. Euphoria had gone. It had melted away among the shelves and the bright shining chrome things and the nuts and bolts and the plastic kitchen utensils. Had disappeared behind the collapsible white Japanese paper lampshades shaped like globes which had just come in. It had been replaced by quiet joy, by dazed wonder at the steady ticking of her life.

Stuart was smiling at her side. He was a nice man, Stuart, dark and helpful with receding hair and pale hands. He wore a wide shiny wedding ring.

'Good morning, Mrs Flynn. How's the Valor?'

They both looked at the line of heaters, sturdy and reliable as keepers of the watch. She thought of William.

'I haven't used it yet.' She was about to tell Stuart it hadn't been cold enough but he was already nodding. He knew this, he could feel warmth all around him. There was a pause as they stared at the nearest Valor. Stuart rubbed his hand over it, his palm caressing its steel flank.

'Was there something else?' he said after a pause.

'I need a replacement sponge for my squeegee.'

In an instant his hands were full of them; hectic green, pink, yellow and turquoise replacement squeegee mops leaped from his fingers. 'Which?' he asked.

He cared too much. Sophie could not tell him that she did not care. That it was irrelevant. That they were all hideous and she didn't care and that if he knew about her he would be surprised.

Her hand flicked, a dismissive wave.

'Blue.'

'Blue it is. Sold to the lady in the paper, what was it again?'

'Hat.'

'Hat.' Stuart's hand slapped his knee. His laugh turned to a cough. 'Pardon,' he said, one hand to his mouth. Now he was on another tack. 'Have you got one of these, Mrs Flynn?' The hands assembled a new refinement of the squeegee which enabled you to clean the shower after you had finished. Stuart dismantled sections, reassembled, wiped pretend walls. He glanced at her over his shoulder to see that she had got the picture.

'You mean you clean the shower yourself, Stuart?'

'Well, of course,' said Stuart, his ring glistening. 'Otherwise my wife would have to, wouldn't she?'

'Yes.'

Clutching her wrapped sponge she farewelled him.

Devonport was not busy. Cars lined the main street, rather old model cars on the whole, low-rumped and squatting, the sun burnishing their roofs. There were few pedestrians. Occasionally one waved, called a greeting across the road. Some of the local people were concerned lest the recent building of the Harbour Bridge would reduce Devonport to a sleepy hollow, as it was now cut off from the mainstream traffic to the North Shore by the demise of the car ferry. The phrase 'sleepy hollow' was heard often in 1962, and seen in the local paper. It was worrying for local shopkeepers, but Devonport was an agreeable place to live. A few artists lived nearby, a potter or two, a bearded Titan who twisted wrought iron, a man who was about to tackle stained glass. Sophie and William did not know or patronise any of these creative people but they knew they were there and were reassured. Artists thrive in sleepy hollows.

There were other advantages. The man in the garage was kind to naval grass widows because he used to be in the Andrew himself and his wife wouldn't know a bee from a bull's foot once she'd lifted the bonnet. The hardware man was generous with his hire-purchase terms. The village atmosphere was enhanced in even more cosy ways. The wife of the grocer, for example, made home-made fudge which was delicious but you had to be quick on a Monday.

A trail of children from the local kindergarten chattered past hand in hand, shepherded by an untidy blonde in yellow. The children wore bright cartoon clothes; reds, greens and squeegee pinks. Everything was cartoons now. Even colours were obvious, easy to label. There was no room for doubt, for subtlety, for the shimmer of crossweave. For camouflage.

A line of straw hats bobbing across the chemist's shop had not been removed though summer had long gone. A large photographed dog and cat still asked each other, 'Will we be free of fleas this summer?' They were too late and again Sophie did not care. The chemist waved, pristine in high-necked white. 'Got the eye drops for Rebecca?' he called.

'Yes, thank you.'

'Good, good.'

And still she remembered and still and still. They were out of peanut butter. She turned into the grocer's for a jar of crunchy. There was no fudge. 'Those days are gone,' Kel the owner told her. He nodded his head across the aisle to *Fruit and Veges*. 'Noelle's full time now,' he said. Noelle, hearing her name, lifted a cabbage in greeting. She was telling a customer that their holiday at Whangamata had been lovely even though they didn't get the weather.

Sophie headed up the hill. Bertha, that's who she needed, Aunty Bertha.

The old man was panting against his letterbox.

Sophie stared at him. 'Mr McNally?'

He nodded, speechless.

'Are you all right?'

'Of course I'm all right,' he gasped.

Tetchy. An odd word, tetchy. Men, even men as obviously decrepit as Mr McNally, are expected to soldier on, to pack up their troubles in their old kitbags and smile, smile, smile. To be a man. 'I haven't seen you for a long time,' she said.

He was silent, marshalling his breath. 'Has your sister found her, her cat?'

First William, then Chester. Absence of mind is no excuse. She shook her head. 'No. No, she hasn't.'

'I'll keep an eye out.'

'Thank you, thank you,' she said to his departing back, his straightened shoulders.

Aunty Bertha's house had grown from an ancient cottage. A top storey plus verandah had been added and later the pepper-pot tower. Bertha had turned the house into two flats, accepting the outside staircase for her better view which, as people told her frequently, was breathtaking. The harbour and the city lay spread before her, ready for inspection twenty-four hours a day. When Bertha clambered out of bed in the middle of the night she invariably checked the view on her way back from the bathroom. On waking she told the city it wore the beauty of the morning: silent, bare.

Bertha had been an artiste, a solo artiste. She had danced the whole world over and had photographs to prove it. Large black-and-white ones from the thirties lined the walls of the over-crowded room: Bertha as a fan dancer in three-inch heels man-handling two enormous ostrich fans with decorum; Bertha in top hat, tails and shiny black shoes, leaning on a malacca cane and/or tap-dancing with widespread flying arms. One of the largest showed a virtually naked belly dancer from the casbah. A more sober Dutch girl in winged cap and phoney clogs had an unexpected cleavage.

Bertha had had many faces but all of them were aloof. Unsmiling as a figurehead, her face was pickled in the cool chic of her period. She was slim as a bean.

The decor of the flat was mixed. The living room was equipped with large Edwardian cabinets with carved excrescences and a three-piece suite in pale blue which bounced.

The verandah (now enclosed) was hung about with faded sun hats and baskets. Straw hats and floral hats, shapeless hats and an ancient solar topee were piled on a cluster of pegs. Rough baskets of rope-like strands lay on the floor beside ones woven from threads of raw silk. There were three Maori kits. Bertha Boniface's catchment area had been wide. 'My baskets,' she said, 'are the story of my life.' Plus her assegais and her carved prow figure from a Solomon Island canoe and her Nigerian toy tractor made from tin cans and her Algerian scarves. Bertha had been a woman of the world.

She greeted Sophie with enthusiasm, her vast form heaving as she slapped her hands about searching for her smokes. She was fond of her nieces and showed it, enfolding them in her arms and kissing them on the mouth with damp enthusiasm. Her denim trousers came from a menswear shop in Karangahape Road. Thank God, said Bertha frequently, for fat men.

'It's high time we went fishing, Soph,' she said. 'Plenty of kahawai at Devonport wharf at the moment. We'll take a sandwich.' She lit a cigarette, inhaled deeply. 'Yes?'

'Yes,' said Sophie, soothed as always by Bertha's views of the essentials of life. She fished all the time now, had done for years. There was nothing like it in her opinion.

There was no way to tell her. Not at the moment. How would you start. 'Bertha, the thing is Bertha . . .' Bertha would understand. Who better than this loving woman of the world. But not at the moment.

'Bertha,' she said after a pause. 'You know Mrs Featherston, don't you?'

'Lettie? Of course. We crouched in her basement clutching each other night after night in the Blitz. Whole streets disappeared! Beds left hanging,' laughed Bertha, her eyes bright with the pride of the survivor, the ex-combatant. 'Lionel was at sea.'

Captain and Mrs Featherston were well known in naval circles. The Captain was a retired Royal Navy man, immensely old and regarded with affectionate admiration by all, especially since the present Commodore had arrived. The Captain had saved Lieutenant Sand's life during the war though Sophie had not heard how. The Featherstons had come to live in New Zealand after their only daughter Rose married a young New Zealand naval officer on Scheme B. Both Rose and her baby died in childbirth which was virtually unheard of, but this tragedy had not sent her grieving parents home to Southsea as expected. 'The sun helps,' the Captain had said, 'and Bertha Boniface is a good friend to Lettie.'

'What is she like? Really?'

'Why do you ask?'

'I've been invited to have a meal with them. With the Commodore.'

Bertha's face was thoughtful. 'Lettie is very fond of the Commodore.' She sniffed, banged her wrists. 'Never there when you want them, handkerchiefs.' She flicked her nose on her wrist. 'Yes. She loves him.'

Sophie leaned forward. 'But what's she like?'

Bertha stubbed out her cigarette, grinding it to extinction in a large Dewars Whisky ashtray. 'I was Rose's godmother,' she said. 'Sad. Very sad.'

FOUR

Celia's voice fluted down the hall. She stopped at the door, brought up all standing by Sophie on her knees surrounded by a flood of orange towelling. Her mouth was full of pins, one hand flapped a tissue-thin pattern. She nodded in welcome, her eyebrows working in support, attempted some comment from the side of her mouth, gave up, spat the pins into the palm of her hand and sat back.

Celia picked her way round the edges, lowered herself onto the sofa and put her feet up. She was at ease in other people's houses.

Sophie attempted diversion. 'How did the lunch go?'

'Ah, the lunch. The lunch was all right.' Celia's lunches were pleasant occasions. She was an excellent hostess who never cooked, a source of pride to herself and suspicion bordering on disbelief to other wives. 'She told me,' said Sophie's neighbour, wide eyed, 'she can't even boil an egg!'

Sophie, her hands deep in offal, smiled. 'Oh dear.'

Nancy Ogilvie's head gave a quick sideways movement of concern. 'I *know.*'

Celia yawned. 'Dear old farts,' she continued. 'Average age a hundred and seven. All senile except the Featherstons, but sweet as nuts.' She stirred slightly. Fifty, Celia had decided, was different from forty-nine. Her recent birthday had acted as a *memento mori*, a reminder of the inevitable way of all flesh. A reminder also of the bloody age gap. She was four years older than Harold, a fact of no concern to her except at birthdays. And yesterday's lunch hadn't helped. Even her superb legs seemed to be packing up, getting puffy at the ankles. 'Oh shit,' said Celia.

Sophie was now piecing pattern sections onto burnt orange, her hands were busy soothing wrinkles, aligning, getting it right.

Celia peered down at the orange stuff.

'You haven't said what it is?'

Sophie pinned around a curve. 'I am making a cover for a lavatory seat.'

'What?'

'You heard.'

Rude as well as nuts. Celia stared at the crown of the head presented to her.

'But those things are insane.'

'I know.'

'Well then?'

Sophie's mind was ticking. You are a spoilt woman. You, you friendly twit, should be making this obscenity, not me. I am stuck with this idiocy because you are an idle slob and couldn't make it anyway. And why should I? Except that the rest of us must pull together, must we not. Help out. Stand by our men, God help us all.

She stood up, tripped over the cord of the Singer, clutched the edge of the dining table and righted herself with dignity. The ferry's wake was alive with gulls who usually have more sense. They follow fishing trawlers where the pickings are better, not the wide-bottomed resolute Kestrel which offers little return. Sophie stood straight. She looked magnificent.

'He thought it would cheer the place up. For the friendly Asians. Asian.' Her eyes turned again to the gulls. Wheeling, aerodynamically perfect, they can rob in mid-air.

Celia's finger stabbed at the virulent orange. 'Did he . . . Did the wretched man . . . ? He asked you to make it?'

'Yes. Your husband.'

'You mean *Harold* asked you to construct this . . . thing?'

'Who else did you think?'

'Edward, of course. The Commodore.' Celia swung her legs onto the floor. One suede toe touched the orange tide. She withdrew it quickly.

Sophie had not noticed before how large Celia's face was. There was too much of it, too much left over round the edges. Her hand still held the old table where she fed her children good nourishing food, where she ironed, sewed and wrote to her husband William.

'As if the Commodore would!'

Celia was now enjoying herself. She shook her friendly head. 'Oh Soph,' she said. 'Oh Soph, darling.'

Sophie stared at her. Looked at her for some time and found her wanting. 'Excuse me,' she said. She stalked into the black-and-white skid-marked pseudo-marble hall, sat on the pseudo-oak chest, glanced at the small leather book marked *Telephone* and dialled.

'Captain's office,' said Kate Calder.

'Sophie Flynn speaking, Kate. Please may I speak to the Captain?'

'The Captain, Mrs Flynn? Now?'

'Yes please.'

'Just one moment, please. I'll try.'

'Sophie, my dear.' Reassuring, deep and sonorous, Harold Pickett's voice flowed up the hill at her. 'All well, I hope.'

Now you fool. Now.

'I'm just ringing to say, Captain, that I won't be able to make the toilet set for the downstairs cloakroom.'

Pause. 'Oh dear,' said the Captain of Philomel. The voice sharpened. 'May I ask why not?'

'I have decided,' said Sophie, her eyes on the albatross chick for June on the calendar opposite, 'that I don't want to.'

'But you said you would.'

'Yes. I have changed my mind.'

The voice was icy. 'I see.'

He didn't. He never would. She was unreliable and unworthy of a position of trust. Possibly difficult. A stroppy wife even. Sophie's heart lifted. She had ditched the bribe of good opinion. She did not care. She was fizzing with excitement, her toes clenched.

'So what do we do now?'

'Celia's here at the moment. I'll put it all in a plastic bag plus the pattern and ask her to take it home to you. I'll leave the pins in if you like.'

The voice rose, 'Good God no! I'll send somebody later.'

'I can leave it in your letterbox.'

'No, no, no.'

'Thank you. Goodbye, Captain.'

'Goodbye.'

Sophie replaced the receiver with care, smiled down at it, touched it again. Grey, shiny and reliable. A good thing. If Celia had not been marooned the other side of an orange sea of unmade toilet requisites in her living-cum-dining room Sophie would have hopped on one leg rejoicing. Hopped the length of the hall in celebration.

Celia was standing at the French doors onto the verandah. She turned with a sigh.

'They're hypnotic, aren't they? I could watch them for hours.'

'The gulls?'

'Yes.' Celia scratched her scalp with her second fingernail, the rest of her hand clamped rigid above. 'Wouldn't it be awful to be a bum seagull?' she said.

'What did the Commodore want?' said Kit licking his knees. He liked the salt taste.

'He was reminding me about the dinner tonight.'

'Are you the Commodore's lady for taking now Lieutenant Commander Banks is home again?' asked Rebecca in passing, having brought in the washing like a good girl.

Sophie looked at her wise child.

'He always has a lady for taking to things,' explained Rebecca helpfully.

Kit stopped licking. 'Is Lou babysitting?'

'Yes.'

'Good.'

Lou (I can't *stand* Louise) and her boyfriend Evan contributed to the wellbeing of Calliope Road. They were so handy. Evan, the more beautiful of the two, managed *Choice Meats* across the road. His striped apron, his low-slung scabbard for knives and steel became him. He was a large gentle man who dropped off Arnie McNally's chop or sausages on his way home even though *Choice Meats* did not deliver.

Lou, an efficient hairdresser and a keen businesswoman, ran deeply incised rings round Evan and loved him dearly. She kept *A Cut Ahead* spotless. Her horizontal surfaces were uncluttered, she was lavish with towels and generous with sweep-ups. You never had to wade through the last cut's leavings at Lou's. Large photographs advertised haircare products. Eyelashes fanned below tangled ringlets, short cuts swung sideways, their image frozen till the fashion flopped. Beehives were in; not only a hairstyle but a way of life. Occasionally owners could be seen at traffic lights attempting a lift with both hands to let the air in. Others, like Lou's, stayed rigid from week to week.

Lou's lipstick was pale. Her hair was pink this week, last week electric blue. Before that apricot. 'What does your mother think of all your different hair colours?' asked Sophie. Lou's eyes were puzzled behind their palisade of loaded lashes. 'What's it got to do with my Mum?' she asked.

The front door was open. The Commodore walked in and stood watching in silence. Sophie was standing in front of the chest in a patchwork skirt and white shirt. Kit, one foot either side of the telephone, fumbled with the catch at the back of her neck.

Cultured pearls were a good buy in Japan (William). There was silence; Kit's breathing was getting heavier.

'May I help?' said the Commodore.

'No,' said Kit. He jumped down, nuzzled his bullet head against Sophie's stomach for a moment and ran down the hall. 'See you,' he waved.

The Gasworks straight was lined with pohutukawas and Norfolk pines in memory of men killed in World War II. Several of the trees were struggling; some had been replaced, leaving painful inconsistencies of height and size.

He glanced at her.

'I like being here,' she said.

'Sophie.' His left hand lay on her knee. The imprint of his hand remained on a patch of brown velvet as he changed gear. 'Sophie,' he said again.

'Talk to me. Tell me what you're thinking about.'

Edward Sand was a man who liked women. Their differences fascinated him, their multitudinous diversities. Their walks: the loping strides, the scuttles, the swing of buttocks all pleased him. And their hair, endlessly dissimilar and always interesting. Tied up in knots or falling free; permed to the bone or hanging, differences pleased him. He watched them. He also liked talking to them. He liked their quickness, their ability to leap from branch to branch and return to the original topic refreshed. Some, like Sophie, seemed genuinely interested in almost everything which was a bonus. He liked her very much.

'I've just been rereading Cotton's *Geomorphology*,' he said dropping speed. The Gasworks straight was notorious for traffic cops. 'Have you read it?'

'No.'

'Wonderful stuff. I never travel without it. Some day,' he said, 'we'll camp on a homoclinal ridge.'

Her lips, he noticed from a brief glance, were shining. 'Yes,' she said.

The pretending has always been part of it. The willow cabin. The love nest. The cave in the mountains warm with skins.

'Yes,' she said again.

He was willing to talk, to discuss, to share. With women. With her.

'Have you read *Madame Bovary*?' he had asked her after a recent mess dinner. Sophie had not been at his table. She was a junior wife.

'Yes.'

His eyes were kind. 'Do read it again. It's worth it.'

Madame Bovary at a mess dinner.

'You don't have to of course.'

'No. No. I mean . . . it's just.' Her hand waved at the men in mess kit, their cummerbunds, their wives, the chat and the chat and death at the end. 'It's a mess dinner,' she explained.

'So?'

William appeared alongside. 'Bandy did well, didn't he, sir?'

'Bandy? Oh yes, yes. All of them. Excellent.' He paused. 'Why do you imagine the RNZN band is wedded to "Lemon tree very pretty", Sophie?'

Sophie snorted. 'I don't know.'

The Commodore moved away smiling.

'Why do you always have to *snort*?' said William.

'I don't know,' she said. 'I really don't know.'

The Commodore had been rereading *The Phaedo*. Did Sophie agree with the critics who said that Socrates' calm acceptance of his imminent death was because of his faith in the life hereafter?

'I haven't read it.'

'I'll leave it in your letterbox.'

She had found it there next morning in a plastic bag with two dead oleander petals left over from summer like the cat and the dog and the hats and the blowfly.

They were back with Socrates by the turn-off to the bridge.

'Christians would say . . .'

He swung a startled glance at her. 'Don't say that!'

'Why not?'

'Be one if you must. But don't . . .' His shoulders twitched beneath pinstripe. 'Soon you'll be talking about devout believers.'

'If I want to talk about devout believers,' she said as the car slowed down for the tolls, 'I will.'

He had a pleasant laugh. 'Good on you.'

They soared over the bridge with the sense of wellbeing experienced by those who remember the queues for the car ferry. 'I remember them,' he said, 'but Clarissa and I were in the UK when the bridge was built.' His dead wife was English. Clarissa. You cannot say it without a slight hiss in the middle but in fact the only person Sophie had heard say the name until this moment had been herself. Clar-iss-a. She murmured it on occasion. Clar-iss-a.

The Featherstons' house in Herne Bay was an old villa behind a high fence. The Renault made a sweeping crunch around the circular gravel drive and came to rest in front of a weatherbeaten black door with a ship's bell alongside.

Captain Featherston opened the door. He was short and spare and bald. His legs jigged with the excitement of greeting them. He took Sophie's hand briefly, a gentle English touching. 'Welcome. Welcome. We have met? Yes. Yes. Of course. Come in. Come in.'

But it was the Commodore the Captain loved. Their hands clasped, the shining eyes blinked with joy, the soft-shoe shuffle increased in momentum. He almost skipped. 'How good to see you, m'boy. How good to see you. Come in, come in, Lettie will be delighted.'

The entrance hall was square and dark with panelling. Panelling was a problem to some in the early sixties. It was dark and confining when the wished-for look was air and space. It enclosed and closeted. It did not reflect light, it absorbed. And yet it was present only in solid well-built houses. To rip or leave? No such thought had entered Captain and Mrs Featherston's minds. Age and declining health had brought them beyond such considerations, had brought them to the haven where if things dropped off they picked up the brass handle, the wooden finial, the broken pieces of an old plate and stowed them away, preferably in a small drawer in the piece of furniture from which they had fallen, and forgot all about them. Lionel and Lettie had long since ceased to hope for experts to repair. The rectangular room was covered with skittery old rugs with holes in them which crept about the floor or else lay supine, flat as a fawning gun dog at fault.

Beyond a table covered with papers, in front of an ashy fire the colour of dead roses, Mrs Featherston sat upright in a chair with arms. She also was delighted to see her dear boy and told him so several times, the slack underside of her upper arms wobbling as she reached to embrace his neck.

'Ah, Mrs Flynn,' she said eventually, extending a flaccid hand.

Her hair was white and thick, coiled about her head and secured with a single comb. It was well trained, there were no loose ends. Her ears were neat, finished with a tiny pleat of skin where they joined her face. Her hands also were beautiful, swollen at the knuckles but smooth and unmarked, their only ring a wide gold wedding band. Why bother to get the rest enlarged. It would have been different if Rose had lived.

Her pearls were large. These were not the product of oysters interfered with by man. These came from oysters in the wild; feral oysters, the pearls from which had been brought home to his bride by a sailor sixty years ago. Baroque gleaming things surrounded the neck which had more skin than necessary.

'And what is your opinion, Mrs Flynn?' said the Captain, placing his wife's sherry glass on a small table beside her hand and sucking his finger.

Sophie had been too busy looking. 'Sorry?'

'These visits. Do you think there's much point in them?'

'I hope so, but I don't know enough about what goes on at them.'

He nodded kindly. 'How could you my dear? How could you?'

Mrs Featherston lifted her glass. Her eyes, the same colour as her Flor Fino, were watchful.

'Edward was telling me Philomel's about to be visited by a VIP from a friendly Asian power.'

'And his consort,' murmured Sophie. She had returned the orange towelling. The pins were her own.

The Captain was not interested in consorts. 'Quite. But is there any point?'

Sophie bent forward. 'For visitors or visited?'

'For anyone?'

Sophie tried harder. 'I saw a book in the library the other day. In the returns, about Windsor Castle. In one of the pictures they were getting ready for a State banquet for the State visit of the head of state of a friendly power. For thirteen hundred people.'

'That's slightly different,' said the Captain, one navy canvas shoe tapping the wooden floor. The Captain had also given up on shoes. He had discovered canvas ones and was delighted with them though Lettie, he told Sophie later, was not so keen.

'Only as regards scale, surely,' said the Commodore.

'The table is so wide,' murmured Sophie, 'that there is a footman in the middle polishing, as well as one each side. He kneels on a cushion with white things over his socks.'

'Oh,' said the Captain.

Mrs Featherston hauled herself upright on the wooden arms of her chair. The Commodore leaped to his feet. The Captain gave a mini-heave and subsided once more. Sophie did nothing. Normally she would have insisted on assisting but she did not know the drill (William).

She did nothing. The men talked.

Mrs Featherston reappeared after some time. 'Come along,' she said, her voice brisk with the slight edge of the sick-of-it cook. As she walked to the dining room her right hand touched pieces of furniture as she passed, checking the disposition of her aids.

She admired Sophie's skirt. 'I speak as an expert patchworker,' she said. 'Some day I shall show you my rag bag.' Sophie thanked her.

They got on to World War II with the grapefruit; the blunders of strategy on land and sea, the problems of supply in the Western Desert. Was Wavell a scapegoat? Yes. No. And what about

Montgomery? Military genius or charlatan with luck?

The Captain had retired from the navy in 1937 and rejoined when war broke out.

'Offered my services to the Admiralty straight away,' he explained to Sophie, 'thought they'd say Good God, no. No room for deadbeats.' He chortled with happiness. 'Not a bit of it. Landed up on the Murmansk run. Commodore of a convoy for God's sake.' His eyes watered at the memory. 'Great days. Cold though. Very, wasn't it, boy?'

'Yes,' said Edward, putting down his spoon.

'Is that when you saved Edward's life?' asked Sophie.

Mrs Featherston stared at her disembowelled grapefruit.

The Captain looked shifty. 'No, no, earlier. Pulled him out, just pulled him out in time. Nothing more.'

Sophie knew about the war at sea. She had absorbed naval histories over William's shoulder, had studied photographs of ships blown up, of lone merchant ships which couldn't keep up and had to be left behind while the rest of the convoy steamed away over the horizon. Men were sliced in half, blown apart like their ships or drowned in their thousands like seabirds in oil.

'Yes, great days,' said the Captain, choking at the memory. 'Amazing luck getting another crack at my age.' He stowed the last of his juice. He had eaten his cherry first.

Sophie watched the Commodore. His face was lit by the straight flames of two tall candles as he sat listening to the old man who had had a good war and saved his life as well. His face was still, not a joke in sight. She had always suspected there were two Commodores. His 'Ha ha's at the bar and his 'ladies for taking' were a shield, a carapace to hide the better half. She had always suspected this, ever since she first saw him. She drew a deep breath. Her heart expanded.

The Commodore leaned forward. 'What's happened to the Stubbs?' His head gestured to an oil painting of a horse which hung on the wall. The Captain clasped the arms of his chair. 'Told you he'd spot it, didn't I, Lettie?'

There seemed little wrong with the horse, except its attenuated shape and the weird swooping curve of its neck.

The Captain, his cheekbones gleaming in the soft light, turned to Sophie. He gave a quick wave at the horse. 'Edward thought "Cracker" should be cleaned. We weren't too keen, were we, Lettie?' Mrs Featherston's napkin scrubbed her lips, either in agreement or dissent. 'Had a man up. Beefy sort of a cove from those people in town. Drove one of those . . .' His hands now indicated length: 'cigar cars.' Stood at the door over there, way over there, and said, "That's not a Stubbs."' The Captain sniffed. 'I didn't say if you can spot a non-Stubbs from fifteen feet you shouldn't be in a tin-pot little auctioneering business down there between the oil tanks and the marshalling yards. Didn't say that. Thought it, though. He did come nearer, of course, eventually, crawled all over the poor boy with his eyeglass, gave me a ludicrous price for cleaning him and left. Glad to see the back of him.'

The Commodore was still puzzled. 'But why did you remove the Stubbs tally?'

'He said it wasn't.'

'But he may not be right. Probably isn't. Jumped up little . . . Why take *his* word?'

The Captain's voice was shy. 'Difficult to say. Couldn't have the poor boy . . .'

'Flying false colours?' The Captain inspected Sophie. He shut the eye with the faster ripening cataract and stared at her face, misty but appealing in the soft light. He nodded. 'Yes.'

The Commodore tried again. 'But it's not false colours!'

'Might be.' He turned to Sophie again. 'One of my forebears was a stallion groom for some old baron. His widow didn't want the painting apparently. Nice isn't he, old "Cracker"? But think about it. Would you give your Stubbs to your stallion groom, Mrs Flynn?'

Nice man. 'But it wasn't then, was it?' she said. 'It was just a good painting of a horse your ancestor loved by a man called Stubbs. There hadn't been time for it to have become a *Stubbs*, if you see what I mean.'

Mrs Featherston touched her hair. 'No,' she said.

'I do. I do.' The Captain jigged happily in his chair. 'A thought, definitely a thought. You may well be right, my dear.'

The Commodore lifted his palms in defeat. He smiled at Sophie across the deep pools of light.

Mrs Featherston wound herself upright and inched round the table collecting discards. Sophie leaped up, the Commodore raised one hand and patted the air.

'No, no, m'dear,' said the Captain. 'We try to have two people sitting at the same time. Damn difficult to achieve.'

Sophie sat. The workers returned, the Commodore wheeling a squeaking trolley with dishes. Mrs Featherston served the casserole, peering at dismembered chicken legs before flinging them onto plates. They munched chicken chasseur beneath the wild-eyed stare of the archaic horse.

'What's this business of Kennedy increasing the number of advisers in Vietnam?' said the Captain tackling a leg. 'What's an *adviser*? You know, Edward?'

Edward chewed for a moment. 'One who advises.'

The Captain was unimpressed. 'Hhh. Increased to sixteen thousand last year I read. That's a lot of advice. Who asked for them?'

Edward looked him in the eye. 'The South Vietnamese. Diem.'

'Is he any good?'

'Who else is there?'

'Mmmn. Tricky, the Americans. Tricky lot. Never know which way they're going to jump. Not entirely. As for their Intelligence.'

The Commodore's glance was sharp.

'And what about this Nhu fellow?' The Captain shook his head. 'You know Truman was determined to keep out of South-East Asia at all costs.'

'So is Kennedy, from a fighting war.'

The Captain smacked his tongue against his front teeth. 'God, I hope so. Look at the French. Bogged down completely.' He gave another quick sniff. 'Sixteen thousand,' he said sadly. He was silent for a moment. 'Looks like UK investment down here's going up,' he said switching tracks. 'That's something for them, I suppose.'

Sophie stirred slightly on her chair. Them. Down here. 'Our birth rate's up again,' she said firmly.

'They always say that,' said Mrs Featherston, gloomily peering and flinging onto the Commodore's plate once more.

'Oh well, Lettie and I'll be under the sod soon,' said the Captain, obviously unconcerned at the prospect. There was a tiny pause as three of them remembered Rose, but not the Captain. Or if he did he had the sense to carry on like the Commodore after 'lurden is bight'. It is the only way.

They ate their baked custard and returned to the drawing room, Mrs Featherston gliding and touching as before, the Captain soft-shoe shuffling in the rear.

The Commodore carried the coffee tray, navigating with care past a top-heavy vase of agapanthus, daisies and dead hydrangeas which teetered on a small chest with a brass handle missing. Mrs Featherston raised her hands for the tray, her face serious, sacramental, a queen accepting her orb.

She made conversation. Children? Did Sophie have any? Yes, two, Rebecca and Christopher. 'Ah,' said her hostess.

The Captain jumped. 'What? What?'

'Mrs Flynn has two children,' said his wife.

'Oh.' The Captain shuffled himself into his chair and tossed a cushion onto the floor. It lay within the circle of light from the lamp, a deep square of apricot flooded with gold. 'Yes,' he said, and leaned back.

They talked once more about the visit of the friendly Asian power. About the Queen's visit next year. About the approaching visit of a Cat class cruiser which would be flying the flag of Rear Admiral Sir Thomas Tower who the Captain thought might be a son of Tommy Tower who was his Captain in HMS Something before the war. And wasn't there an Australian frigate due soon?

'Yes,' said the Commodore. 'Yes, quite soon.'

Silence drifted across the room. The Commodore excused himself and departed, his shadow dancing beside him on the wall. The door clunked.

Sophie smiled. The Captain stared at the ceiling. 'Yes,' he said again.

Mrs Featherston picked a thread from her wool jersey, made a half-hearted attempt to throw it on the fire and failed. Her frock was soft and draped, designed to soften sharp-angled age. The scent of the daisies was strong and not pleasant.

'You have a lot of papers,' said Sophie in desperation, nodding at the table in the middle of the room.

Mrs Featherston agreed.

'Are they all English?'

'Yes.'

'Oh.' The piles of papers heaved slightly before her eyes: the *Daily Telegraph*, the *Spectator*, the *Sunday Times*, the *Financial Times*. *Country* bloody *Life*. 'There's a lot of reading in them,' she said. She heard herself saying it. Dear God in heaven.

'We like to keep in touch.'

'Of course.' But it is a puzzle, is it not. Not the keeping in touch which is understandable, but the creating of an enclave where everything including the brand of mustard and the things you put on your toast at breakfast, the different things you put on your toast at teatime and the papers you read and the thoughts you think are not the thoughts of here. It has been going on for a long time, this enclave-building, sometimes against almost insuperable odds and in life-threatening situations this fear of going troppo has persisted.

Sophie saw herself discussing these thoughts with the Commodore on the drive home across the harbour, saw the streams of coloured lights jigging on the water. Heard his voice and smiled yet again.

Mrs Featherston smiled a faintly puzzled one back and closed her eyes.

The Captain's were already shut. He slept like the small hairless animal he was. He made snuffling noises. His mouth was open, his head back. His wife's sleep was more tidy. They were both dead to the world.

Sophie was bored. Where was the Commodore? He had now been gone for ten minutes which seemed a long time.

She picked up the topmost *Country Life* which had a yuletide-log gathering scene on the cover. She moved with care. The tedium is more obvious if you're caught in mid-snatch.

She read about wassail and the customs of the yule log, but her heart was unstirred. Her eyes kept returning to a small stuffed head (chamois? springbok? wildebeest?) which hung in a shadowy corner of the room. Even in the dim light the hair was soft and fluffy, the expression resigned as an early St Sebastian's. Nobody presumably, however keen on the killing, would want stuffed terror on the wall.

Sophie studied the Houses for Sale. She checked out a fully refurbished Regency house in the Vale of Aylesbury and an important Grade II Georgian country house in Sunningdale, Berkshire. The *Country Life* bird of the week was a crossbill. A snaggletoothed ivory fish on the opposite page had a voracious appetite.

Fifteen minutes now, which was ridiculous. The Captain's head had slipped forward, his wife's still rested against her cushion. Her profile was pleasing; aquiline nose, closed mouth. The Captain gave a small bark, an old dog dreaming. Sophie returned *Country Life* to the table and tiptoed from the room. The Commodore might be flat on the floor in the cloakroom. She ran across skiddy rugs, her heels clattering. The door was not locked. She was in another type of air lock, an ante-room to the lavatory which smelled of rubber boots and coats, both of which were present. There was a small handbasin with brown soap and a nailbrush. The face in the mirror above was troubled. She rattled the door. 'Edward. Are you in there?'

She rattled the handle again and flung the inner door open. Her image of slumped collapse was so vivid that the empty gleaming space was a surprise. She leaned against the wall, confronted by fading ships' photographs of rows of men with folded arms staring straight ahead through seventy years. There was also a sepia photograph of either a very large water rat or a low-slung dog.

Her faint panic had gone and about time too. Obviously, for reasons known to himself but not her, the Commodore, after pumping ship (William), had gone elsewhere. It is absurd tracking down a fellow guest in someone else's house but she was saved by a thought. The Captain and Mrs Featherston seem a little tired and perhaps they should slip away? Sophie wished to slip away very much indeed, to be together and alone. She left the lavatory. Nothing. Not a sound. She headed in the direction of the kitchen through a long narrow room lined with wooden cupboards and an old-fashioned safe with trickling water. Three pewter meat-covers hung on one wall. There was a wooden slide into the dining room and a closed door. For some reason she knocked. 'Come in,' called Edward.

His pinstriped jacket hung over one chair, a checked gingham apron frilled about his waist, his hands were immersed in soapy water. He placed a clean plate in a wooden drying rack by his left shoulder and smiled. 'Hullo,' he said.

Her inept shyness disappeared, the chill of Mrs Featherston's reception was irrelevant. She picked up another tea towel. 'Hullo.'

The Commodore was busy with a pot scrubber on the base of the casserole. His bald patch was an inch in diameter.

She took the casserole dish from his warm soapy hand. 'Why didn't you tell me?'

'Drain it a minute.' She smiled, turned it upside down, watched it slide on the ancient brown salami terazzo. Domesticity in the desired is endearing.

'I thought I'd come out for a few minutes. Break the back of it for Lettie.'

All by himself, scraping and scrubbing in this bleak outpost of the Empire.

'Why didn't you tell me?' she said again.

'No, no, I wanted you to enjoy yourself.'

'They're asleep,' she said, polishing a long-stemmed glass and longing for the Renault. The round wooden clock above the stove was ticking their lives away in finite bites. This life, she had learnt at Sunday school, was as the flight of a bird across a window, a brief glimpse, a moment of transition compared with aeons of life hereafter. Her love for Edward deepened. This good man had demonstrated unselfishness and caring for others in the here and now when there was so little left.

He turned to her, suds dripping, eyes shining. 'Both of them?'

She moved nearer. 'Yes.'

'Poor Sophie,' he murmured, wringing his white crochet dish-cloth and shaking it. They were close together as Mrs Featherston entered. They leaped apart. Mrs Featherston was not pleased. She was displeased and said so, punting up a more admissible reason for her displeasure. 'I would have thought, Edward, that you of all people would have known . . .' She glanced at Sophie. '. . . I dislike guests coming into my kitchen. It's so . . .' Words failed her.

The Commodore charmed her with shared memories and recognition of the customs of his country and the quaintness of some. 'I promise I won't do it again,' he said.

Mrs Featherston touched his shoulder briefly. 'I'll forgive you this time.' They left her stark kitchen to its quiet defeated gloom and faint whiff of compost bucket.

Captain Featherston was stamping himself into wakefulness as they re-entered. He stomped one canvas shoe, then the other, scrubbed them on the wrinkled rug beneath his feet and slammed his pink hands on his knees. 'Ah,' he said. 'There you are.'

Sophie's thanks were over-effusive. The Captain's farewell was as exuberant as his welcome, his face and hands still shone. Mrs Featherston's was cool.

They swept out the circular drive and drove towards the bridge.

'Whacko,' said Sophie.

His smile was beautiful. 'What?'

'I like it here.'

The car sped past solid well-treed houses.

Edward took her hand and placed it on his thigh. It lay at rest, oddly separate from her but at ease. 'Dearest Sophie,' he murmured.

'Tell me about Sufism,' she said as they swept past the Herne Bay Baths. The night was still, cloudless, a full moon was sailing above North Head where the tunnels are. The kaleidoscope reflections glinted on the harbour as she had known they would.

'I don't know much,' said the Commodore and told her.

They crossed the bridge at a glide, sailing away from the ridiculous confusions she had extracted from an evening of pleasure.

Edward turned towards Takapuna instead of Devonport. Sophie did not comment on this error. He pulled the car to a halt at the end of a blind road facing Takapuna Beach. Small waves slapped the sand; Rangitoto was a black cut-out against dark sky. 'Darling,' he said.

Sophie, who was aware of betrayal, turned to him. Snatching and grabbing in their fierce joy they reached for each other, their mouths busy as their hands. 'My darling, my sweetest love.' The moon shone.

Her breasts were covered by his bent head. 'Christ, we can't stay here,' he muttered as two shadows slipped past the car, 'the whole of Philomel'll be rooting down there.'

She did not laugh. It was not a joke. After some time he leaned back. 'What are we going to do?'

Indecisions, guilt, irrelevancies would have to wait. 'We'll go home now,' she said, 'and later we'll have to get away somewhere.'

'Home?'

'Mine. Ours.'

His voice was desperate. 'We can't.' This man was not using her for an easy lay (William). She knew he was not. She would go to the stake for this belief but that is easy to say is it not. Her legs navigated the gear lever as she leaned across to kiss the shape of his mouth. His cheek was rough, he had not had a second shave this evening. 'Would you do that,' he said, 'go away somewhere?'

Her hand was in his hair. 'If I can get someone to mind the children.' It was now stroking his face, lingering on the cheekbone which was not shiny at all, exploring the dip beneath, tracing the mouth with one finger.

'You would?'

'Yes.'

'Where? Where would be safe?'

Nowhere.

'I'll think of somewhere,' she said. 'Up north. The hot pools.'

'I'll park the car along the road,' he said on the Gasworks straight. 'Wait till I see the babysitter leave. That's her old Hillman, isn't it? The red one?'

'Yes.'

'Then I'll walk back.'

'Good.' How simple life is when you plan ahead. 'Good,' she said again.

Lou had also gone to sleep. Her mouth was open, her legs spread wide, her snore a muted whistling. Her crocheted squares lay beside her splayed bare feet which were tipped with silver. When she has enough ecru squares she will crochet them together to form a double bedspread beneath which she and Evan will lie for ever. It is tomorrow's heirloom today. Lou has sixty-five squares already. She counts them every day. She can understand misers, she says. And squirrels.

Sophie rubbed her sleeping shoulder till she woke. 'Oh,' said the babysitter. 'I must've dropped off.'

'Lou,' said Sophie handing over the money. 'Would you, and Evan, if he'd like, would you babysit here—for a whole weekend?' Lou's eyes were remarkable. They were not large and her round face made them appear smaller. When she smiled they were invisible. But they were so bright, of such a deep fierce blue, outlined with such thick black twigs of mascara they appeared to glitter at the beholder. Her mind was busy, the tip of her tongue visible.

'How much?'

'I'd have to work it out.' Hardly a bean, hardly a bean in the house till the next allotment. 'I'm going to get a job but I haven't anything yet,' said Sophie, 'so it couldn't be for a few weeks.'

Lou's raisin eyes were sharp. 'Mum's veins are on the blink again. You could shampoo and hand up the pins on Fridays for me till it's even, if you like.'

Sophie felt like hugging her. All you have to do is grip, nudge, shove the world. 'Great,' she said. 'Wonderful.'

Lou's tiny white hand pressed one side of her lilac-blue head. The fingers ended in pointed scalp-scratchers. She looked at Sophie thoughtfully. Why didn't she dump the kids with her neighbour, Nancy, as per usual.

All the Road wives were Lou and Evan's clients. The relationships were relaxed. Lou was formal only with Mrs Pickett. Not because she was the Captain's wife and awareness of hierarchy was endemic in the road. There was something about Mrs Pickett. A presence.

Lou yawned in Sophie's face and departed, clutching her fee and her squares in a white pillowcase to keep them clean.

Sophie stood in the draughty hall. Dirty weekends and bits on the side were not the words she needed.

Celia had lent her *Tropic of Capricorn* recently, which she found interesting. Did all men, well, go *on* about women all the time like that. She asked William. Did he?

He looked at her above the *Advertiser*. 'When there's a new intake of Wrens I sometimes look at their legs. Just a quick glance.' He folded the paper. 'The last lot were a disaster.'

Sophie sat on the pseudo-oak chest.

'You look like a nun,' said Edward at the open door. 'A nun listening.' He clamped her wrist, pulled her upright.

An arrival's anchor chain rattled. A nearby cruise ship was leaving with a wail of despair. The binoculars on the window sill remained untouched. Pacific Star's pilot would have to do without Edward's surveillance. His mind was reeling with astonishment as they fell to the floor. What the hell was he doing. Commodores don't, can't, don't. Not with wives. Not naval wives, junior or senior. Not *wives.* He was ambitious. Keen. The top job was within his grasp. Wives were not on.

He pulled himself back from her, leaned on one elbow, studied her smile, eyes, breasts.

He heard his voice. 'I love you.'

'I know.'

'And you have good nipples.'

'Doesn't everyone?'

'No.'

He pleasured her. Gave her startling unexpected treats. They loved each other. They gave their all.

They lay spent and gasping on the haircord. 'Ssh,' said Sophie.

His eyes were closed. 'What?'

She was kneeling, her ear to the floor.

He opened his eyes. She had a beautiful bum. He put out one hand.

'No, no, listen!'

He rolled over. Listened. Nothing.

'What the . . . ?'

She leaped to her feet, grabbed his jacket, fumbled with the locked French doors and ran down the verandah steps. 'Ches, Ches. I'm coming. I'm coming.'

He followed her, his hands fumbling with shirt buttons, his eyes flicking at the darkened houses alongside. She was invisible but still calling. A door slammed open in the decking below, a shape shot across the dark lawn followed by Sophie still calling. A sudden dog yapping. A light next door. God in heaven. He backed indoors.

Sophie ran up the steps with the distracted cat yowling in her arms, murmuring, loving, caressing the thing all over his pinstripe. Her face was pink with joy. 'Isn't it wonderful! I'll go and feed him.'

Edward turned off the overhead light. The Ogilvies' light had been a signal, clear as the yellow-blue-yellow of Flag D for Danger. It also increased his excitement, his amazement at this woman who rolled around fucking him silly and fed cats.

This woman was different, this woman was worth it, he could *live* with this woman. Gratitude, wonder, plus the whiff of gunpowder from next door seemed to be producing some sort of frenzy. He loved this woman for Christ's sake.

She came back after some time, naked except for his double-breasted cat-haired pinstripe. He moved his head above the tented shirt, startled by the instant return of longing. The jacket ended neatly at the junction of her infinite legs.

He almost stumbled towards her. 'Not a nun in sight.'

She smiled, unbuttoned the jacket, welcomed him. 'He's all right now,' she said.

'What?'

She moved against him. 'Chester.'

'Oh good,' he gasped. 'Good.'

'He's been lost since Sunday.' She nibbled his ear.

'Jesus,' he moaned.

'I know. But he's all right now.'

FIVE

'*Tea*! ' bellowed Kit from the door. Sophie burrowed deeper. She wished to dream. Three hours was not enough. She was unwell.

Kit bounced, his arms wide for the kiss he was almost too old for (William). The tea spilt. She closed her eyes.

'Mum.' He was now dancing beside the bed. 'Come *on*—and what's Chester doing here?'

Dear God. She blundered down the hall, pursued by Chester dancing on his hind legs, shadow-boxing the air for food. The telephone rang for some time. She handed it to Kit. 'She'll be asleep. Tell her we've found him and he's all right. Come on, Chester.' He zig-zagged between her bare feet, his meows tearing her brain.

Sophie was abstracted, almost vacant at the kitchen bench. Images of last night filled her mind, left her with her mouth open and the Vegemite knife poised above half-spread brown. Rebecca and Kit made no comment. A vertical mother is operational. All children know this, as do their fathers. Sandwiches were snatched, hugs returned. Time was precious. The best bit is before the bell goes.

Edward stood at the back door, half-hidden behind a raft of

bronze chrysanthemums. The peppery smell filled the space, overpowered the soap powder. He shoved them at her laughing, one hand knocking the tiny card envelope. He had no time either. He was due at Whenuapai at oh nine double oh for a wash-up of the joint exercises. He stood for a second, one palm flat against the side of her face. 'Soon,' he said and was gone.

Sophie sat on the red painted stool, the inside of her head a Wall of Death with motorbikes. He would have had to have been in Devonport at sparrow fart (William), buy the flowers, a risky process in itself in a sleepy hollow, then stop in her drive, knock on her open door, risk observation from all quarters to deliver these long-lasting sculpted heads. This token of regard. Her fingers snatched at the card's envelope. She tore it open, a famished carnivore getting to the heart of the message. It was brief but adequate. Enough in all conscience. 'Sweetest love,' it said.

She shoved it between her breasts, the miscast heroine of a busty romantic epic. The pasteboard was sharp. She could feel it as she heaved the whites into the washing machine and immersed the flowers up to their necks in cool cool water. They filled the bucket. They were abundant. They needed stripping, their stalks must be cut.

Liz strolled down the hall. 'Hullo,' said Sophie, her hands moving with the precision of a sapper's on her unexploded bomb. She waited for the inevitable question, felt it homing between her shoulders. 'Who are they from?' said Liz.

Sophie turned to her friend. 'William.'

'Good heavens.'

'It's one of our anniversaries. You know those weird ones.'

'No.'

'Tin and paper and stuff.'

'And this is?'

'I can't remember.'

Liz flicked the topic away with one hand. 'Have you seen Celia lately?'

'Yes. Haven't you?'

'No,' said Liz, scrutinising the whites now slapping about in the Bendix.

Sophie's reeling head cocked to one side, a pre-strike thrush with problems. 'That's her now.'

Liz disappeared, graceful in retreat to the whirlygig clothesline and the box of feijoas rotting by the back door.

Sophie's fingers touched pasteboard. 'Hullo,' she said. 'Liz has just left.'

Celia marched ahead of her and reached for her cat mug. 'She's a fast mover that one. How were the Featherstons?'

Chester caressed her legs, twined and recaressed, patted a paw against a knee.

'He's Mary's.' Grand Central Station was now clashing with the Wall of Death. 'That's her now.'

Mary dashed past them to snatch Chester in her arms; to moan with relief, to bury her head in his neck, to adore. 'Where was he? Where, where?'

Sophie's voice was cautious. 'Under the house.'

'But he must've been there on Sunday. How did you hear him and not us?'

'I was lying on the floor in the sitting room.'

Celia centred her mug. Her finger traced the line of the uplifted leg. Her eyes were down. 'I'm so glad he's safe,' she murmured.

'Come and tell Arnie,' said Mary.

They dumped Chester on the way, waved at Evan and Lou, exchanged good mornings with the wife of a Sikh bus driver who was pegging her husband's wide white trousers on the line.

So that's how they work, is it. Six foot at the top, then tapering. She must tell Edward. Everything was to be shared, rejoiced in, taken to lay before the object of her desire like a bower bird's loot. Sophie sniffed the bright air.

'I've got a job,' she said, one hand on the galleon gate's latch.

'What?'

'I'm going to hand up the pins for Lou on Fridays. While her

Mum's on the blink.'

'God, you're a nutter.'

Arnie's front door was open. They walked down the dark hall to the kitchen.

'Arnie,' called Mary. 'We've found Chester.'

The voice from the bathroom was faint. 'Don't come. I'm not well.'

A door slammed. They moved into the fernery, stared at each other and back to the door.

'What's wrong?' said Mary.

'Go away! Go away.'

The sounds were not reassuring. A lavatory flushed, taps ran, there was lurching, bumping, then total silence. Mary's face was white.

'I'm a nurse,' lied Sophie and opened the bathroom door.

Arnie stood with his head hanging, his body slumped against the handbasin, his arms bent with the effort of supporting his body. His face was grey, sweating.

'Go away,' he whispered. 'I'm not well.'

'I'm a nurse,' said Sophie again. Nurses, like cops and Salvation Army, are allowed. Sophie shut the door on Mary's face. Arnie's striped winceyette pyjamas lay around his feet, his withered hams were stained with brown. The lavatory was not good, nor the floor.

'I had an accident,' he gasped.

'It's all right,' said Sophie and got on with it. The silence was broken by his shame, his apologies, his broken gasps.

'Sssh. Sssh, Mr McNally.'

His gasp turned to a hiccoughing sob. 'Arnie,' he said.

'That's better,' said Nurse Nurse as she dried the shaking legs. 'Where do I find pyjamas?'

Sophie and Mary sat either side of his bed. Mary looked slightly green. The perfect balance of her small high-cheekboned face seemed to have slipped, become flawed.

'Who's your doctor, Arnie?' said Sophie, adjusting the chenille bed cover with a professional tug of one hand.

His eyes were closed. 'I haven't seen one since they killed Win.'
'There's nothing in the house except the heel of a loaf and some milk,' said Mary.
Sophie bent forward. 'Come and stay a few days with me and the children, Arnie.'
The block-like head moved.
'Just till you're better. I'll get you on your feet in no time,' said the pro.
Arnie's eyes opened. He passed his hand across them, pressed briefly and stared again. 'No, Mrs . . .'
'Sophie.'
'Sophie,' he murmured tasting it, 'Sophie.'

'What are you *doing*, Soph,' said Mary as she slammed the gate.
'You heard.'
'Is this some Christian kick? The man's not an idiot.'
'There's no one else.'
'So who are you to sweep in like Madam la Fat?'
'He can't look after himself at the moment. When he can . . .'
'He probably wants to die anyway.'
'Like that? Starving in his own shit?'
Mary was silent.
'I'll get him organised with Dr Pleasance. Get Meals on Wheels started again.' Sophie's finger touched a small galleon. 'But you'll have to look after him if he's not a hundred per cent by Queen's birthday.'
'Why?'
'I'm going up north.'
'Who with?'
Sophie studied her sister. Mary had ditched a good job and was thus suspect, irresponsible and untrustworthy (William). Sophie had not bothered to argue. She knew Mary. Had always known her. She touched the length of hair beneath the pepper tree.
'With Edward Sand.'
'Huh?'

'The Commodore.'

'Oh my Gaad.'

'Shut up, you smug little twit.'

Mary's mouth dropped. 'Come and see Bertha. Quickly.'

She dragged her along the road, ran up the stairs. 'Bertha,' she called. 'Bertha, we've found Chester.'

Bertha lifted her arms and slammed them on her knees, a type-cast Italian momma unexpectedly encased in denim. 'Where is my boy?' She was moving with speedy grace (once a hoofer always a hoofer) to the outside staircase.

'No, no, later.' Mary dropped to the floor, reassembled her limbs. 'Wait till you hear about Soph.'

'Sophie,' snapped her sister.

'Sophie, Soph, what does it matter?'

'It matters to me and I'm it.'

'What's got into you?' Mary paused. 'Don't answer that.'

Rage clenched her insides. 'How dare you!' yelled Sophie. 'Take something good and true . . .'

'Good and *true*.'

'What do you know? What do you know about anything? Nothing. Not a thing. I don't bitch about Ben.'

'Soph-ee,' said Mary moving towards her.

'Bugger off.'

Bertha stepped between them. She loved both young women with unflagging warmth. They were her best thing. She looked at Sophie's radiant face. This was not the face of anger. Presumably the man lived nearby who was causing this incandescence, shining the hair, transforming the child into some other being. And so vulnerable. So hopelessly bloody vulnerable. Bertha hugged her. 'What's going on, Sophie?'

A tanker gave a sick-cow bellow. No one glanced at it. Sophie's eyes were on Bertha as fan dancer. 'Did you love more than one man, Bertha?'

'Good heavens yes.'

'Did Bryan mind?' Bryan Boniface had been Bertha's tea

planter husband. Mary swore he was an apocryphal figure, not worthy of Bertha's robust past.

'I can't really remember,' said Bertha, picking her way briskly through the overstuffed room to the kitchen and real coffee with hot milk for comfort.

Sophie moved to the sunporch. The mangy lawn below had not greened up after summer. Mary licked her lips.

Bertha's voice called from the kitchen. 'But then we didn't have any children,' she said.

'You know Ben and I'd be happy to mind the kids,' said Mary, one sandal caressing Chester's belly.

'You don't like Edward.'

'What's that got to do with it?'

'Everything.'

Mary's mouth tightened. What was going on. Soph of all people.

'So how'll you get the money to pay Lou? Queen's birthday's the week after next.'

Sophie's smile embraced Calliope Road, shone on the windows of *A Cut Ahead*, gleamed from Evan's sluiced pavement. 'Lou's going to give her time on tick. I'll make it up later.'

Arnie McNally lay thinking. The high-ceilinged room was still and sunless. There was little furniture: a wire-wove double bed, a chipped and varnished chest of drawers, a bedside table on which Sophie's bowl of bread and milk lay untouched. Bread and milk. Sweet Jesus. It was seventy years or more since Effie, the next one up, had shovelled it into his hungry little gob and he'd begged for more and there was never enough with nine kids and a stinking getty out the back. The white cotton curtains stirred, the chenille tufts lay in rows beneath his hands. There were no photographs or pictures in the room. He had shoved them behind the Patient's Effects suitcase, shut the door on them. The room was empty except for a half-dead old bugger who used to be Arnie McNally from Tyneside. He'd got away though, hadn't he. Got away from the cold and the bleak streets and the hunger. And now look at him. Arnie laughed. A sound between a creak and a groan filled the empty room.

He put out a hand. 'Win,' he said. 'Win.'

He went with Sophie the next day. He trusted her. She made no fuss and nor did he, as long as she promised to take him down once a week to water the ferns.

'But Mary'll do it, Arnie. She's practically next door.'

'No.'

'Just as you like.'

A sensible woman. And sonsy with it.

The cardboard suitcase was installed in a small room beside the bathroom. There were no more accidents. Arnie slept, drank soup, talked to Kit as he became stronger. They yarned on the verandah. He wouldn't touch William's binoculars. He reviewed the harbour daily with his own ancient pair. Spare, rudimentary, uncluttered as a Victorian naturalist's microscope, they hung from a cracked leather strap around his neck.

'Why have they got string on the case, Arnie?' asked Kit.

'Ropework, boy, ropework.'

'Did you do it?'

'Yes.'

'Neat eh.'

Rebecca ignored him. He took too long in the toilet and she couldn't understand him anyway.

Sophie sat on the front steps with William's blue envelope unopened in her hand. Bertha's words had stayed with her. Her love for her children was fierce, self-excluding, die-for-them stuff. Living for them was trickier. But it was just a question of working things out. She stretched her legs to the sunlight, a green girl remembering. Even the first kiss had been memorable, a tentative brushing movement of the lips, an osculatory exploration, a beautiful build-up. Not just a damp clamp, though that happened later, before further exploration which continued, she remembered, for some time. It had not been a quick peck behind the Chapel of St Christopher. Quite the reverse.

He rang her every day. When the telephone rang, Sophie knew instantly, inevitably, and every time a coconut when it was Edward. They did not talk long. The times, usually during school hours, varied. They did not say much. Hullo, they said. Hullo. They didn't talk about themselves. She didn't know what they talked about. Sometimes he told her something he had discovered and vice versa. They had a code. When he first suggested it Sophie thought it was slightly, well, nuts. 'Tap your fingernails on the mouthpiece,' he said. 'How many days?' Now, tense with excitement, she signals the countdown. Fourteen.

She opened her letter. William's last one had not filled her with longing. During a run ashore William and the other officers had timed the local hula ladies' hip movements on their stopwatches. She saw the scene clearly, the strong brown knees of the men of the Royal New Zealand Navy visible between white shorts and long white or blue stockings and the ladies dancing so skilfully and smiling withal. Saw the coconut palms and the lapping surf. There were 140 hip movements per minute, wrote William, which is a lot of hip movements. 'Much love, William.'

William's writing was legible, crisp and clear, the stamp placed foursquare in the corner. A stamp placed upside down was an insult to the Queen, according to his great-aunt Una. Information which Sophie had found interesting at the time and smacking of graven images.

William wrote of the training programme at sea and how well his ship had done in the combined exercises especially the night trials, and how pleased William was and how the Old Man was also. William told her how the young sailors from Tamaki were shaping up on their first time at sea (good), about the outbreak of cockroaches in the galley (bad) and his dislike for the engineer who is a shit but don't hand it on. I know what your hen parties are like. How are the kids? Much love to you all, William.

Last year before Christmas Sophie and her neighbour had made an abortive attempt to sell some of their old wedding presents. They had stood in the queue for the ferry gangway clutching Pusser's Green suitcases, watching the water slapping the barnacle-encrusted piles beneath the wharf. A small child in gumboots swung whining on his mother's hand. 'Mum,' he begged once more, 'I *want* it, Mum.'

'That's your trouble,' she snapped. 'You want the lot, don't you.'

But don't we all, lady. Don't we all. Trikes, bikes, chuddy, love. We all take our pleasures differently.

They were surrounded by grey-haired women in spectacles with pudding-basin haircuts. Four, five; too many for comfort. A man with a beard stood staring with his mouth open. It had been a relief to get off the boat.

Sophie answered William's letter. She did not tell him that she had been unfaithful. Un-faith-ful. She did not tell him she had slept with another man. She did not tell him their marriage was over. She would tell him later. She would tell him when his ship came home. She sat at the battered table which he was going to restain as soon as he got round to it and sucked a yellow ballpoint. There was another cruise ship moored across the harbour. Passengers paid hundreds of US dollars a day and cruised for thirty. Arnie and Sophie had agreed the money should be redistributed. They had also agreed this was unlikely to happen.

She told William about the parent-teacher evening and Rebecca and Kit's satisfactory reports. She did not tell him the headmaster had said Kit would not set the world on fire because she did not believe it and how could you possibly know at seven. She was not concerned by this comment but William would be. She would tell him later. She told William that the Scarlet Runners had now withered completely and she would dig over the vegetable plot ready for planting. William was keen on his vegetable garden. He was more assiduous than she at disposing of excess. He strode along the road night after night in the peak season dispensing largesse and avoiding waste. Sophie was unfussed by rotting plenitude. Mouldering fruit and the sharp wasp-attracting tang of corruption were familiar as household words to her. Piles of green torpedo-shaped feijoas rotting beneath the tree on the front lawn and by the back steps worried her not at all. Waste was a fact of life. William fought it tooth and nail.

'We have an old man called Arnie McNally staying with us for a week or two till he gets on his feet,' she wrote. 'He used to be on my Meals on Wheels run. Chester has been lost but is found again.' The biro leaked purple, a thick oozing trail of demise.

'Good to hear the exercises are going well, particularly the night ones,' she wrote with a replacement from the bookcase.

'Love from us all. Sophie.'

Arnie came in from his rest, his slippered feet soundless on the haircord. One of the slippers had split. Sophie was staring straight ahead. He watched her for a moment.

'What is it, lass?'

She swung round. 'Arnie,' she said. 'Oh, Arnie.' Her eyes were huge. 'The parents' evening was awful,' she said.

He lowered himself into a chair, a reverse levering process which took some time.

'Last night?'

'Yes.'

'Tell me.'

'It was . . .' She couldn't say boring. It hadn't been. It had been, no, not alarming, how ridiculous. But something. Arnie, Rebecca and Kit had minded one another. She had been home by eight-thirty.

'There are men, there are women and there are parents,' the head told the mother in front of Sophie, who wanted her son put up a class because his teacher did nothing but play 'Coming through the Rye' all day on the recorder.

Gin a body kiss a body
Need a body cry?

Of course not. That is the thing about obsession. Everything is filtered through it. The Art Work papier-mâché policemen in Rebecca's classroom leered at the maidens beside them whose sexpot lips and black-ringed eyes relayed the message back. The white mice were hot as monkeys, Sophie knew they were. She could hear their frenetic rustlings amongst the torn scraps of paper in their cage. White mice are too naked and too quick and pink as well.

The colour, the exuberance of the paintings in Kit's room seduced her. When do they learn, these painters, that arms should match, that eyes should tally and lips must smile?

There were no problems with Rebecca, the head told her, but she knew this already. 'As for Christopher—remember the school motto: "They who do their best do well." He probably won't set the Thames on fire, but he's a nice lad.'

'Why the Thames?' snarled Sophie.

She walked home up Calliope Road through air which was too warm for winter.

The light was on in the Commodore's study. Nothing stirred. She glanced up and down the road then walked with head high, up the curved path to the front door. She was on business bent. She rang the bell, kept her back to the road and sweated. Edward still had his pen in his hand. 'Sophie!' He pulled her in, shut the door, gaped at her. 'My dear girl, you can't come here.'

Arms splayed against the door like a forties film heroine, Sophie nodded. 'I know.'

'Tollerton's just this minute left.'

'I came on business.'

He smiled. 'Navy League or Welfare?'

'I haven't thanked you in person for the flowers.'

'Oh,' he laughed at her breathless wit and welcomed her. 'That's all right, then,' he said. 'So long as it's business.'

'Are you sure you know what you're doing?' he said later. 'This old man? How're you going to get rid of him? And anyway. I mean, he's *there*, isn't he?'

'I know what I'm doing,' she said. 'And yes, he is there.'

'Come fishing, Sophie,' said Bertha. 'I want to talk to you.'

'No thanks. Come and meet Arnie.' The meeting was a success. Arnie had fished at the wharf till his legs gave out on him. They discussed bait, the vagaries of the tide, the seasons. Did Arnie think piper fish were worth the effort? 'No.'

Bertha agreed. 'Though they're fun for kids when they're running.'

'When,' said Arnie. He was dry, dry as parched riverbeds, the only hint of a joke the glint in his watery blue eye. His chuckle was a dry gurgle and worth waiting for.

'My dear, we screamed,' reported Bertha inaccurately.

'Where's Arnie?' yelled Kit each afternoon before he ditched his school bag.

'Here, boy, here.' Behind jigging the cushion of his chair sideways in excitement, Arnie waited on the verandah.

'Did that tanker go out?'

'Not yet.'

'Good.'

They watched a Chinese junk sail up the harbour, remote and mysterious as someone else's dream. They put down their binoculars, turned to each other and smiled.

'Any good?'

'Aye.'

Arnie's presence acted as a buffer, a shield. He defused gossip. When Celia or Liz appeared, he heaved himself upright on stiff knees, bowed his head in greeting and departed to his room. They came less often. Celia appeared to have lost her grip on who was fucking whom. Gossip is not confrontation. You don't have to see them at it.

'Celia's stopped coming,' she told Edward. 'And Liz.'

'Good.'

'Is Celia happy, do you think?'

He paused. 'How many days?'

'Twelve.'

They had forgotten about Sufism.

They made plans.

'Arnie?'

'Yes?' He was mending his slipper, restowing the extruded horsehair with an awl and sail-maker's palm collected from his ditty-bag in the dead fernery.

'Will you go and stay with Mary and her friend Ben for Queen's birthday?'

'I'll go home.'

'No! Not till you've been assessed. Dr Pleasance said.'

He stared at her above his glasses. 'How many days?'

She moved her head, momentarily punch-drunk, momentarily defeated by the phrase.

'Three.'

'Three it is. There's the phone.'

Mrs Slater from Holy Trinity Brass was in a panic. Eunice Glover had come down with a lurgy and she knew it was short notice but could Sophie slip down?

Bit of a problem there, Mrs Slater. I have sinned and am no more worthy, see. 'Now?'

'Well, yes.'

'All right. If you're stuck.'

The Vicar was confiding his love of chokos to two polishing heads. Chokos were his favourites. Mrs Webster and Mrs Slater glanced at each other above their blackened rags. Their lips were pursed. They found chokos tasteless and bland. Sophie could see it in their shared rejection, their dismissive twitchings, their head shakings. They took Mr Farrell's divergence re chokos personally. They themselves scarcely bothered to pick the chunky green pendants from the vines which tumbled over their respective woodsheds each summer in evidence of the bounty of the Lord.

'Perhaps,' murmured Mr Farrell deprecatingly, having caught their drift, 'they are an acquired taste.' He thanked them all and slipped away. Mrs Webster gave Sophie some clean rags. Did Sophie know that the right hand of a pair of rubber gloves usually wears out first if you're right-handed and the thing to do when this occurs is to turn one inside out? They left soon afterwards. They had done their bit.

Sophie restowed the cleaned vases in the dusty room beside the vestry and washed her hands. The shadowy reflection in the mirror was dislocated and out of place, a face glimpsed below water. She shut one eye at herself.

She sat in the back pew of the church, her eyes on the small red light at the end of the nave. The brass gleamed. The Adoration of the Magi window was hectic: blue, carmine and livid green. There was a memorial to the fallen.

Old Mr Farrell lurched from the vestry, still in his rusty black cassock. His movements were fast but the mechanism was faulty. He crashed up the wide chancel steps to the altar and flung himself on arthritic knees, his arms stretched wide as he prostrated himself before his risen Lord on Wednesday morning in the empty church of the Holy Trinity, Devonport.

Mr Farrell had not glanced anywhere but straight in front of him. All his attention had been fixed on getting to the altar so he could give thanks with an extravagant rapture which Sophie had never seen Freddy Farrell (William) display before his congregation. A theatrical Wise Man's gesture; Melchior, or more likely Balthazar, at the satisfactory conclusion of the search. Mr Farrell had kept his faith alive, steely and strong as the bridge. Its brightness had remained undimmed through vestry squabbles, doctrinal difficulties, badminton every Thursday and the successional problem in the Mothers' Union. Mr Farrell knew that his Redeemer lived, like Padre Bell but more so.

The Vicar dragged himself upright from the altar and turned to begin his heave down the nave.

'Sophie, my dear,' he called, 'is that you?'

She had forgotten about their shared long sight. They had joked about it. Wondered to what useful purpose they might put this useless gift.

'Yes.'

They met mid-nave and held hands. Mr Farrell's face, old, tanned and hooked about the nose, was anxious. 'Are you all right, Sophie?'

Sophie blinked. The thing is Mr Farrell I desire a man other than my husband. I lust after this man Mr Farrell. And what's more I'm going to keep doing so.

Mr Farrell was waiting. He had had a good war, Mr Farrell, had won gongs and been ordained later. This old man had known it all, had known the brutality and the valour, the scream and stench of war.

'There's a fly somewhere,' said Sophie.

The lean carved face was puzzled. Their hands still held. 'Fly?'

'Can't you hear it? A blowfly buzzing.'

'A spider perhaps? He's caught it, I mean.' The Vicar stared up into the dark timbered roof in search of spiders.

'Possibly.' The moment had passed. She had avoided confession.

She would not burden Mr Farrell with her lewd thoughts, her gross desires. She had never had any intention of doing so. They were not his part of ship.

The combined exercises with the Yanks and the Aussies had gone extremely well. There is a buzz, wrote William, that we may be given a pierhead jump to Hawaii instead of coming straight home. For further in-depth exercises with the Yanks. The situation in Asia, well, never mind. William would like to give Sophie a big hug and kiss. Only a few more weeks now with any luck. Fondest love. William. PS. Hey you kids, I hope you are helping Mum. If we make it to Hawaii, I'll bring you a pineapple apiece. Pineapple Poll, eh Becca? Much love, Dad.

'What's a Pineapple Poll?' said Rebecca straightening the

knives and forks Sophie had flung on the table.

'A dance, isn't it?'

'Tap?'

'No.'

'Oh.'

When Rebecca was little and William was at sea for months, she and Sophie had had a nightly ritual. Rebecca had kissed her father goodnight. Cherub lips made aquarium kissing motions against the cold glass behind which William smiled in cap and doeskin. It didn't work though. Rebecca became confused when the tall dark stranger returned. Sophie found her alone in her room in her pink pyjamas with feet, kissing the glass Daddy. Sophie hid the photograph beneath outgrown baby clothes in the small white chest of drawers painted by William before Rebecca's birth. He had left the wooden knob handles till later so he would know whether he should paint them pink or blue. He was glad it was pink.

SIX

Edward made the booking at the motel. Sophie would take their car which was anonymous, or more so than the Commodore's Renault. William was proud of his new Holden. It was the first new car he had owned—an automatic with good road-holding capabilities which handled well and had plenty under the bonnet.

There remained the rendezvous.

'The bakery in Belmont?'

This was no time for jokes. 'Try harder,' she said.

'I like the yeasty smell. I worked in one after school. Ed Sand the baker's hand.'

'Try harder.'

Lane's Bakery was not a good meeting-place. It was too exposed, too populated, too like the rendezvous it turned out to be as wives and mariners joined the queue for their Viennas, their half barracoutas, their occasional Sally Lunns.

Rebecca and Kit stood dancing and waving farewell beside Lou who had mapped out a programme. It was full of delights and did not include Church Parade.

Sophie stood beside Outsize Books in the Takapuna Library and waited for her lover. She was relaxed. 'Nobody's going to look at you,' her mother had said when Sophie panicked before school socials. A useful memory.

He came through the door smiling, his Pusser's canvas grip an exact replica of William's.

'Hullo.'

'Hullo.' Joy, pure flagrant joy descended, enriched, socked it to her. She kept her head. 'I'll go out first, give me a few minutes.'

The car joined the programmed queue of holiday weekenders heading north through the Bays. Edward's eyes flicked past the miles of ice-cream slab houses as they passed: vanilla, peach parfait, banana, a chocolate mocha surrounded by a sprouting ponga log fence.

'I've never had an automatic. Ever have problems remembering to fling away your left foot?'

She shook her head. 'Nope.' A camping ground loomed and disappeared. 'We stayed there once,' she said.

'What was it like?'

'Not good.'

Not good at all. William had bought a small second-hand tent and insisted they had a dry run before tackling the East Coast. He wished to make sure all was shipshape. He wished to check the guy ropes and procedures for loosening them if necessary, to make sure there were the correct number of tent poles, flys and pegs. The four of them crouched side by side in the damp tent (don't *touch* it), gazing across to the camps of the regulars, the long termers, the bronzed hairy men and friendly women in their homes away from home who laughed and drank beer and had fun surrounded by wooden cupboards and useful gear. 'Will it be like this at Anaura Bay, Mum?' asked Kit as their neighbour Ena tottered back red-faced from the communal kitchen clutching an enormous frying pan of steaming chow mein. 'No,' said Sophie, 'no, it won't.'

It was idyllic. The children had a pup tent and William and Sophie made love once or twice. A fat moon beat a path to the island. She could see it when she sat up.

*

They were both quiet on arrival.

'Well,' said Edward outside the door labelled 'Reception'.

He came back swinging the room key. 'Three. Clarissa's lucky number.'

Sophie was startled into nonsense. 'She had one?'

'Yes. Fortune tellers, astrologers, the lot.'

'Oh.'

They loved each other. Astonishing things, amazing unforeseen things happened. He begged for more and gave them back. They lay in each other's arms on the wide bed afterwards listening to the silence of their own world.

He turned to her. 'You are the most honest woman I have ever known.'

She laughed aloud at the absurdity. A pohutukawa tree waved near the window. A car changed gear.

'Tell me,' he said later. 'Why did you marry young Flynn?'

'William.'

'William,' he said kissing her nose.

'Because he asked me.'

'But you were only nineteen.'

'Yes.'

He lay back, his eyes on the reproduction of a red-robed dancer flamencoing her head off on the concrete wall opposite. 'Mad,' he said.

She had loved him. Of course she had. The honeymoon had been a disaster, but she had become used to living with this amiable stranger who desired her. He was a decent man, a man of good character and entirely self-oblivious. He did not question or whinge, had not an ounce of this who-am-I, what-is-life stuff, no crumb of self-doubt had ever reproached him. He was steadfast. The fact that he had no more understanding of her than an armadillo confronted by a yellow-eyed penguin had not worried her after a while. He was fond of her. What passion or interest he had left over from his real purpose in life was hers. She was lucky.

He was a good father. He practised drop kicks with Kit and was proud of Rebecca's propensity to win things.

She had hoped to absorb some of his strength and give some of hers in return. He had looked puzzled when she mentioned this thought.

'Your strengths, Soph?'

There were private hot pools, a dining room, oleanders waiting for the summer. Everything was as it should be.

'Tell me about Clarissa,' she said later.

'What do you want to know?'

'Everything.'

They had met during the war. Clarissa had been a Wren in Malta and much sought after. 'Wrens were pretty thin on the ground there. A lot of pulling rank went on. She was intrigued by the wild colonial boy. I climbed a tree to her room. Insisted. Was determined.' He shoved a hand through silver hair. 'I don't know. It was . . .'

'And then what?'

'We were married in March. It was cold. Freezing. Stone floors. The whole place is designed to be cool in summer.'

'Then?'

'Ah, then.' His hand flopped against her, tightened on her thigh. 'Why do you want to know?'

'Because.'

Because you loved her. Because anything about you, anything in your past, your present, your future is essential to me, is mine. If you have a photograph of yourself as a child I wish to own it. I need this image, however small. And I will keep it, like all secrets, secreted about my person where else.

'The first change she made was to call me Edward.' He grinned. 'I'd always been Ed. She thought she could reconstruct me, knock me into shape, ditch the bush and buff up the brawn. I didn't realise at first what was going on. She was subtle, never corrected me in front of her friends, never made a fool of me until they'd gone.

Then she would explain, gently, lovingly, and at some length, which button I'd got wrong.'

'Button?'

'Done up. Left undone.' He lay silent, watching the faded memory of his pale wife. 'You can't imagine how insidious, how soul-destroying it is to live with someone who's waiting for you to make a balls-up so she can explain exactly where you went wrong. And the insane things she fussed about. I didn't give a stuff about any of it but the sensation of someone waiting for you to crap out . . .'

'I know.'

'It killed it. Love. Sex. Everything. I found myself watching her as she prepared to sacrifice her life, to give me the benefit of her arcane knowledge. "Oh darling, not those shoes. Cap. Tie. Jacket." It was twenty years ago, remember.' He was silent once more. The room was still.

'You do love me, don't you, Sophie?' he said at last.

'Yes.'

His sigh was deep, recognition of atonement. 'Good.' His eyes closed. 'How are we going to do it? Live together. Without destroying people. Us.' He hesitated. 'My job.'

'I'll think of something.'

He reached for her hand. 'That's all right then. Good old Soph.'

'Sophie.'

'It doesn't sound right, Sophie. Not for the sweetest little fucker in the forest. Soph's better.'

'No. Not Soph. Come here,' she said.

She had to know. 'Did you leave her? Before she died, I mean.'

He frowned slightly, his eyes blank as lapis.

'Yes.'

Her voice was light, casual. He didn't have to tell her. 'Then?' she murmured.

'She killed herself.' He leaped off the bed and strode to the shower. At the door he turned. 'Gas.'

Captain and Mrs Featherston knew, he told her later. No one else. It was a long time ago.

The mattress, she noticed as she straightened the mangled bed, was named Desire.

The hot pool was good. They slid against each other, nibbled predatory as eels and drifted apart. Her breasts were misplaced water wings. They enjoyed themselves, stayed in too long and crawled out water-logged. Clar-issa. Clar-iss-a.

The next-door pool was also occupied, complete with the requisite laughter and splashes and murmurs. Sophie listened, her pink ears flapping.

They had agreed in one of their final telephone conversations. They were not going to be furtive. They planned to spend their lives together. Later they would work out ways and means to accomplish this without pain or damage to a living soul. It would all work out. This weekend was an exploration, they did not hope for landfall this time. He mentioned, she remembered, the Transit of Venus.

They walked along the beach. Clarissa joined them.

'I mean she must have loved me.' He touched Sophie's cheek with one finger. 'I've never discussed it with anyone, you see. That's why you're getting both barrels. And why did I let it get to me?' He turned to her in bewilderment. 'Why did I let her?'

'You loved her. She loved you.'

'But why . . . ?'

'Some people are remodellers. They see the potential. Know best.'

'Manipulating, soul-destroying . . . oh, Sophie.' He whirled her around; a sand crab disappeared in panic. 'Promise you won't knock me into shape.'

'All right.' She licked her finger, flattened a rogue hair in his right eyebrow.

His face was tense. He really wanted to know. He wanted the

truth. 'Was it my fault?'

She didn't ask him what he meant. 'No,' she said. 'No, it wasn't.'

Clarissa was dead.

The wind changed, long plumes of spray blew back from breakers, sand whipped their ankles. They were on to the Dardanelles.

'Balls,' he said. 'The ANZACs didn't forge their national identities in the hell of Gallipoli or anywhere else. Churchill saw a chance of success for himself. Simple as that.'

'We shall not flag nor fail.'

Another crab appeared, pincers guarding stalked eyes. Edward's foot stamped. The crab dived. 'He had his points.'

'The thing is,' he said, abandoning the crab and the topic, 'I can't live without you.'

Gulls slip-streaming above the spume screamed their dissent. The wind freshened.

William had never tried to change her. 'It says here,' she had said to him last year, flapping one of Celia's magazines in his face, 'it says here that the secret of a happy marriage is communication, talking things through. I think,' said Sophie, her hands clasped in emphasis, 'I think we should "communicate" more.'

William was checking the sports news. He was worried about the navy's chances on Saturday. It was their backs. He slapped the paper flat, lifted it again. 'All that happens when we communicate,' he said, 'is you tell me what's wrong with me.'

Smiling, demonstrating her acceptance of his telling point, she tried again. 'All right. But there must be things you don't like about me. Tell me!' She cajoled. She could remember cajoling. She knew how important it was.

'I'll think of something,' said William. He told her later. She snorted. And sometimes braked when she should have changed down.

*

'I'm going to communion tomorrow,' she said later. Edward turned to her, his fingers splayed on the greying fluff on his chest. 'Why?'

'To give thanks,' she said inspecting her thumbnail.

'But you're spending the weekend fornicating. Backwards. Sideways.'

'I know.'

His finger touched the side of her mouth. 'You could go into a sideshow—Sophie, the slowest smiler in space. Doesn't adultery affect the situation? Sin? All that.'

She tried to work it out. 'The fact that I'm here with you . . . That's wrong. I choose to ignore it because I love you. But that doesn't mean . . .' She sat naked and cross-legged beside her lover on a mattress named Desire, trying to find the words.

'*Dieu me pardonnera, c'est son métier.*'

'Who said that?'

'Heine.'

'Tell me about him.'

'I don't know much.'

The congregation at the little church was sparse. The Vicar beamed at his scattered flock. 'Welcome,' he cried.

He invited them each to greet the person on either side of them. There was no one either side of Sophie. She turned to smile at a man and a woman in the pew behind her. They were identical as bookends; small, ruddy and carved from tweed. They glared back at her. Fellowship was not what they had in mind. They believed, perhaps, that God is a Spirit: and they that worship him must worship him in spirit and in truth. An occasional cup of tea in the parish hall afterwards was as far as they were prepared to go.

There was no one in front of her either. The yellow chrysanthemums on the altar were backed by variegated flax and pittosporum, the brass shone, the wind tossed behind lancet windows. The epistle was from the Colossians, the Gospel from St Luke. New residents to the parish were invited to fill in a card at the back of the church and make themselves known to the Vicar. A slip indicating that more people (preferably younger!) were needed on the grounds roster slid from her hymn book. Also the news that the Queen's birthday service at eight a.m. would be taken by the Very Reverend Jim Batton from our sister parish in Western Australia.

'Alleluia!' cried Mr Batton. He was a large man bursting with goodwill. Alternatives were unknown to him. No sense of misgiving or despair had ever brushed him. His face gleamed, but not with the scrubbed spare glint of age. Well-larded certainty illuminated the Vicar from across the sea.

Behinds wriggled on polished rimu as the congregation settled for the sermon. A man in the pew opposite Sophie closed his eyes the second the Vicar reached the pulpit. Mr Batton, his hands clasped on its carved front, smiled at them yet again. 'Alleluia!' he cried. He continued to exhort them, to lead them, to explain to them the wonder of the Risen Lord. He told them about the stone—the one at the mouth of the tomb. He told them about the rolling away of the stone and the linen clothes lying. He told them about the disciple whom Jesus loved outstripping the others in his haste to tell the world. All this they had heard before and were pleased to hear again. The Reverend Batton continued. 'Those of us who are here, who are gathered here today in love and fellowship, we *know*.' His face twinkled above them, his eyes darted. 'Every man, woman and child gathered together in his name within these four walls *knows* this story to be true. The truth of the Resurrection. The most important truth in the world.'

But do we? How can we possibly? All we can know is that a large man sweating in a nylon surplice is telling us so. Sophie gave a minuscule shake of her head. What about Faith. Grace. All that.

He got worse. He lifted his hands; avuncular, smug, entire as a hot cross bun, Mr Batton shone at the faithful far below him. 'And you know,' he confided, 'I feel *sorry* for those who know not faith. All those who scoff at the Christian religion and there are many of them. Those who are lost to the love of God and walk not in his ways. Who lie and cheat and fornicate and know not his love.' His arms were outstretched. 'I am *sorry* for those people. That is what I feel for all those people out there. *Sorry.*' The minister paused, overcome by the impact of his own words. His hands rose beside him, the surplice sleeves slipped back. 'I am *sorry* for them,' he said yet again, nodding his head in stately confirmation.

Sophie's mind was busy. His smugness, his unctuous conviction that he was right and would continue to be so for all eternity and that those people out there could never be, bruised her heart. His faith was repellent. She did not wish to share it. She wished to doubt.

Staring up at him she was filled with an extraordinary lightening of spirit, a soaring upwards from the clamp of certainty, from the conviction onto which he now moved, that those who were gathered together inside St Whatever's would ascend into heaven and eternal bliss and the rest of the north and the world beyond would not.

He was sorry for them but there it was. They had had their chance.

Light filtered into her mind, illuminated the dark patches, the bits used for thinking.

The Reverend Batton's philosophy was not Christ-like. His convictions could be paraphrased, and had been by William. 'Shove off, Jack. I'm inboard.'

What did the resurrection of her soul matter. It was a deceiving lying soul. Why should the fact that its attendant body had climbed out of an adulterous bed and ambled down to Eight O'Clock mean it should be saved. She was sick of her soul. It was not worth fussing about. Thoughts of rejection, liberation, release were thundering in her head. Drenching showers of disbelief filled her mind. She had shed the life hereafter. To hell with it. The Vicar lifted his hands to her thumping heart to welcome it to communion. 'We do not presume to come to this thy table, Oh merciful Lord, trusting in our own . . .'

She did not take communion. Nor did she leave. She sat in her pew and waited for the end.

She tried to avoid the Vicar at the door. He seized her hand. 'Alleluia,' he cried yet again.

A small boy in a Superman cloak pedalled past her at speed. He swung round at the corner and charged at a little girl on an even smaller trike. She backed, turned, attacked. Antlers clashed. One of them yelled.

Edward waved from the hot pool. His body sank.

'Don't put your head under!' yelled Sophie.

He laughed, spluttered, stayed up.

She had once seen a slide of infected spinal fluid, had watched the amoeba flow after its own ever-changing shape. So beautiful. So lethal. Never put your head under. Not in a hot pool.

Her legs wrapped around his. Buoyed up by water she was light as a feather from Bertha's fan.

'Nice,' she said.

'Yes,' he said, reaching for her as she drifted towards the outlet. 'Very nice.' She drifted beyond reach.

'What's Mrs Featherston like, really?'

'Lettie? Why on earth?'

'I just wondered.'

'Oh, a fine woman. Very strong character. Lionel'd be lost without her.'

The comment was unsatisfactory. Even though she no longer cared, was strong, had put on the whole armour of love, Sophie did not wish to hear it. She wished Edward to find poor old Mrs Featherston who disliked her wanting in some minor detail. Floating on her back beside him, Sophie had her second revelation of the day. Love is not enough. Nor sex. Nor understanding, nor sheer bloody joy. Insidious, invasive as pathogens, she wished to flow into her lover's mind, to absorb, to be part of it.

To make her home there. She had another thought. This need for wholeness is why people believe. It was not a new thought, but it was the first time she had thought it and it pleased her. It was a clean hard thought. Clear-sighted. It stood upright. There was probably a poem about it. But not a hymn.

Holed up in their unit they continued their explorations.

'Coming for a walk?' he said later.

'No, I need a shower.'

He came back sooner than usual, his hair wet from the rain. 'Guess what?' said Edward, and did not wait for an answer. 'I've just seen Liz.'

She was upright. 'What!'

'With Harold Pickett. Coming up from the beach. Towels and things.' He took her hand in his. 'French farce stuff, eh, Soph?'

Her knees folded. Liz, Liz of all people, Liz with her adoring husband, her slavering dog, her cool hand on the tiller of life, of getting there. 'We'll have to go.'

'No, we won't.'

She looked at him, her face blank with distress, then remembered. The Commodore, like William, had been trained to stand his ground, to keep his head and never ever to run away. He had been trained to win. To stand.

'It's mad, insane . . .'

'Worse for them. They're both married.'

'But you're the, oh bugger it, you're the Commodore.'

'And he's the Captain.'

'I'm going.' She began snatching at bits of clothing, still-damp stockings from the doll's bathroom, a pair of pants.

'Sophie.'

'I said I'm going. I'm not going to be part of some . . . some sort of . . . Philly orgy. What are you *doing*? Is this just . . .' Her voice broke. 'Is this just some sort of *weekend* to you? Is that all?'

'Darling heart, calm down. Let's take a rational appreciation of the situation, shall we.'

'Stop talking like William.'

'Watch it, sailor,' he said mildly. 'The situation is that Kelson and Pickett are staying at the Hot Pool Motels and so are we.

Right?'

She nodded, her nose damp with misery. She grabbed a handkerchief and sat on the bed.

'So all are equally guilty in the eyes of your God. Right?'

'He's not my God.'

He refused to play. 'In the eyes of the world then, as if they'd fuss, or the Service, which might, all four are equally guilty.'

She was still mopping.

'So no one will shop any other one. So why should we run away?' Edward lay full length on the bed, surveyed his kingdom, touched her.

'Because I couldn't stand meeting them. I don't care how idiotic it sounds.'

He smiled at her, 'You couldn't?'

'No.'

'Well, we have a problem. I'm not leaving.' His eyes shone, he was enjoying himself.

'*You* have a problem. It's my car.'

'I'm senior to Pickett.'

She did realise he was joking. They rolled together laughing. Ed and Soph were at it again. He sat up, laughter gone once more as he continued his sitrep.

'It's highly possible we won't even meet.'

'Oh, for heaven's sake.'

'We haven't so far and it's Sunday. Presumably they came up here on Friday. We've never seen them in the dining room, have we?'

'No.' Her only memory of the dining room, apart from the inevitable candle in a Chianti bottle on each table and indifferent food, was a skeletal woman in white and a bearded male. Each time they left their table she stood waiting for him, glued his palm to hers and marched out.

'They're probably holed up in their room like us. It's quite simple. We carry on as we have been.' He was at ease with the world and his plan of campaign. 'The Pickett/Kelson combo is no threat.'

'I couldn't bear it.'

'Sophie.' He took her face between his hands. 'You know I love you.'

'Yes.'

'Well grow up.'

'If by growing up you mean not being ashamed at betraying my . . .' She aimed the archaic phrase between his eyes. '. . . my marriage vows, then I'm not sure I want to.'

'Ashamed? Oh God, yes. Don't get me wrong. I'm all for shame and guilt. There isn't enough guilt in the world.'

'Very funny.'

'I mean it. The world wouldn't operate. We'd all be monsters. We need it.'

'Well, that's great because I've got it.'

She turned away, reached for a pillow and sat on it, her face flaming above her pale body.

'Sweetest heart. You're sure it's adultery that's worrying you? Not the being found out? Retribution and hellfire? Relax. Either God's a busy man or else he doesn't exist.'

No one's going to look at you.

'That's not what I'm talking about,' she snapped.

He was thoughtful, smiling, more relaxed than ever. 'You never know . . . Them being here too. It adds a certain frisson.'

'Oh, shut up.'

'Yes, well. We'll wait and see.'

They walked down the corridor to the pool. He was swinging his towel, flicking its end. Sophie was some distance from him.

Liz Kelson and Harold Pickett appeared around the corner, their eyes on each other, their arms entwined. Harold stopped dead. For a dazed second Sophie thought he might spring to attention, salute. He was ludicrous, which helped. A pathetic stock figure. Liz was calmer. Much much more calm. 'Good God,' she said. 'Sophie.'

'Hullo.'

Liz's hands moved. 'Hullo, Edward,' she said.

'Hullo there,' said Edward and laughed. Liz took him up. Harold, after a pause, joined in, but his laughter was not carefree. The corridor was an echo chamber filled with sound. It rebounded against the walls and crashed again. Laughter bounced around them in the narrow space. It was Liz she had heard in the hot pool the other night.

Sophie sagged against the wall.

'Well,' said Edward. 'What do you suggest we do?'

'Have a swim,' said Liz. 'Come and join us.'

Sophie heard her voice among the lost echoes of laughter. 'No.'

'Come *on*, Soph,' said Liz. 'It's 1962, for God's sake.'

Harold Pickett looked ill. Sleek but ill. He was not in command, of either the situation or his thought processes.

Edward was looking at Sophie with affection. It was her decision.

'All right,' she said. 'Why not.'

'We won't look,' said Liz.

But they would have to. Rabbit-scared but stone-faced, Sophie undressed slowly in front of them. The men slipped into the steaming water. Liz turned her back to remove her clothes. Sophie turned her front. There was nothing furtive about her. She removed each garment, folded it as though it was precious and removed the next. She stood upright. She did not smile. This was not a striptease, this was a demonstration. Of something. She was not ashamed of her trembling, near-hefty body.

And things only matter if you think they do.

Liz glanced at her; mouth tight, eyes quick, the woman whom Sophie had loved, had bounced around like an effusive untrained puppy, was displeased.

Taking her cue from her erstwhile disciple Liz straightened her shoulders and walked the four steps to the pool.

'No soap,' said a sign at the end.

It is virtually impossible not to relax in a hot pool; slow-moving limbs, dark genitals lay hidden. Tension in the enclosed space drifted upwards with the steam and the silence.

She heard Edward as they dried themselves. 'Come for a drink later.'

Damn.

'How much later?' said Liz, her glance slipping from one man to the other.

'What's the matter with you?' she muttered to Sophie as they walked along the corridor.

'Why?'

'I've never seen you like this.'

'You mean I've stopped smiling?'

'What a moment to choose.'

Sophie used to like drinking in motel rooms. It seldom happened, but she had enjoyed a faint feeling of decadence even with William. It was no longer faint, this feeling. Alive and well, decadence had put out suckers, had infiltrated the concrete foundations of their weekend.

If this was licence, Sophie did not think much of it. This was not what she joined for. She joined to lie with her lover because she wished to be part of him. To enfold him. He smiled at her as she sat with a gin in one hand, staring at the lavatory with its seat up. She shut the bathroom door. No one else seemed to have noticed and she was after all the hostess. Memories returned: chaste food-ridden parties, rocking the night away, Liz demonstrating the Twist. She laughed aloud. Harold Pickett lit a cigarette with fussy hands. He was not enjoying himself but he had had a thought — a conversational cushioner.

'By the way, Sophie,' he said. 'Don't worry about that little . . .' He recrossed his legs. 'Kate Calder has it in train.'

'What little?' said Liz, recrossing her legs in imitation.

'Nothing, nothing,' said Harold, smoothing his smooth hair.

You cannot. But you can, can't you? Kate is in the Service. And she cannot refuse. Sophie squeezed her eyes shut. There was grit behind them, grains of rage for Kate who might not mind at all but damn well bloody well should.

She put her feet together, sat straight-backed and prissy. 'I don't think you should have done that, Harold,' she said.

They left eventually. Edward took her in his arms. Doors flung wide, curtains billowed, doors crashed; cameras panned across the ceiling of their concrete bunker.

They slept afterwards. Hot pools are soporific, as is gin.

It was almost dark when she woke. She licked his ear. 'Are you awake?'

His eyes opened. 'Yes.'

'I'm leaving tomorrow. Going somewhere else.'

'Why?'

'I'm going.'

He put out an arm. 'May I come too?'

'Yes.'

'Thanks.'

The hand now lay on his chest. The index finger moved up, down, up, down as he spoke.

'They're putting you off, are they?'

'Don't be nuts. But you see, I love you. It's not just a dirty weekend.'

'How do you know theirs is?'

'I don't.'

He kissed her idle hand, watched her face. 'Never mind, darling. Of course we'll leave if you want to. Now that I know Pickett is scared shitless.'

They had not worked out their plan for life. There had not been time. They stayed the night in a motel further down the coast. The wallpaper was upside-down cocktail glasses and dead fish, the beds were single. Rain fell down. There was no answer when she rang home.

It was still pouring next morning as they left. Wind lashed the beach, rattled the unpainted corrugated iron fence, swept scuds of rain across the flooded road.

An old couple stood in dun-coloured parkas and squashed hats, marooned in a sheet of water outside the motel. Mad crone's hair flew from beneath her brown hat, her face was red with wind and too much mirth as she tried to capture an escaped gumboot. She leaned against him as he tried to help. He bent to shove, to encourage, to laugh and shove again. They stood clutching each other, their cheeks wet, she still on one foot, the woolly-socked one hanging. Weak with mirth she gave up and stood flat-footed in the water, her rogue boot the smoke stack of a coaster adrift. They embraced in mid-pool.

Glamour is the joy of being envied. She had read it somewhere.

SEVEN

Sophie saw the white sling and froze. The car door was left hanging. 'What *happened*!'

They stood waiting for her at the top of the steps. Lou backed by Evan, Rebecca and her sling, Kit beside her. They were lined up waiting.

'I burnt my arm,' said Rebecca.

'She saved the house and everything. She saved it. Wow, Mum.' Kit's eyes were wide, the shit-scared eyes of a small boy. 'Wow,' he said again.

'Tell me, Becca.' She shook her head at Lou's dough-faced sulk, at Evan's creaking attempt to explain. 'Tell me,' she begged, taking the child in her arms with care.

Rebecca disintegrated. She hid her face on her mother's chest and wept. 'Why didn't you come, Mum?'

'We couldn't get you. Not last night. We rang and rang the motel,' said Lou, demonstrating responsible behaviour while she had a chance. The ground ahead was more shaky, a track through thermal mud pools.

'I rang at six o'clock,' said Sophie, the memory backed by dead fish and cocktail glasses. 'There was no one here.'

'We were along at the base by then. The young doctor was very nice. Fixed her up in no time, didn't he, dear?'

Rebecca, her head still buried, nodded.

It is not Lou's fault. I am not allowed to hate her. It is not her fault. There are no thunderbolts.

'Come on Becca. Come and tell me all about it.' She looked at Lou. 'I'll . . .' She would think of something to say later. 'Come on, come on, Kit.'

An arm round either child, supportive, protective, Sophie guided the pyramid-shaped tableau of motherhood down the hall.

'Shit,' said Lou to the stephanotis by the front door.

'She's upset, love,' soothed Evan. 'Stands to reason. She'll come right. It wasn't your fault.'

The fat for the chips had caught on fire. It had happened in a flash.

'But what were Lou and Evan doing?'

'Oh, you know. Fooling about.' Kit picked at his bare foot. 'Yeah. Fooling around. You know.'

Leave it. Leave it. Leave it.

'And?' she said.

'And Rebecca carried the pot out and the flames were shooting up and she turned off the stove even and she got it right out the back door and then whoosh the wind blew back up her arm and she screamed, didn't you Becca, but she got it out all by herself.'

Rebecca, three years older and bossy as stink, was transformed. Kit's face was white with memory.

'Where were Lou and Evan?'

'Oh, they were flapping around. But Evan was good with the water wasn't he, Becca? He ran cold water on it and the skin all peeled off. All hanging like cobwebs in the bush. You should've seen it Mum.'

Rebecca, self-contained, competent Rebecca, still lay in her mother's arms.

'Mum,' she said.

Kit gave his mother a puzzled glance. He hadn't asked before, not the exact location. 'Whereabouts up north were you, Mum?'

'Not very far.'

He patted her knee. 'Any good?'

Mary, Ben told her yawning, was down at the wharf with Bertha. She caught her foot as she climbed out of the car, stumbled on a rubble-filled crack in the concrete. Lime had leached out, transforming the nearby grass strip to brilliant green. She must tell Edward. She blinked, her hand still on the car door. She would not tell Edward. That stage had passed. They were beyond bower-bird exchanges which are not given by the female anyway. He did not know about Rebecca yet. Nor did William. How could he.

Ben was pleased to see her. He was always pleased to see this amiable woman whom he found exciting. He would have shared this thought with Mary—they explored their sexuality and desires with enthusiasm—but he disliked the thought of her reaction. The pause, the disbelief, the sibilant explosive, 'Soph!' The laughter.

'Hi, kitten hips,' he said, one hand on each to heighten the joke. Sophie kissed him. She liked him. It was just a question of keeping William and Ben from converging too often, of keeping them trundling along their own particular branch lines with an occasional nod in the direction of the opposing track.

'How's Arnie?'

'Great. Great guy. Enjoyed meeting with him.' He paused, his smile gentle. 'William know he was in a naval mutiny?'

'No. Nor did I.'

'Ask him about it. Come in, come in and see what I'm working on.' He led her by the hand, side-stepping layered piles of loot fossicked from the Devonport tip: a giant cog wheel from a medieval torture rack, a broken Aztec Gold plank with an interesting knot, the bottom half of a traffic light. 'You should see the packing shed in Greytown, Ben,' she said.

'I look forward to that.' Six foot four, skinny, courteous and elusive as his past, Ben led the way. His past was elusive merely because he never mentioned it. It had no interest for him, it was over. He had trained as a painter in New York and won a valuable, in fact munificent, Young Artist's Award. He had been surprised, but not as surprised as his critics felt he should have been. He had seen an article in the *National Geographic* about New Zealand rain forest, liked the look of Fiordland, and came. He met Mary on the ferry, moved in with her and had not been south of the Coromandel. He would one day. There was plenty of time.

Their bedroom always gave Sophie a slight frisson of unease. It was chaos in action, a pit to fall into, a cave plus midden. Coffee-dregged mugs lay on the floor either side of a mattress on legs. Above was a yellowing sheet of calico printed with a languorous Christ in ecstasy, blue eyes rolled upwards, thorns askew.

'I wish you'd take that down,' said Sophie.

'Yeah, but look,' Ben waved his arm. In the corner of the room stood an old wicker chair; legs splayed, hocks spavined, it was falling apart. Tendrils of unravelled fibre hung in coils or rolled about the paint-spattered boards trapping dust. 'Look at it,' cried Ben. 'What do you reckon?'

Hard to say. 'You've spray-painted it then?'

'Yeah, but . . .' He was determined she should understand. 'It's the idea see. Every time something wears out,' he slapped his ripped jeans, 'I mean completely, I fling it on and then spray her again. It's the build up, the texture as well as the original concept, the overview, the "*Ceci n'est pas une pipe*" bit.'

'Oh.'

'We've got to go backward, to learn how we learned originally. OK?' Ben's sleepy charm had gone, the febrile driven nutter had taken over.

'I don't know what you're talking about.'

'Surely even you know art and religion were once inseparable . . .'

'Thanks.'

He didn't even hear her. 'It's only now that art's cut off, marginal, irrelevant to the real world. What I'm trying to do is to get back to . . .'

He gave up momentarily, banked his fires. He carried the old guy's suitcase to the car, shook his hand and went back to work. He didn't want it too vertical, this sculpture. The strength was in the spread.

If Arnie was pleased to see her he didn't say so. 'Stop at my house, would you, lass?' he said.

The house was dry but airless. Arnie, pretending not to puff, tapped his way up the hall with a staff labelled *Milford Track* in pokerwork which Bertha had unearthed from behind some major baskets.

'Look at that,' he gasped.

More showing forths. The fernery was no more. Not a pot, not a failing or expiring fern in sight. The white slatted boards were bare. 'Where are they?' said Sophie.

'I'll show you. I want you to help.'

She gave him her hand going down the steps. His grip was a manacle biting her wrist. 'This way, this way.' Past the pittosporum, on past the ragged grass where the sparrows had given up waiting for crumbs, on beyond the clay sods and stones of the defunct vegetable garden, they zig-zagged their way to the tangled mass at the bottom which hid the view, a rampant jungle of banana passionfruit vines, datura, withered choko and Old Man's Beard. Arnie held back the green hanging curtain with Bertha's stick and stood gasping. The pots of withered ferns were lined neatly inside a beer crate.

'Empty them.' His eyes were half closed. 'Please empty them. No puff. Got no puff. Ashes.'

Mary had told her about the ashes. 'On the ground?'

'Aye.' He handed her the trowel he had brought from the fernery. 'No puff,' he said once more.

She levered the plants out, shook out the loose stones for drainage and laid the dead ferns in a row.

'They were rootbound, Arnie, that's what killed them.'

His voice was fierce. 'She said it was the ashes.'

'Mary?' Sophie laughed. 'Don't worry about Mary. She doesn't know anything.'

She scattered the remaining contents of the pots at their feet. They stood half hidden by greenery, silent and at ease.

A blackbird practising for the mating season cranked up a few notes on the lawn behind them.

'Do you want to say . . . ?' The phrase 'a few words' got stuck somewhere. 'Do you want to say anything?' said Sophie.

'No.' A long pause. 'You can if you like.'

Nothing came. The army of good words had deserted, shoved off and left her undefended. 'How about "Go forth into the world in peace? Be of good cheer . . ." that one,' she said at last.

'The Commissioning Prayer? God no.'

She took his arm as they crossed the rough broken ground, guided him past a trench of rotted compost. 'If it was the navy,' she said, 'we'd have a lively tune now.'

He was pleased, his smile so wide it revealed a blackened molar. 'To march off to? Yes, that's one thing they do get right.'

The French doors rattled as the squall hit the harbour. 'If I was real Geordie you couldn't understand a word I said. Not a word,' he said smugly.

She inspected the base of the iron. It needed a rub of something. 'Tell me about it.' Her hands were quicker than the rest of her, he had noticed that before. He was glad to be back. Mary and that daft lag Ben had been kind and they hadn't fussed when he had gone home day after day escorted by Chester picking his way on bun feet. But what a set-up. What a crew.

'No, I won't tell you. You wouldn't understand.' He watched the iron steaming over bright trousers. Win aged fourteen had gone in daily to wash and iron for a lady who had remained unglimpsed for ten whole years. A lady with a rich husband and babies and nannies and staff and the lowest of them all was Winnie. A lady with flat-irons and goffer irons and ruffle irons to be heated on the range and run back with before they cooled and the resident housekeeper threatened her with instant expulsion.

'When were you and Win married?'

He didn't mind that one.

'1920. June 1920.'

'You were a sailor, weren't you?'

'I joined as a seaman boy.'

'When?'

'And I was kicked out after the strike in '31. "Services No Longer Required." They called it a mutiny! The Invergordon Mutiny, that's what they said after.' His hands tight with rage, his heart thud-thudding, Arnie glared at her. 'Mutiny!'

'Tell me about it.'

'Read it yourself! It's all there—not what happened. What they say.' He was furious with her. 'Read the bloody thing!'

'I will.'

It was no use. How could she ever understand? It had been a strike like the miners. What did the bastards expect. Three bob a day instead of four for an able seaman and worse for older married men with children and some families near sinking as it was and every penny precious. No man would stand for it. None. 'Twenty-five per cent cut! I'd have been working a year, more, over a year for nothing.' He spat it out. 'How'd you like that!'

She opened her mouth. He was on his feet, his face distorted with the impotent rage of frailty.

'Don't say it,' he snapped. 'You'd never understand with your fancy iron and your fine house and your . . .' He stopped, appalled, put his hand on hers. 'Not you, not you,' he panted. 'Them.'

She shook her head, smiled. 'Stop talking. You'll make yourself ill.'

Rage had saved him in '31 when he was left outside the dockyard gates with a rail warrant and thirteen bob to last a lifetime. And luck. He had got a job as a deckhand on a tramp. Over forty years old. No questions asked or answered. Had saved every penny and Win was lucky as well. The unseen lady had allowed her back to her cubbyhole.

They had survived, arrived here almost destitute with all their savings gone as well as the money for the baby who never came and so what after a while, though never like that for Win. Things were beginning to pick up in '33. He joined the Labour Party the week they arrived. Had worked on steering committees, got their men in '35. They had made a new life. Services No Longer Required.

Sophie noticed his slight grudging smile. Arnie had worked something out. He could stay here, pay board and stay. The husband was in the navy. The navy owed him a life. RN, RNZN, what did it matter. They owed him. And he was tired, tired rotten. Age had caught up with him, dampened the fire in the belly but left it smouldering. His smile widened. Perhaps that was what was causing his heart to flap like a wounded seabird. And the hiccoughs.

Encouraged by the smile, she tried again. 'And the upholstery?'

'We didn't have a skerrick when we arrived. Bought stuff from the mart. All its innards sticking out, stuffing, horsehair.' His eyes were bright. 'You know that Old Man's Beard down the back?'

'Yes.'

'Reminds me of our first sofa, the fluff does. Stuffing hanging out all over the place. A pound. That's what we paid for it. A pound. More than that to get it home and Win said, "Right, I'm going to upholstery classes to learn how," and I went along too, why not?' He shook his head. 'Filthy, it was, filthy, you never saw such muck but it came up fine. The teacher came from Glasgow. Gave me a job after in his own business. Then later Win and me had a bit of a shed down the village. Tin it was. Tin. Tin and ply. We had it for years. Win did the books, she was quick with figures. Had a feel for them.' He was running out of puff. 'It wasn't all synthetics then,' he gasped. 'I can tell you.'

She folded a pillow case. Quick, neat and sonsy. 'Stop talking,' she said again.

'It's healing very well,' said the young medical officer. He placed a large brown hand on Rebecca's shoulder and pressed slightly.

Sophie awarded her daughter a blue budgerigar for courage.

Rebecca liked Bluey, except for the ugly warty-looking bit above his beak.

'Why does he have that, Mum?'

'Because he's a budgerigar.'

Rebecca would have arranged things differently.

Celia, legs up and head back, was pleased to see Sophie on Friday but displeased by her technique. 'Harder, Sophie, rub harder. Not your nails, woman. Your fingers. And something's leaking.'

Sophie restowed the towel, tightened the plastic wrapper. The mock bow-tie was centre front, the buttons of the pretend tuxedo straight. 'Aah, that's better. In KL they massage your head into your shoulders. Heaven.'

Lou clicked past for bulk shampoo which she diluted more than specified behind a bead curtain out the back. 'Have a good Queen's birthday, Mrs Pickett?' Celia's face was expressionless, laid out like a shield below the wet hair streaming down the chute behind her. Her unblinking eyes stared upwards at a large piece of beige canvas painted with purple and green bacilli which hid a damp mark on the ceiling. Evan had perpetrated the thing and put it in place. Celia preferred the mark. It had the deeply indented Terra Incognita coastline reminiscent of old maps with cartouches and puffing cherubs; an interesting stain with room for the imagination.

'Yes, thank you, Lou. Bliss. My husband had to go to Waiouru unexpectedly.'

Sophie's hands stopped rubbing for a second. Paul Kelson had been in Waiouru at Queen's birthday. A busy effective operator reeking of complicity, she rubbed on. 'Some visiting fireman from somewhere,' continued her friend. 'I lay like a log; egg on the knee, cat on the bed, book in the night. Bliss. What about you?'

'Oh, Evan and me babysat for Sophie, didn't we?'

A gleam, a gleam of malice in the palisaded eye? Sophie rinsed, wet hair streamed. 'Yes, I had a lovely break up north,' she said.

'All God's chillun got breaks,' murmured Celia, upended but

gracious beneath the purple and green camouflage of *A Cut Ahead.* She kicked her legs.

She knew. She had challenged Harold on his return and he had told her, as always. As always she had been filled with contempt. As always he was abject and contrite. He told her about Edward and Sophie, which compounded her scorn for him with concern for Sophie.

The first time had left her reeling. They had been married how long? A year, two years, no more. They had come home to Hampshire while he did his long Communications course. It had been good to be back. Celia enjoyed life in New Zealand but as Mother said, there was no place like home. Father's assistance and Mother's background knowledge found them a nice little place in the village. There were snowdrops. It was heaven. Harold insisted on cleaning the dolphin knocker he had brought back from Malta. The cleaning woman left streaks and he couldn't stand sloppy bright-work. Even their neighbour was pleasant. A divorced woman with problems including Ariadne, a ten-year-old bedwetter, and Tim, a bleached distraught thirteen-year-old who kept running away from Downpark. Celia was fond of their mother, Halcyon. She was a nice little thing.

The bitter grief of first betrayal had faded eventually.

This defection, Celia decided, was different. This time she would leave. Celia lay with her feet up working out how to leave the bastard. She would go. She would take her money and run. She would leave the ageing roué still performing his ritual ball games to an increasingly uninterested circle of females and run while there was still time—before he packed up on her and duty held her back. Leave him on the beam end of his naval pay, shorn of first-class skiing holidays and bespoke suits, strapped for cash for his new Snipe. Leave him unadorned and ill-equipped, his charm creaking at the après après ski. And the après pool. Why had she not left him years ago? Celia moved beneath the plastic red bow-tie and the tuxedo, astonished at her own . . . at her own what? Her tolerance? Forbearance? Or possibly (she was an honest woman) her lassitude, her shameful idle lassitude. Originally, after her first raging despair, it had been for the girls' sake she had procrastinated, had pretended the fireside game of Happy Families was being played with a full pack. But Blanche and Rowena had never been close to their father. Close. What a word. And they loved England. 'Why can't we *live* here, Mum?' Well they would, all three of them. Celia, who hadn't run for years, felt her legs twitch. She wished to be upright and on the move. She wished to be gone. She wished to see Liz who was beneath contempt.

Sophie wrapped Celia's hair in a towel. Drips of water ran down the client's neck. Everything takes practice, even wrapping heads. Celia touched Sophie's damp hand briefly. Her nails were pink. 'Be careful, darling,' she said.

Hair still warm from the dryer, Celia walked up the Kelsons' path. 'Yoo hoo,' she called. Caesar bounded down the hall to greet her, rolled on his back, swept his plumed tail from side to side in a wide arc of welcome for his good friend, Celia. Celia straightened to meet her hostess. 'Elizabeth,' she said. 'May I come in? Thank you.'

She walked past the wary face into the drawing room, inspected an invitation on the mantelpiece, put it down again. It was not interesting. She turned to the woman and smiled.

Liz attempted a return. She heard her voice, high, unfamiliar. 'Would you like a cup of coffee?'

'Coffee? No, I don't think I want any coffee, thank you. Not here.'

They stared at each other. Their eyes held. Blue snake, brown rabbit.

'Why are you here?' said the voice. Celia leaned against the mantelpiece to tell her. 'Your husband is a fine man,' she said.

Liz's nose moved. 'Aren't they all?'

'No, not all. Most, but not all.' Celia buried her nose in a vase of half-dead roses, sniffed hard and lifted her head to smile once again. 'Like the wives.' She sat, slid her legs sideways, adjusted a pleat. Liz stood.

Celia told her what she thought of her. In words graphic, blunt and mainly monosyllabic she made her meaning clear. Liz grasped the door jamb. She was in need of support. 'Don't tell him. Oh, dear God. Please, please don't tell him,' she whispered.

Celia looked at the stricken face before her. Looked at it with calm interest. 'Tell Paul?' she said. 'Why on earth should I tell Paul? That's your job.'

She turned and left. Escorted by the still ecstatic Caesar she strolled down the path between Paul Kelson's roses. A few ragged blooms remained, a full-blown Iceberg, an imploded Peace. He was going to prune them next month. Celia lifted her head to the scudding clouds and thought about Sophie.

'Yes, I see what you mean, you can't trust the woman. But what are we going to do?' The voice was tense. She could see the slight frown, the tightening around the mouth. 'No babysitter, that old man . . .'

'Arnie.'

'How are we going to *meet*? I'm not joking, Sophie.'

Sweet Jesu, nor am I. 'I'll think of something.'

It was unexpectedly difficult. Where could they go? The Esplanade would be suicidal, the Mon Desir not much better. There was no bush, no tangled hideaway of passion vines and withered chokos, no deep track into indigenous rain forest or exotic podocarp. The North Shore does not welcome homeless lovers. Not in winter.

They fell back on Nancy Ogilvie's son Michael and the Holden at the beach. 'I'm too old for this,' said Edward digging a lost spanner from beneath his spine. Sophie lay on top of him.

'Don't you find it exciting?' she murmured.

'Yes, but painful.' There was no moon.

Sophie had an idea. Driving home after leaving Edward in Devonport as a precautionary measure, she had an idea so spell-bindingly simple, so precise and tidy, that she pulled into the kerb and sat grinning at the pepper-pot tower of Bertha's house.

She would ask Arnie tomorrow.

*

Kit got in first. 'Arnie,' he said, pouring tea from the two-man pot. 'Would you come and be my Old Person at school?'

Crumpled and unshaven in his tartan dressing-gown, Arnie peered at him.

'Why?'

'We're doing old people. It's a project. It's meant to be Grans and that but we're allowed anyone if we haven't got a real one.'

'What do I have to do?'

'Just be there.'

'And be old?'

'Yes.'

'But I'm only seventy-three.'

Kit was silent.

Arnie watched the sudden shyness, the downcast eyes.

'And I don't like being old. I'm no good at it.'

'You get a cup of tea after.'

'Oh, all right. All *right.*'

'Gee thanks, Arnie. Mum'll run you down, eh Mum.' He put a hand on Arnie's shoulder. 'You don't have to do anything,' he said kindly.

'Arnie?' said Sophie as they drove home up the hill.

Being old had exhausted him. He sat clutching the safety belt in his hand, too tired to fight with the thing.

'Aye?'

Her eyes were straight ahead as they should be. 'Would you let me borrow the key to your house sometimes?'

The band of his old man's hat was sweat stained, his face hidden.

'Why?'

'I . . .' God in heaven, what am I doing. You know what you're doing. Do it.

'I want to meet someone there. At night.'

'What d'y'mean?'

'Oh Arnie, what do you think I mean?'

The mouth was working, chewing on something distasteful.

'Your fancy man.'

'Arnie!'

'You don't like the word then?' Every line of the face tugged downwards. The fist on the safety belt was clenched.

'No. I don't.'

'There's other words much worse. But you'd like a nice one, is it? Try paramour. You want to take your paramour and lay on my bed?'

Insane images. Bears, beds, a golden head. Her hand signal was precise as she pulled into the curb. He had shrunk. Shrunk to a tough old nut enclosing a kernel of outrage. 'There's right and there's wrong,' said Arnie.

'You're just the same as all the rest of them!'

He was not giving an inch. 'Hh.'

Her eyes snapped back at him.

'Who makes the rules? Who says? Who? I've only met one man in my whole life who ever left room for doubt, for differences. The essential *differences.* Who realised that we're all hopeless. Incomplete. That we don't know. And that's the man I'm going to sleep with and I wouldn't go inside your house if you paid me and I never will again and it was stupid of me to suggest it and . . .' Tears, dumb infuriating tears, swam in her eyes. Her sniff was long and disgusting. She turned on the ignition, a small sound in the sparking silence. Beside them Evan was writing the specials on the window of *Choice Meats* with white paint. Mid loin and leg were both down.

Arnie transferred the safety belt to his left hand and laid his right on her knee.

'Go away!'

Her neighbour Nancy Ogilvie gave an exaggerated leap from the path of the car as they turned into the drive. She waved a book in greeting. 'What a bit of luck I waited,' she said. 'I've finished your *Madame Bovary.*'

Arnie disappeared.

Sophie wiped her nose. 'Did you enjoy it?'

'We-ell. Everyone in the group really hated her.' Fresh-faced and lissome as an advertisement for female deodorants, Nancy tucked a curl behind one ear. 'And we were all so sorry for that poor little Berthe, I mean. And she never went *near* the kitchen.'

'I must reread it.'

'Why don't you join the book group? You do have to read them. That's one thing about it.'

Sophie shook her head. 'No thanks. You've done her now.'

Nancy's hair stirred in the breeze from the harbour. She had heard rumours. Had denied them hotly. 'Soph!' she had laughed. She put out a hand to her friend. 'Soph, you do know I'm always there, don't you. If you want me.'

Sophie looked at her. Sweet as a hand-picked Cox's, Nancy smiled back. She is a good woman, she is kind, she is generous. She is a friend. I could kick her.

'Thank you. But you always have been, haven't you?' She paused. 'Can Michael babysit tomorrow night?'

'I'll ask him,' said Nancy and left through the gap in the fence.

Arnie was waiting for her in the hall. He held out his keys—two long-shanked old things, stylised symbols of security for locks that could be jemmied in minutes. They were attached to a tattered label marked 'House'.

She shook her head. 'No. No.'

He put his arms around her, rocked slightly but stood his ground. She was inches taller. 'It's all right,' he said. 'It's all right, lass.'

'It bloody is not,' she pulled away, defiant, dangerous, her hair hiding half her face. 'But it will be, you see.'

Arnie said nothing. The boy. What about the boy.

Rebecca, as always, had changed the telephone calendar. July was a porcupine fish.

'How's Arnie?' said Celia.

'He's all right.'

'I thought he looked a bit po-faced yesterday.'

Like the porcupine fish. 'He's all right.'

'Good, good. The thing is, Sophie. I've taken a nasty turn.'

Sophie's feet moved. Celia's nasty turns occurred seldom but their shock waves were wide.

'I've decided it's time the naval wives *did* something. So we're all going to dress up and sing songs and do the tea next month at the Eventide Rest Home in Takapuna.'

'Oh,' said Sophie. 'Are we?'

'Yes. Matelots. Harold's getting the rig.' She laughed, a strange throaty sound. 'Harold,' said Celia, 'can deny me nothing.'

And Kate Calder can organise it.

'It's my swan song,' said Celia cheerfully, 'so it'd better be good.'

Swan song? Sophie did not ask.

It was good. Celia insisted it was good. Like many lazy people she was a good organiser, an efficient delegator who kept her finger on the pulse of other people's efforts. Fat wives and thin wives and callow wives and old Singapore hands poured or squeezed themselves into a variety of bell-bottomed trousers and prepared to sing their hearts out at the residents of the Eventide in Taka. They had been drilled, they had rehearsed, they had grizzled and laughed till they wept. Liz was absent.

'To think she's missing all this fun,' said Nancy. 'And she must've said she wouldn't. Imagine.'

Nancy played the piano, Celia conducted, the audience sat and waited. Paper hats had been provided.

The majority of the audience were old women. One or two smiled, one or two whimpered, one wept silent tears down her mauve front. A few old men sat at the back. An ex-bowler in a blazer covered with badges and mementos of past triumphs slept with his head down.

This is where I am going to work thought Sophie loving them all, their smiles, their stubborn unbreakable gallantry, their rage. As soon as I've paid off Lou, I'll be there. A member of the staff sat at the back knitting something pink. I'll ask her later. Where is the Matron, I'll say, I wish to work here.

'They only come for the tea,' muttered Tricia, the wife of the electrical engineer in William's ship. She was a flat-faced woman much given to busyness. She reminded Sophie of Erin, though no one could call Sophie's father a shit. No one.

The room was large, the television—a source of new pleasure or more bewilderment donated recently by Rotary—sat on a dais by the window. There were many small tables, each one topped by a narrow vase of pink or yellow artificial roses. The young Queen, tiaraed, sashed and smiling, gazed at them from the far wall.

The chairs had been rearranged on the red and purple swirls of the carpet. 'I want the telly,' yelled a man in a red baseball cap labelled 'Uncle Sam Goddam' in gold. 'Where's the telly?'

'Sssh,' said Celia, waving a friendly hand. 'Wait till you hear us.'

'Where on earth did he get that *thing*,' said Tricia.

'I suppose someone sent it from the States.'

'What's it got written on it?'

'Uncle Sam Goddam,' said Sophie exercising her long sight.

'It shouldn't be given house room. Not in a place like this. You'd think the Matron . . .'

Celia's hand lifted. 'Ladies?'

They worked up gradually. They sang 'Clementine'. 'Oh my darling, oh my darling, oh my *darling* Clementine,' they begged the phlegmatic, the gammy knees, the sea of faces before them.

'*Bring* back, *bring* back, oh bring back my bonny to me,' they sang, swaying from side to side as they pleaded. Several of the faces before them perked up. This was better than usual. Of course it was. Celia had organised it. Her hair shone beneath the fierce overhead light, her hands insisted on excellence. The naval wives tried hard, loving themselves and their captive audience. Sophie glanced at the transfigured face of the wife of the Captain of William's ship beside her. The woman was glowing with animation. 'Cockles and mussels alive alive Ohhhh,' she breathed, leaning back slightly as Celia's hands sprang wide for a clean cutoff.

She turned to Sophie in excitement. 'Isn't this *fun*,' she cried.

The wife of William's Captain was not well known. She lived in Kohimarama and was rarely seen on the North Shore. When duty called she appeared, was pleasant and friendly and departed as soon as possible. It was the first time Sophie had seen her rooted to the spot, not transitory—not eyeing the door marked Exit for escape to the balmy joys of Kohi. 'I've some amazing photos,' she whispered to Sophie, 'I'll show them to you and Tricia later. Of the cruise.'

Celia's hands were lifted in supplication once more. They burst into their finale, their set piece, their triumph. Their favourite song of all.

All the nice girls love a sailor
All the nice girls love a tar;
Because there's something about a sailor
Well you know what sailors are;
Bright and breezy
Free and easy
He's the ladies' pride and joy
Falls in love with Kate and Jane,
Then he's off to sea again.

Twenty large and small, willowy and short-arsed wives, volunteers to a woman, hand-picked by Celia from those not gainfully employed or possessed of mewling infants or tone deaf or stroppy, sprang to attention and saluted the audience.

'Ship ahoy! Ship ahoy!' they roared.

They were a success, an enormous success. Tears of happiness were shed, hands were grasped. 'You were lovely, dear, lovely.' 'It took me back, oh my darling girl, it took me back.' 'Never, never, never,' sobbed a lady as she clutched Sophie's hand and the nails dug deep. She would not let go. 'Never,' gasped the lady in the paper hat. 'Never.'

The tea and buns were an anticlimax.

Tricia was cutting cake. She had a good eye; each slice was identical. 'Whoever brought cream sponge?' she muttered. 'They can't cope with jam, let alone cream. Not in a sponge.'

They can, they can. And who are They, and why can't his cap curse for him, here of all places. Here and everywhere for always why not.

'I've got some amazing photos to show you, Sophie,' continued Tricia, manoeuvring between tea drinkers. 'Amazing.' She paused, her eyes on her guests. 'Look at them, just look at them. They bring *bags*, they're that greedy. That's all they come for, you know. We're all busting ourselves for weeks on end and look at it.'

Celia appeared, her face distracted. 'Sophie, come with me.' She led Sophie out onto more swirling carpet and into an empty office. 'Matron's had to slip down the corridor.' Celia nodded at the telephone. 'Now don't panic, it's not the children. It's Arnie. He's in hospital.'

Arnie lay in a small ward, empty except for a barrel-chested man with a plastered leg reading the business page. He nodded at Sophie.

'Asleep,' he said.

Arnie's eyes opened. His smile welcomed her. 'I had a wee turn,' he said. 'Better now.'

She held his hand, noted the ridges and the valleys, the synclines and anticlines of the ancient form. She sat straighter. 'Tell me,' she said.

He hadn't felt too good. 'Didn't want to give you or the boy— or Rebecca,' he added politely, 'a fright if you, you know, came in and found me, so I rang the ambulance. I said you were at Eventide. They asked, see.' His hands moved. 'You'd better get home, lass. They'll be home soon.'

'Yes. How do you feel now?'

'Capital.'

'Oh, Arnie.'

He could have got himself dead. He knew he could have got dead. There was always something.

He closed his eyes.

Sophie kissed his cheek, waved to the rugby injury and left.

Sophie cancelled Michael for babysitting. She and Edward made love in the double bed. It was good.

'What time do they wake up?' he murmured when they woke next morning.

'Not before five. Six.'

He glanced at his watch. 'I'd better go.'

They lay hand in hand staring at the ceiling. 'You'd be proud of me. Slipping along the fence line in the dark like some bloody marine. If I had a black balaclava I'd be a pro.'

'I'll knit you one.'

'And combat fatigues?'

'OK.'

He kissed her. 'Darling Soph.'

'When does Arnie come out of hospital?' he said afterwards.

'Not long. It was very slight, a mini-stroke. He doesn't have to go over the other side to Auckland Public.'

His palms slammed the bed either side of his body. 'Oh, good. Good.'

She rolled on to her stomach to tell him, 'And my parents are coming to stay.'

'Great.'

He leaned nearer. He could scarcely hear her. 'And then William comes home,' she said.

EIGHT

'Mary, you can't.'

'Who says?'

Who says. Who says. 'I do,' said Sophie. 'She adores you. You can't just shove off.'

Mary leaned her hands either side of the sink, her eyes on the crawl of rush-hour traffic over the bridge. 'Ants,' she said. 'Streams of good little worker ants all going home to Mum. Christian socialism, that's ants. All for one and one for all.'

'Will you listen to me!'

'I am.'

Can/Can't. Did/Didn't. The impossible endless jockeying, the jousting of siblings.

'You knew they were coming this week.'

'Yup.' The casual defection was deliberate then. Sophie was hotting up. Mary watched her. Memories of former skirmishes surfaced. Every sign was known. Pink for danger.

'Why do you have to go now? Ben's just got back.'

'He wants to buy a bit of dirt. He wants to . . .' Mary's hand waved, her voice dropped to a husky baritone, 'get down, man.'

Palms upwards, fingers rigid, Sophie gave it to her. 'If you're not back by the end of the week you're a selfish shit.'

Erin shook her behind free from clinging Terylene. 'You mean she's not here?'

She leaned against the car, wiped her forehead with a sunburnt arm. She had taken over again at Hamilton. He was hopeless in traffic.

'Where then, where is she?'

'In the Coromandel. She'll be back on Thursday.'

'Thursday!'

Sophie knew long before her father had told her she was not the daughter her mother had had in mind. Keith Driscoll had dried up Erin's tolerance for the indecisive, had left her bleached as a bone for dreamers.

She needed a quick competent helpmeet and confidant, a sure ally in the battle against ineptitude. She needed in fact Mary, and had rewarded her accordingly. It was quite understandable.

Fruit, chutneys and jams from the boot were received with thanks. Erin, breathing heavily, mounted the kitchen steps to restow. Their labels must be visible. How else could Sophie avoid confusion between apple, pear ginger or green tomato; between quince conserve or jelly? She said nothing more about Mary's defection but, ignoring Sophie's protests, flung herself into her holiday tasks. Ironing and 'altering', mending and gardening engulfed her days. She played Strip Jack Naked with the children, suspected them of cheating and accused them accordingly. Asked them archaic riddles about chickens and roads, about blushing lobsters and Queen Mary's bottom which bored or puzzled them.

'But why did he blush, Nana?' said Kit. 'Because bottoms are rude, dummy,' said Rebecca.

'Oh that.'

'*Sa-ad movies*,' yelled Rebecca, leaping to turn it up, 'always make me cry.'

'Turn it *down*,' moaned Erin.

The withered flower head of the tuberose puzzled her. How on earth had Sophie managed to get a tuberose to flower? 'It was here when we came.'

'That explains it.' Erin did not like chokos. Or the banana passionfruit. 'Tasteless, completely tasteless.' William's onions were worse. They smelled. And repeated, she said darkly.

She watched the children and ached with love.

Keith Driscoll lay in the front room on the four-man sofa William and Sophie had found in the Mart. He placed his behind up the Commodore's end, a piece of newspaper under his feet on the other, arranged his pile of books beside him and settled in for a long haul. Once an hour he heaved himself up, drifted to the verandah and lit his pipe. He was not allowed to smoke indoors. He read six hours or more a day, his sandy curls just visible from the doorway, a faithful searcher after truth. He extended his range on holidays. He read histories, especially those of the Spanish conquest of South America; biographies, particularly contemporary accounts of plant collectors or religious fanatics; and detective stories, but only by women. He was a happy undeserving man. His faults, thought Sophie, were of omission not commission. He wouldn't hurt a fly. Her former faith in the Risen Lord had puzzled him. He was sceptical of answers but interested in extremes. 'Some day, Sophie,' he had said years ago, 'we'll have a good talk about it.' They never had.

He lay at ease all week, his banana shirt open-necked beneath his cardigan, and read. 'I don't know how you can read all day, Dad,' said Sophie from the doorway. Keith lifted his head politely, dragging himself away from *The Hookers of Kew* and the discovery of the delicious little *Rhododendron mirale* at 17,000 feet.

'Oh, but I change books, dear. I don't read the same book all day.' He shook his head as though she had offered him praise which he could not in all conscience accept. 'I couldn't do that,' he said lying back once more.

'Soph has always been so *vague*,' laughed Erin at the kitchen table with Celia whom she admired because she was fun like Mary and got through her morning chores so early.

Celia was not interested in Sophie's vagueness. Not this morning. Previously she might have discussed it, swapped examples, followed it through. Her fingers could not keep away from Punch and Judy. They were on their heads again. 'You New Zealand women are all so competent,' she said, accepting a second mug of coffee.

Erin agreed, her strong weatherbeaten face smiling. She did not realise that Celia would not care to be thought competent. That competence is for the lesser birds, the low-flying millions streaming and wheeling in programmed flight across the world. Eagles fly high, birds of paradise need space to display. They do not flock. They do not wheel and turn on command. They are free from the compulsions of the herd.

'I've popped in to pay my respects,' said Nancy Ogilvie.

'Oh,' said Erin, her face doubtful. Wasn't that when you were dead?

Nancy was worried. Her husband John was the Officer of the Guard.

'Guard?' said Erin.

'The Guard of Honour. For the visit of the friendly Asians on Friday.'

Erin refrained from sniffing. 'Oh, that.'

'And he's left-handed too,' worried Nancy. (Sword drill is more difficult for the left-handed; William.)

John Ogilvie was an old salt. Like his wife, his image seemed born to sell. Fish fingers perhaps, or Navy Cut tobacco. His beard was trimmed, his cap angle rakish, as he rolled around impersonating himself. His sea-going days were past. Like the fish fingers.

Owing to essential commitments, the guard had had very little practice and a less than a hundred per cent perfect guard would reflect on him. Nancy took John's professional concerns personally. Any remark other than ecstatic about the performance of the guard would be taken as an insult to her, like a businessman's wife fussing about the floral arrangements in the foyer for which she is in no way responsible. A dead flower in the foyer indicated incompetence, lack of attention to detail, was an insult to her husband and thus to her. They are loyal, these wives.

Nancy glanced at her Seiko. 'I must dash,' she said.

Sophie scrubbed kumaras and thought about Edward. Her mother sat foursquare beside her, a hand on each knee, her head forward. The time had come.

'And what's your sister up to?'

'You must ask her yourself, Mum.'

'You must know.'

'I know she's given up her job. I know she lives with Ben.'

'And what's he like?'

'I like him.'

Erin's sigh was dragged from deep inside her. All gone. All of it gone. The scholarship, the bracket clock, the research fellowship, her pride in her clever daughter. Where was it all? Where had it all gone, as though it had never been? Erin shook her baffled head.

'The feeding patterns of scallops', that was what the paper had been called. She knew it by heart, had told them at smoko. 'Feeding patterns, my foot,' she had laughed. It had been an extension of Mary's PhD thesis. Had had practical applications. Was of definite value to the fishing industry. Not some cockeyed ivory tower nonsense. Her own daughter had dissected scallops, examined their gut contents, correlated her data and been of some *use.* And been happy. She knew she had been happy.

'Why?' begged Erin. 'Why?'

Mary was right about her mother's bottom teeth. They were enormous, each one separate from its fellows. Had they always led such individual lives? There was no one to ask.

'I don't know.' There must be some crumb of solace, some anodyne comment Sophie could make to soothe the pain. She tried. 'She told me once,' she said, 'that her colleagues liked her because she was zero competitive.'

'How could you be competitive in scallops' guts?' cried Erin.

'I don't know, Mum. I just don't know.' And wait till you find out about me. Sophie's top teeth closed on her bottom lip. She had had a pleasing thought. Erin would not care about her. Not deeply. Not with heartbreak. Hostages to fortune also have their hierarchies. Some are more expendable than others. But what about the grandchildren?

Erin, having professed lack of interest, decided they might as well see the parade in honour of the friendly Asian and his consort. Keith opened his mouth and shut it again.

It was a cold day and the band played as the seats around the football field filled with the entitled. The friendly Asian was small and slim and looked as wistful as Keith Driscoll, with more reason. His country was threatened, neighbouring states were in turmoil all about him. Presumably he believed in the domino theory like Mr Dulles. Had he found the talks in New Zealand a help?

His consort was beautiful; unsmiling but that was as it should be. Consorts, however beautiful, do not smile at such times. Her husband was escorted by John Ogilvie, drawn sword upright in his right hand, as he inspected the Guard of Honour. Nancy was tense. Fiona Banks stood beside her husband Graeme looking bored in a woollen shirtwaister and multi-drop earrings. The band played a selection from *My Fair Lady*. The Commodore was far away, over the other side.

John Ogilvie and his escorted walked slowly along the guard. The VIP stopped occasionally to make a comment to a sailor. He then nodded and moved on. They were up to 'I could have danced all night' before the Officer of the Guard accompanied his charge back to the dais and saluted him with his sword in a series of stern forceful gestures. John Ogilvie's quick about-turn was both respectful and final. His main task was done. The friendly Asian had been returned. His slight form, a mere wisp of martial splendour, took the salute as the guard and band marched past. Bandy has done well once again, as have the guard. The whole ceremony has gone well. It will be discussed with approval later. Usually guards do well, but not always. The ability to mount a good guard is a point of honour and engenders pride in one's ship like being Cock of the Fleet for games.

Sophie's mother's yawn revealed her bottom teeth. Her father's gentle face was impassive; he knew that time was on his side. The ceremony could not go on much longer and *The Hookers of Kew* was waiting. He had reckoned without the reception in the Wardroom.

Sophie had known since the gulls first snatched the scene from behind the Memorial Chapel of St Christopher and screamed it abroad that she was no longer a nice girl. The buzz (William) would have got around. Sophie Flynn was flinging herself at the Commodore. Even if it had not been true it would have got around. It would have buzzed, undergone parthenogenesis and buzzed some more. It would have sported, developed two heads, become obscene and common knowledge. Sophie accepted this. She was ready for knowing looks. The semi-smiles and turned heads of the road disturbed her little. She was prepared. Armoured.

She had braced herself at Eventide rehearsals for mirth or innuendo. 'Your friends may laugh, ha ha ha ha / 'cos friends are funny that way.' She knew too many old songs. They informed the silliness of her life. But laughter had not happened. Possibly it was the masking, the disguise of bell bottoms and clean white fronts, of wide collars and cap tallies. Or the common purpose. Arnie's reaction had been a shock. But she should never have been such a fool, such an idiot, as to make the suggestion to him. She had in fact asked for it.

Her reception in the Wardroom after the ceremony in honour of the leader of the friendly Asians and his consort was different. Amid the coffee cups and the clink of teaspoons and the friendly exchanges between friends and acquaintances, alongside the laughter and goodwill Sophie became aware of this. Wives were displeased. Her affection for the Commodore had gone too far. A joke, after all, was a joke, and excess was more than. Faces turned, chins lifted. Eyes of dumpy wives and tall, of the elegant and the flung-together, slid past her. They did not see her as she stood beside them. Her conduct was unbecoming from one of their own.

Celia was not fussed, nor Nancy who had chewed off her lipstick in five seconds and looked fresher than ever. Sophie's smile was serene. She introduced her parents to Tricia's back, 'This is Tricia Wellbone, my mother and father. Tricia's husband is in the same ship as William.'

'Is that right?' said Erin to the startled face.

Keith was looking desperate. He nodded dumbly.

Tricia was trapped. Sophie drank her coffee. Her smile deepened. She had worked it out. Men were present. Aberrant behaviour from a former member of the group must be seen to be rejected. The shallow root systems of female loyalty can be disturbed by the presence of men, say what you like.

Filled with tolerance towards the good, Sophie watched Tricia who was now impaled by Keith on Chapter Five of *The Hookers of Kew*. A particularly interesting one entitled 'A Viking Funeral', which, he told the now blank face in front of him, did sound odd, but if she took his advice and read the book as soon as possible, she would understand why it was called that. Chapter Five he meant.

Erin had moved on.

'Excuse me,' said Tricia and slipped away, her amazing photos of the Island Cruise still unshown.

The men were friendly as usual. The navigator with the tic told Sophie about his patio. He was still building it, had been building it for some time. He thought he might be able to square it off on his next leave. He told her about the amount of shingle and cement required, his reinforcing and his problems with the boxing. The site had not been easy but he had got there in the end with a bit of help from Barry.

'Barry?'

'My oppo.'

'Oh.'

Barry had knocked one up at Browns Bay. The navigator told her about the joists; where he had got the timber for the struts. How much he had paid for it. How he had eventually decided on teak for the decking. How Lorraine had thought it was too expensive and in a way she was right but, as he had told her, they were getting it labour free except for the beer, ha ha, and when you put that sort of time into a job you feel you've earned the best, if she saw what he meant.

Sophie looked at the lean tanned face working away in front of her, followed the lines, the deep tracks either side of the nose. She wanted to put her hand on the blinking twitching eye, to calm, to heal, to tell him it would be all right. His patio, the teak, Lorraine. Everything. It would all be all right.

'And anyway,' he said taking her empty coffee cup and putting it on a nearby table. 'You don't have to stain teak. So it's worth it in the end. Excuse me.'

Sophie congratulated John Ogilvie on the performance of the guard. Nancy stood beside him blinking with pride and concern. It was lovely having John home from Waiouru but Michael was playing up worse than ever. She had been appalled at his appearance the other day on the Stanley Bay Launch; hair, shoes, everything. 'Your father won't put up with this,' she had warned him. And he hadn't. And the house was creaking with the strain and the fights and Bettina looking scared with her period just started and Michael refusing to mow the lawns or even come out of his room half the time. 'He's sixteen, dear,' Nancy kept saying.

'I know he is and look at him. Look at him!'

Last night as John snored beside her and Nancy watched the fanlight above the drawn curtains change from black to grey to pearl she had a thought. A thought so shameful she had destroyed it at birth like some desperate tragic girl. It was easier when John was away. It was much much easier. Last night had been . . . Nancy, sick at heart beneath salmon pink, blinked again.

'You've had your beard trimmed, John,' said Sophie.

'Someone in the family's got to keep up some sort of standard.'

'What a pretty jersey, Mrs Driscoll,' said Nancy smiling, smiling and smiling again. 'I love fine knitting myself, I mean it takes longer but . . .' They turned away.

'I read such a brave thing the other day,' said Sophie.

John looked wary.

'It was about a bearded lady. I mean a real one, long ago in a sideshow. And every year she had her beard trimmed by the circus barber in the latest fashion. Say Vandyke or Spade or one called Double Twist or something. I can't remember all of them. But don't you think that was a fine thing to do? Changing the style each year, I mean.'

John Ogilvie's beard jerked backwards. His laugh was loud. 'A man, you bet.'

'No, no.' Sophie shook her head. Her hair fell forward. She was very serious. 'No, it wasn't. And when it went grey she just left it. She didn't bother styling it any more. It was thirteen and a half inches. The longest it had ever been.' She looked at him, beseeching him to understand grace under pressure.

'Excuse me,' said John Ogilvie. Sophie allowed herself a glance at the Commodore as he waved the friendly Asian and his consort forward to admire the view.Sophie watched their backs. Noted the slim silk elegance flanked by doeskin. Had the consort's heart been gladdened by the tarted-up toilet? Did she smile Kate's work to see?

Even Harold Pickett's back view pleased Sophie. He had been a liberator, an unknowing catalyst, a growth enhancer.

They turned. People were presented.

The wives did not reject the Commodore. Sophie watched the smiling faces, the animated movements of the heads. The pleasure. The deference. The pride even. She heard Erin's voice across the room.

'Ah, Commodore,' she said. 'I'm Erin Driscoll. I believe you know my son-in-law.'

Liz's eyes also slid, she looked beyond and through her friend. This one was tougher, more incomprehensible. Why had Liz gone dog on her? They were both miscreants. Both beyond the pale.

Both, if you could stand it, in the same boat. The logical answer did not taste good. The buzz, the scuttlebutt, had been heard. Sophie's flag of flagrant excess had been read by all. Evasive action must be taken. The area was mined.

Liz's emerald-green jacket was too long, out of proportion to her skirt. Sophie disliked the collar, the colour, the fit. She realised with a small stab of pleasure that her rejection of this garment was suspect. She had gone off its owner. We are all mad. She laughed aloud. 'Hullo, Liz,' she said. She introduced her parents with a rush of affection for them and the grey earth slog of their lives. Her father might be useless but he worked hard and could make things grow. It was just people he couldn't do.

Liz chewed her lip, smiled. Paul Kelson appeared beside her and told Sophie's parents yet again how much he liked New Zealand. Her mother as always was delighted. Don't bother with Rotorua she told him, there are far more exciting places. Had he thought of the Milford? Paul's laugh was full of pride for the high-stepping filly at his side as he explained that hiking for four days didn't sound quite Liz's do. Liz's eyes were on the Official Party who were leaving the Wardroom. 'Excuse me,' she said, and moved to speak urgently and with force to Harold Pickett who should still have been hovering in attendance giving his support to the Commodore and his undivided attention to the VIP and his consort. They were his guests while they graced the Wardroom with their presence. His expression was intense, serious. This was no idle chat. Celia put her coffee cup on Steward Benson's tray.

'What fun,' she said.

The white ensign was snapping above the signal tower as they left the Wardroom.

Sophie glanced back. 'It's funny how it's called Philomel, isn't it?' she said.

Her mother's eyes were on Keith's departing back, the hand reaching for his pipe. 'What? Why?'

'Because Philomela had her tongue cut out.'

'What!'

'No, no, it's a Greek legend . . .' The face beside her was red, the eyes fierce. 'Never mind,' said Sophie.

'You're so *vague.*'

Her father strode ahead along Calliope Road. His spare scarecrow shape loped past *Choice Meats* and *A Cut Ahead*, mouth puffing, arms swinging like an Early American windvane in the fresh winds of freedom.

Erin shook her head. Even to look at him irritated her. The fact that he could snatch happiness from life despite her drove her mad. She had no time to read. Never had and never would. Never.

'I must go and see Arnie tomorrow,' said Sophie.

'Don't expect me to come. One gaga old man's enough for me. How did you get yourself in this mess in the first place? How are you going to get rid of him?' Erin's eyebrows raged at her daughter.

'Mary'll be home soon, Mum.'

'What's that got to do with it?'

The dockyard hooter sounded. Cars began streaming along the road beside them. Erin raised her voice.

'And what about the children? What about Rebecca? She's growing up. What sort of a man is this Arnie? You know nothing about him. Nothing. What about Kit even!'

'Mum, don't . . .'

'Don't? My own grandchildren and it's Don't?'

Erin, toes outwards, hands clenched, had thought of something cheering. He could dig over the vege garden for his daughter.

They turned into the drive in silence. Not an oleander petal in sight. There was a letter from William.

What's this about an old man? How are we going to get rid of him? It looks as though the buzz about Hawaii is right. Even so, that's only four more weeks. William cannot wait. And he will not forget the pineapples.

Erin had not asked William's reaction to Arnie's presence. Erin did not like William. He was spoiled. People picked up after him in those boats. He was spoiled rotten. She routed Keith from the sofa, flung him into the garden with a spade and began to iron. She was an angry ironer. The board rocked beneath her but she would not give up. 'It has to be done,' she said. Sophie left her mother to her rocking rage and sneaked into the garden. Such words attend her mother—'sneak', 'creep', 'slide'.

Her father stood hidden behind the banana passionfruit smoking his pipe. The tension engendered by the reception and her mother's rage disappeared at the sight of the furtive puffing old man. 'Oh, Dad!'

'Hullo, dear,' he said mildly.

'Let's sit down.'

Her father looked surprised at the suggestion but conformed as always. Vines lay around them, shielding them from the impact of anger. The ground was parched; black ants flowed along their trails, several heaving and tugging at a shared leaf. 'Clever, aren't they?' said Sophie.

'We don't have them at home,' said Keith which was no answer.

'How are the packers? Have you had a good year?' Sophie knew exactly what sort of year they had had from her mother, but never mind. They were relaxed, she and her father.

'Esther's very well,' said Keith.

'Still biting her nails to the quick?'

'She doesn't do it with me.' Her father's eyes watched the long concrete drive as he knocked out his pipe. 'Not when we're alone together.'

The casual announcement of infidelity was astonishing. Sophie had no words. Even if she had, would she challenge him? Would she say, 'You can't have an affair with that sad little misfit, that fey lady.' For one thing there was no point. He probably had been for years. And what could *she* say? Sophie put out her hand, her disloyal mother-rejecting hand and placed it over the brown scarred one which lay beside her. 'Oh, Dad,' she said.

After some time she heard him give a half-cough, a winding up to speech. 'I gave your mother a transistor radio the other day. A lovely little one. All for herself. I put it on the bed. She was very surprised.'

This was too much. 'Oh for heaven's sake!' Sophie leaped up. She was shaking with anger. 'Come on.'

He was surprisingly nimble. 'Mind the ants,' he said. They both stepped over them.

'Of course,' said Erin, attacking his pyjama top with quick stabs of the iron, 'you realise that we'll stay with you when she gets back.'

'Why, Mum?'

'It'll be filthy,' said Erin with the unconscious wriggle of satisfaction of one who knows her subject. The chaos in which Mary chose to live since her defection had been sighted before, marvelled at and grieved over. 'She was always so *tidy*, and now look at it.' Mary's present way of life had the anthropological interest of that of a distant tribe—the Dyaks perhaps or the Mud Men of the New Guinea Highlands: fascinating if you could stand the shock, but not to be stayed with. 'And anyway,' she continued, 'we can't stay with that man there. So we'll just sleep here and go along by the day. It'll be company for you at night.'

Erin waited for her sister, her own sister, not to come and see her. She waited with the same impatience she waited for Bertha not to thank her for the cases of apples she sent her. Apples which Bertha, whose tastes were for the more exotic mangoes, pawpaws and sweet Island bananas, never touched. She left the case opened at the wharf with a card saying 'Please take some'. They disappeared plus the box. She was bombarded by letters from Greytown. Had she received the case? It was now four, five, six days since Erin had taken it to the railway herself. Where was it? Should Erin start enquiries? Bertha rang. Thank you, she had received the apples. Well, that was nice to know. Just as long as Erin knew. Things did go astray. She had only wanted to know. 'It's very kind of you, darling,' said Bertha cheerfully, 'but don't send any more. I can't cope with a case on my own.'

'It's no trouble,' said Erin and sent another next week.

Bertha came billowing down Calliope Road in a ridiculous flowing cape. She embraced her sister. The iron and board disappeared in black.

'Look out!' cried Erin.

'And how are you, luvvie?' asked her sister fondly, thrusting a damp paper parcel of freshly caught kahawai into Erin's hand and extricating her cloak with the other. The double-handed dexterity of the fan dancer had stayed with her.

The rugby injury had disappeared. His place had been taken by a gnome with his teeth in a glass who lay mumbling at the ceiling.

'Good afternoon,' said Sophie. He leaned on one elbow to glare at her.

'I am shat of this place,' he whispered. 'Get me out of here.'

'I . . .' she began. But he was mumbling again.

'Is he like this all the time, Arnie?'

'No. Sometimes he's looking for paradise.' Small, old and battered, Arnie grinned at her. 'I can't help him there.'

Nor me Arnie, nor me.

'What do they say, Arnie? The doctors?'

'Oh, there's physio and God knows. They talk of swimming. I'm a real sailor, I can't swim.' He leaned back. 'But I'm getting there. It takes time, they said. Anyway,' his eyes flickered, 'there's your Mum and Dad.'

'They're going soon.'

It is just a question of my lover, Arnie, and, of course, my husband. The nail marks on her palm convinced her. It was real, this astonishment, this impossible mess.

'How's the boy?'

'He's coming to see you tomorrow. He's got it all worked out.'

'Aye?' He saw the bent head, the concentration, the timetables.

As she was going he grinned, took her hand, pulled her down to him. 'I dislike this place,' he whispered.

*

Edward rang each day. Her parents returned each afternoon 'in time to help', Erin bringing travellers' tales and action, Keith silence and his book.

The telephone calls were less satisfactory than formerly. Sophie desired her lover, ached for him, wished him to be naked beside her or under or over but *there.* Here. There. She leaned against the wall in despair, stuck her tongue out at the bloated puffball on the calendar. 'Uncle Sam Goddam,' she moaned.

'What?'

'I want you.'

There was a pause. 'Tonight,' he said, 'after the Australians' cocktail party. Even if we have to hire the Ops Room.'

She had always loved him.

The quarter deck of the Australian frigate was lined with side curtains lashed to the stanchions in an attempt to keep the wind out. You had to be careful where you put your feet. There were bollards and ring bolts. It was cold. Men in snug doeskins or city suits gravitated to the edges. Women huddled inside this inadequate protection like Western pioneers encircled by wagons. The wind was freshening. The RAN band played 'Moon River'. Tricia, the engineer's wife, was shivering in Thai silk. She had left her mohair shawl in the Captain's cabin. How could she have been such a fool. She will have to send someone for it. But who? Hedley is sweating far away in the South Pacific. She misses him. 'Fool,' she moans.

The young ladies from the Middle Watch of the Navy League also shiver. Some are half-naked with shoestring straps against their smooth creamy or brown shoulders and short skirts beneath. One is in flaming red chiffon with hair heaped and piled and tangled above her head like one of Lou's posters. Another has a cropped flapper haircut. She is small with round red cheeks and bright eyes. She is a sparky lady and looks as though she might come skipping or sauntering on stage dressed as an Edwardian masher with a top hat and cane to tell the party that she is Burlington Bertie, she rises at ten-thirty as if they cared. There is a lot of laughter from the Middle Watch ladies and courteous attention from the Royal Australian Naval officers especially the Jimmy who seems to be particularly good at it.

A small uniformed man standing beside Sophie sighed. He had two-and-a-half gold stripes on his arm. Soft fair hair fell across his face.

'Have you enjoyed your time in New Zealand?' she asked.

'We've only been here half a day.'

'Oh.' They stood side by side in rigid social unease.

'Excuse me,' he murmured and departed. Sophie never saw him again. She pictured him curled up on his bunk with a book. He seemed the type. The canapés were good.

The band was now confiding their lack of wooden hearts. Time passed. But slowly. Sophie was warm in her patchwork and jersey. You do learn some things. She stood and smiled. Where was Edward? One or two of the Middle Watch were getting a glow on. The stewards were assiduous. There were no empty glasses. The frigate was not a long ship (William) and the drinks were strong by civilian standards.

The officers, as always, paid for them. The keen men drink very little and never at sea (William).

The Commodore appeared smiling. 'Soon,' he murmured. Their fingers touched.

The band burst into 'Ramblin' Rose'. Captain and Mrs Featherston were visible across the crowded deck. The Captain smiled and waved. Mrs Featherston nodded.

Everyone leaped to attention for 'God Save the Queen' with that awkward hopping movement which is always more noticeable in women than men.

The stewards had ceased serving drinks. 'God Save' had finished. The party was over.

'You've got your car?' murmured Edward.

'Yes.'

'Park near the Devonport fish and chip shop. I'll send the car back. Walk down.'

'What!'

It would be less risky than the Operations Room but not much.

He arrived without his cap, his Burberry buttoned to the neck, a steaming parcel of fish and chips in one hand. She had a vivid glimpse of a tall tree bending, of arms reaching upwards to Clarissa.

'Best in Auckland so Tollerton tells me.' He laughed at her startled face. 'No, no, weeks ago. Let's go down to the boat ramp. Good place at this time of night.'

It was dark as they drove past Elizabeth House, not a Wren in sight. 'Some day,' he said, 'we'll live down this end. Right?'

'Right,' said Sophie, melting, self-destructing with longing.

She parked facing the black hole of the harbour. The wind tugged the car. It was colder than ever. The lights of Auckland were far away.

He unwrapped the newspaper, sniffed the hot greasy smell as it filled the car. Permeated. 'Fish first, or chips?'

'Fish.'

They lay in the back seat after he had ditched the discards, mopping their shining fingers, their oily mouths.

He belched, hammed it up. 'Oops, pardon.'

'Give over,' said Sophie, her eyes bright with tears.

'I once tried to teach a parrot to belch,' he said. She reached in the space below the dashboard, handed him connubial tissues.

'When?'

'I worked hard on him for weeks. Day after day. Didn't work though. He was a good talker, too.' He thought about it. 'Something to do with his tongue, maybe.'

'What did Clarissa say?'

'It was after Clarissa.' He wiped his hands again, scrubbed his mouth. 'Dear old Cocky.'

'Sophie?' he said later.

Her voice was muffled. 'Yes?' He lifted her head from his chest to ask her.

'Can we go to your house?'

'My mother's in the double bed and my father's in Arnie's room.'

'I want to lie beside you.'

'Yes.'

'I don't want to scramble about in the back seat. Not tonight.'

'No.'

'We did all right on the floor. In the front room. When . . .' The name had disappeared. 'When you found the cat.'

'Chester.'

'Chester.'

'Yes, we did, didn't we?' She sat up, lifted her arms and clasped them around his neck. 'Why not?' she said.

The luxury, the God-given luxury of a whole floor, of carpet, of room to manoeuvre. The hardness was nothing. They fell upon each other like thieves, robbed each other like felons and were generous in return.

'Sweet Christ,' he whispered.

'Nnnn.'

He sat up. She could see him only dimly. They had not left a light on.

'I have to go down to Wellington soon,' he said. Fingers and thumb came up, rubbed the bridge of his nose.

She sat up, knelt before him shivering with cold.

'Why?'

'Routine. Programme meeting.' The hands reached to welcome her again.

'Love you,' he said.

The overhead light was blinding. Keith Driscoll stood aghast, an abject slippered Pantaloon with one hand on the switch. He gaped at the naked figures on the floor before him. His daughter, kneeling on her haunches. Some man. 'I'm sorry, I'm sorry,' he gasped. 'My book.'

Horror leaked from his eyes. 'I came for my book.' He turned off the light. 'Oh my God, my God,' whispered the darkness as he shuffled away.

Sophie was inconsolable. Edward could not help. He had never seen her cry before. Tears splashed, literally splashed down her face. Her mouth was anguished as an expelled Eve's.

'What is it?' he begged. 'All right. All right, it's terrible. Your father—but what *is* it?'

He could get no sense from her.

'No, no, no. You wouldn't understand.'

'Well, tell me, darling heart, *tell* me.'

'It's the apple grader all over again,' wept Sophie.

Her parents left the next morning, Erin driving as usual because of the motorway.

The surge of loss, of something missing, which usually dogged Sophie's farewells with her parents, was absent. She was numb. She no longer clung to the blind hope that one day they would learn to play the game like other families; like naturals.

Erin unwound the driver's window to tell Sophie they had had a nice time. A very nice time. Yes. And Ben. Well, she could only hope. Time they were off. She rewound the window, still trying to say something. Yes, she called behind glass. Lovely. Love to the children. Goodbye. She gave a final wave. Her lips moved. Goodbye, dear. Look after yourself. And thank you.

'Goodbye,' said her father.

NINE

'You don't have to be mad to work here,' said the sign above the poodle-cut head, 'but it helps.' It was surrounded by postcards: the Hawera water tower, lambs among daffodils, the Parthenon. And Peter Pan at the bottom. Peter Pan in bronze, piping away for ever in Kensington Gardens. Sophie sat waiting.

'It's like this,' said the woman, riffling with quick laden fingers through case notes labelled 'McNally, A'. A black Oroton bag clanking with wide gold chains lay on the desk. The shoes had been bought somewhere else. Sophie watched the spectacle frames and counted the rings. Five. Almoners, social workers, whatever they are called now, used to be serene comforting ladies noted for home-made bread at ward parties; soothers and smoothers with an aura of homespun.

'It's like this,' she said again, fixing Sophie with eyes as wild as Cracker's. 'There is no reason why Mr McNally should not go home at this stage.'

'No,' said Sophie. 'Except that he can't look after himself.'

'No, no, of course not.' More riffling, 'But I understand, Mrs— Flynn, was it? Yes, Flynn. And I'm Maureen Ridge. I understand Mr McNally was living with you.'

'Yes. But my husband is coming home from sea and . . .'

'That's nice.'

Sophie took a deep breath. 'Mr McNally came to live with us because he needed help . . .'

'In what way?'

'He was incontinent and starving.'

The shoulders moved beneath the lambswool.

'And Dr Pleasance was assessing him and arranging Meals on Wheels and for the district nurse to call and . . .'

'That won't be enough now, I'm afraid.'

Listen, Oroton, I am very fond of Arnie. He is my friend. He will come home with me. But I have a lover and my marriage is over and how am I going to tell him and he didn't ask Arnie to stay. You sit there in your Cubans dispensing and allotting and making suitable arrangements day after day. As you should. As you are paid to do. You work hard, you will go far, but think, woman, *think*. Some situations are impossible however hard we organise and this is one of them and all right it's my fault but I love him see, not that I would tell you. Not a chance lady. Not an iceball's chance in Hades. Not till the busy world is hushed, the fever of life over, and our work done. Then Lord in thy mercy . . .

She leaned forward. 'Mrs Ridge . . .'

'Maureen.'

'Maureen. There must be residential homes . . .'

'Oh there are, there are. The North Shore is well served in that way, you're lucky over here.' Her hands reached for another file. 'Rewarewa's the nearest. But the problem is that Mr McNally falls between two stools if you see what I mean. He doesn't need hospitalisation but he's shaky on his pins. A very slight residual weakness in the left leg and they have to be pretty spry for Rewarewa.' The voice dropped. 'Just between ourselves, they're not too struck on walking frames even. And they won't have a bar of wheelchairs . . .' The poodle-cut head shook in defeat.

There was nothing to say.

'How mobile is Mr McNally?' she said after the pause. 'Can he get to the bathroom by himself for example?'

More riffling.

'The toilet? Yes, with a stick.' The *Milford Track* staff would come in handy.

Maureen Ridge stared at the face in front of her and gave her verdict.

'If you are unable to accommodate Mr McNally, then of course I must make alternative arrangement as regards placing him.'

Sophie was on her feet. 'He comes to me. To me! But not for ever,' she said pink with shame. 'Not for ever.'

Maureen, calmed by an over-emotional response, adjusted her spectacles once more. Her eyes were stilled, her hands quiet beneath their cargo of rings. 'I quite understand, Mrs Flynn. One's family must come first. I'll make arrangements and we'll discuss it later.'

'And Mr McNally? Will he be consulted?'

The laugh was phoney as Tinker Bell's. 'Of course. But in the meantime . . .'

'He comes to me. Us. Yes. Thank you.'

'And of course they'll probably recommend physio.'

'Yes.'

The corridor shone. Sophie strode out into the real world, the world where she could tell Arnie how lucky he was and get on with it.

He was coming home tomorrow.

Sophie helped him into bed. 'Better now,' he gasped. 'Better, thanks. Better.'

Rebecca had put Bluey and his cage beside the bed to welcome him. 'Bloody bird,' he muttered, turned his face to the wall and slept.

His hands shook with excitement at *The Book of Knots*. 'Mum got it out for me on her card,' explained Kit, demonstrating bowlines on the dining room table. 'It's in Adults.'

'He's back then, is he?' said Edward.

'Yes.'

'Great. And when's William get back?'

'The twenty-fifth.'

'Of course. Of course. Tonight then.'

'He's just come home. He might need me. You know, in the night.'

Silence.

'I know, I know. Tomorrow. Please come tomorrow,' she said.

'It's the Harbour Board annual dinner.'

'Oh.'

'Wednesday?'

'*Yes.*'

'Arnie,' she told him. 'My man is coming tonight.'

He looked away. Picked up his nutty old binoculars, stared at the harbour. 'It's your house,' he said.

His friends came bearing gifts.

Bertha arrived with kahawai. She shook his hand warmly, sat opposite with her denim legs wide and grinned. 'You'd better buck up, Arnie,' she said. 'I'll be needing some help with the whitebaiting net soon.'

'I doubt that,' he said. He was unimpressed, stern, a man to be reckoned with. 'I doubt you mean that, Mrs Boniface.'

Bertha was unfazed. 'Too hearty? You may be right. We'll see.' She turned to Sophie, 'I'm going down to Greytown next week. Your mother has to have her bottom teeth out and poor old Keith, well, you know.'

'She didn't tell me.'

'She didn't want to worry you.'

Arnie left them, a slow rasping shuffle of retreat across the haircord.

Celia brought shortbread. Buttery yet textured, airy yet firm, it was made by Mrs Robinson who cooked. She was the reason why Celia had not yet departed. Celia had had hopes of Mrs Robinson. She was a childless widow, why not join her in Wickham, Hants. Mrs Robinson declined. 'I like it here,' she said.

Mary and Chester arrived with gingerbread. Bluey panicked, flung himself about the cage with desperate cheeps, his wings hysterical.

'Why did you change everything when Ben moved in?' asked Sophie, shoving the cage through the slide to the kitchen.

'Everything how?'

'Dropped your job, changed your life, lay around.'

Mary stretched to the sky, clenched her fists, dropped them. 'Ah, the critical change of pace you mean?'

'Yes.' Sophie's voice was gentle. She was just interested. 'Why so completely?'

'I've always done what I wanted to. No messing about. You know that.'

'Exactly. So why change because of Ben?'

Mary snapped upright in her chair. 'I didn't change because of Ben. I'd had enough of scallops' guts. I knew them, I loved them, I'd done them, I got sick of them, that's all. Or rather, sick of the Yo-heave-ho of the research world. The scramble to publish, to further the careehah, the foot poised on the ladder of break-through.' Her hands were furious, her hair swinging. 'You've got it all wrong! Ben is different from Dad. Right?'

Sophie's smile was forgiving. 'Nutter.'

'Ben is a very relaxed person. Ben is a good painter and he's mucky.' Mary leaned towards her. Rebecca's eyes flecked with gold insisted. 'If I'd cleaned up after Ben, I'd have turned into Mum.'

'Oh.' The back of Sophie's neck prickled. She saw her mother's face mouthing at her through glass, felt her hopeless concern. 'She has to have her teeth out,' she said.

'Mnn, Bertha told me,' said Mary. She was still angry. 'Think about it. What I said.'

'Yes. But . . .'

'But nothing.' Mary was as convinced of her satisfactory handling of her role in life as the Harbour Board pilot in his launch below. 'Use your loaf. There's nothing cute in stupidity, in destroying yourself. In making a desert and calling it a victory or whatever. And anyway we're not at war, thicko.' She changed tack, her voice sharpened. 'And I'll tell you something else.' Sophie recognised the tone. She concentrated on the homeward-bound pilot boat and was silent.

'Your life won't change if you go and live with this rooster. You realise that.'

Sophie flung back her head to laugh. 'Oh, Mary,' she said, putting out a reassuring hand.

Her smile was still tolerant as they walked to the gate. The fair weather of last night's loving was heightened by Mary's absurdity. Everyone should have it, this life-enhancing passion. This glory should be in every home. 'Why do you think Mum stays?' she said, resisting a quick note-from-Edward check in the letterbox. She had not mentioned Esther and Keith's liaison. It was too pat, too much, too mother-bashing at the moment.

'Because he's all she's got. That's all she has to keep her ticking, poor old bat. Just nagging him rigid, running the orchard, having her teeth out.'

'And us.'

'Us? Oh God, yes. Tons of fun there. Chester! Come back.' She sprinted down the road after his gleaming shape. 'Chester!'

'I have to get some sausage meat,' Sophie told her back.

Evan was pleased to see her. He had been even more attentive since the incident which was nobody's fault least of all Lou's, and the rumours were interesting. He stopped hacking a weeping carcass into governable hunks and moved forward smiling, his hands buried in bloody cheesecloth. His renovations in the Ngataringa Bay house were going well he told her, though Wow the price of timber these days.

'Yes,' said Sophie. 'I heard that.'

'Sausage meat, was it?'

Sophie nodded. 'It's for Scotch eggs.'

'Come again?'

She told him. How you hard-boil the eggs, how you must not flour your hands or the sausage meat won't stick, how the egg must be covered completely. All this she told the pale eyes before her, while her heart was beating boom/lurch boom/lurch and the winter sun was shining and she could burst with sheer wanton joy. 'Then you fry them,' she said.

'Is that right,' said Evan, slapping the glossy pink stuff onto a small square of greaseproof paper. 'Not for me though. I'm not an eggy person. Never have been.'

He bent to peer at the scales, wiping his hands yet again. Was Lou an eggy person? Did it matter? Probably not. Not if other things were equal. And far far more important, was Edward an eggy person? Sophie stood very still, drenched in lilac/green fluorescence. She would find out.

She saw the four of them around an unknown table. Edward, Rebecca, Kit, herself dispensing eggs if desired, saw the hands reaching, accepting, rejecting. She dismissed the image quickly. William was an eggy person. Had been from way back.

Evan handed over her change. 'There you go then. Good as gold.'

She worked it out at the empty letterbox on her way home with the makings. Twenty-four days left.

They discussed the future in the double bed. As the days became fewer they discussed it more. They lay awake churning it over, thinking it through. 'I must be there when you tell him,' said Edward. He switched on the light, watched her blinking eyes. A thousand years ago he had thought them faintly cow-like; large luminous and brown, they were the colour of peaty mountain tarns, of brown-gold pansies so help him God.

They were now sparking. 'No, no. Ask yourself. He's been . . .' No one, however deranged, could say the word 'cuckolded'. 'I'll tell him by myself,' she said.

It was a cloudless day. Their ship was coming in. Groups of women waited on the wharf; eager laughing women exchanged anecdotes—what happened last time, how you never get over the thrill of them coming home do you, not really, how it made it all worthwhile and you could say that again. Children ran around in circles, tugged at hands, a small boy had a wee lapse. 'Poor little mite's overexcited on top of the wait,' said his mopping Gran. 'He's not,' snapped his mother and why the hell the old girl had to come every time was beyond her. A small child in pink frills jumped up and down for half an hour, jigging with the wonder of the day and the promise of a hula doll as well. Babies looked blank, small toddlers puzzled, larger more knowing ones caught the infectious gleeful tension from their mothers and circled faster. A tough egg in rompers charged a herring gull. 'Gail,' screamed a tiny brunette to a two-year-old about to fling herself off the wharf. 'It's just the excitement,' said her grey-haired restrainer.

Kit's wide grin was constant. Rebecca was happy.

Sophie felt sick, sick as a dog who'd died, sick beyond word or thought. The effort required to smile increased the nausea. Tricia Wellbone was further along the wharf, talking to the pill-boxed wife of the Captain. She appeared beside Sophie. 'I've just been chatting to Brenda,' she said, patting the breast pocket of her knit which had a tendency to buggle.

'Brenda who?' said Sophie, her mouth dry.

'Oh Soph, you are a scream. Oh look!' A ragged cry went up. Relatives and loved ones waved harder. The frigate was visible slipping around North Head. Long, low and purposeful, she slid past the ferry wharf. Tricia glanced at her watch. 'Only ten minutes,' she said.

The Captain was on the wing of the bridge giving orders. William stood at his side relaying them. Stop both engines. Finished with main engines.

'A perfect alongside,' said a naval officer goofing beside her. He sounded faintly disappointed.

The band played. The herring gull returned. The romper suit ignored it.

'There he is, look. Look Mum!' said Kit. She stared at his beaming face. He couldn't keep still. Everyone was laughing, shouting. More waving, more cries, more delight. 'He'll like the decorations, won't he?'

'You bet,' said his mother. Rebecca was dancing beside her.

Solemn-faced sailors hiding smiles lined the upper deck. They were home. It was good. Lines were thrown, caught, cast round bollards. The gangway was put in place and mounted by the Captain's wife. Tricia was eyeing Sophie. Eyeing her with intent. 'Come on, Sophie, they'll be waiting,' she said, and led the way up the brow to her shit of a husband.

William was waiting, a fine-looking officer, smiling and harassed. 'Dad! Dad!' squealed his children. He reached over their heads to peck her cheek, seized each child to him for one fierce clench and dumped them immediately, his eyes on the gangway. 'Quick, quick, get behind here.' He shoved them behind a gun or something. Sophie was reeling, the children open-mouthed. 'The Minister,' said her husband and leaped to the gangway.

'The Padre?'

'God, no.' She caught the exasperated glance in mid-flight. 'The *Minister*.'

'Oh.'

'What minister?' said Rebecca.

'I don't know.'

They peered around the gun. Escorted by the Commodore and the Captain of Philomel, a large man in a tight suit and a brown hat marched up the gangway. The bosun's call sounded; the Captain, William, the Officer of the Watch and gangway staff all sprang to attention. The brown hat was lifted, revealing tight red curls. The Commodore saluted. He saw Sophie behind her gun. He smiled, a smile of such delight, complicity, recognition of stuff-this-for-a-lark absurdity that she turned away blinking.

The official party moved forward. William came back to his loved ones smiling. 'Well,' he said. 'Great to see you,' he said and kissed them. 'Come on down to the Wardroom.'

'I don't think I want to,' said Sophie.

Blankness, total blankness. 'Why ever not?'

'I don't see much point in being dumped behind a gun one minute because of a so-and-so Minister and then going down to the ditto Wardroom to suck up to him, that's why.'

His mouth dropped, literally dropped, hung loose. 'But I was on duty. And anyway, it's not a gun. It's a turret.'

'Oh, for God's sake.'

'Sophie!'

She saw the children's eyes; wary, flicking from one face to the other and back again. Saw the Doyenne du Comice outside the window. She shivered, touched his arm. 'Do you want to go to the Wardroom, fellas?'

'Yes!' The Wardroom was Coke and potato chips and kindly men. 'Yeah!'

'Let's go.' She took his arm.

'Watch the coaming,' said William. She fell over it and clung harder. He smiled down at her, delighted once more with his warm loving wife who was as clumsy and desirable as ever. 'My God, I've missed you,' he whispered.

'Go down backwards,' he called but they had disappeared. Sophie ducked her head and went down slowly. William skidded down, his black polished feet scarcely touching. He was used to companionways.

'Any problems with the car?' he said as they drove up the hill.

'No.'

He sniffed. 'It pongs a bit.'

'Pongs?'

'Yes. Open a window, Kit.'

The cold air sliced the back of her neck.

'Quick, come and see, Dad. Quick!' they squealed as the car stopped. They dragged him into the sitting room. 'Shut your eyes,' they yelled. 'Now!'

He didn't see it for a minute. The surprise hung high above the long sofa, the few chairs, the Valor for background warmth and permeation. The kids were staring upwards. Sophie's hands were clasped. He looked up. A ragged line of red painted letters spelt it out. 'Welcome Home Dad.'

'Wow,' said William. 'Gee. How did you get it up there?'

'Ben did it for us.'

'Did he indeed?'

They were staring at him now. They had not had enough. Not enough words had been said. 'Do you like it, Dad?' said Kit.

'Yes, yes. I said.'

'It took a long time,' said Rebecca.

'Yes, yes, it would,' He clapped his hands together, smiled at his loving offspring. 'Well, thanks a lot, kids.' He turned to his wife. 'Well, it's great to be home. Great.' The pause was brief. 'Don't you get the *Star* delivered now, Soph?'

She mouthed at him. 'Presents.'

He snapped his fingers. 'Of course. Come on, kids. Come and see what I've got.' He picked up his Pusser's grip from the hall and headed for the dining room.

The pineapples were first. Identical in size, chosen with care to ripen sequentially, they were eyed with suspicion. Was this all?

No. He had done well. Cars and a gun for the boy, a doll which wet itself and said Momma, shell necklaces and candy bars with weird names and exotic shiny wrappers.

'Thank you,' said Sophie. 'Thank you so much.' Thank you for my hibiscus-laden muu-muu and my flask of scent called Extacy. She kissed him. He rolled against her, seized her, slammed his mouth against hers and dug deep. She felt him move against her.

'Here's Arnie,' said Kit.

They scrambled up from the sofa, caught red-faced in their own living-cum-dining. 'William,' she said, 'this is Arnold McNally. Arnie. William. William. Arnie.'

There seemed no reason to stop the insane bleat, the plea for harmony. The two men put out an arm, moved closer. There was no enthusiasm. They were stuck with each other. Fate, Sophie, something untoward had landed them in this unsatisfactory coupling of hands, this mug's game.

'Hullo,' said William.

'Hullo,' said Arnie. He murmured something else.

'What was that?'

'It's Geordie.'

A muscle tugged William's cheek. There was silence. Kit and Rebecca stopped in mid-chew. Sophie touched the table. 'What does it mean?'

'Welcome home.'

William shoved his hair back with a brown hand, uttered a quick yap of mirth. 'Well, thanks. Thanks very much.' He looked at his children, his silent wife, the old man with his stick. What did they want? What did they all want from him, standing, staring, bloody well *looking* at him. 'I'm going to change . . .' he gave a manic grin to show he was joking, '. . . into dog robbers.'

'Bring your washing,' said Sophie.

There was still no wind. Strips of multi-coloured light hung straight, sinking deep into calm water. Neon advertisements, endless, repetitive, winking ads for meat, for flying, for getting away, blinked across the harbour. Arnie had departed. The children were asleep. Their parents sat in silence on the verandah.

'More coffee?'

'Thanks.' She shivered.

'Are you cold?'

'No.'

'We could go inside if you like.'

'No, no, thanks.'

He had thought of something. The coffee mug remained in mid-air, his shadowed face was anxious. 'You don't think Rebecca's too old for that doll, do you? The pisser?'

'She seemed very happy.'

He sighed. 'Good. That's good.' They were a worry, presents. Always had been. He stretched his legs, took her hand. 'Bed,' said William.

'There's something I have to tell you.'

'Tell me in bed.'

'No.'

He glanced at his watch, sighed again. Put out his hand. 'Tell me.' There was a pause. 'Incidentally,' he said, 'did you get the vegetable garden dug over?'

'No.'

'I'll get onto it this weekend.'

'William.'

'Yes?' He moved closer, shoving his deckchair nearer with quick jerking arms and feet. 'Spit it out.'

She had one hand screwed against her mouth, had run a mile. 'I want a divorce,' she said.

He didn't believe it. Not for one second of one minute did he believe it. He almost laughed, searched for her face in the shadows, saw it and didn't. 'Balls!' cried William.

'I . . .'

'I don't believe it.' He was on his feet, lean, tough, whipping about, stirring himself into a rage he didn't feel. All he felt was disbelief. 'I don't believe it.'

She stood up, moved closer. 'William.'

He grabbed her, shook the fool, the wife, the woman he had ached for night after sweating night in the fucking tropics. 'No!' he shouted.

'I'm in love with someone else,' she yelled.

This was too much. Far too much for his lust and his love and his rage which came at last. He shook her again, harder. Her head jerked back, her hair was everywhere. 'I'll kill him!'

Her eyes seemed to be rolling. They couldn't be. Appalled, he grabbed her in his arms, held her to his chest, murmured her name. He lifted his head and hid it again. They stood in each other's arms, shaking with fright.

'Who is it?' he whispered.

It was too dark. But light would be worse. She pulled away. 'Edward.'

'Edward *who*, for Christ's sake.'

'The Commodore.'

This time he did laugh. Loud brutal and crass, the sound shattered about them, made the night hideous and left them breathless. 'That shit,' yelled William. 'Old Groper Sand. The biggest stick man in the business!'

Sophie hit him. Her hand came up and slammed against his gaping mouth. Fair square and hard, Sophie hit him. He was caught in mid-gasp, but managed to sob it out. 'What a fool! Jesus Christ, Soph. What a fool!'

She was proud as a bolt. 'Right,' she said. 'So you won't mind when I leave you.'

'You're not leaving me.'

On and on, round and round, hour after hour, they tore at each other, insisting, hating, despairing. They had never talked so much in their whole lives. What about the children. She hadn't given them a thought had she. Not a fucken thought. You'll have access. Access! Access! These are my *kids*. Catch old Groper taking on a couple of . . .

Lone and broken, William wept. Wept till his face was wet, till Sophie mopped it and lay against his chest. 'Come to bed,' he said.

'No, no.' It was never going to end. Scrambling to her feet, her arms guarding her breasts in maidenly rejection, Sophie tried to explain. She would sleep on the sofa in the front room.

She didn't. They slept in the double bed. She tried to comfort him.

He brought her a mug of tea next morning. Sleep had restored his rage. Disbelief had gone for ever. Why Sophie? Why *Sophie*, in heaven's name? He looked at the heavy eyelids, the dried track of a tear, the skin. She was so fucken innocent. *Groper* had seen this, had known it all. William gripped the bedhead. After a moment he pulled on his clothes, glanced at his watch. Even the kids were asleep. He strode along the road.

The bell rang for some time. William tried again, kept his finger on it till the door opened. The sod stood there. Crumpled grey hair, unshaven in paisley silk (*silk*), the swine looked at him. 'Come in,' he said.

William leaped at him, hands outstretched, head reeling. Kill him just kill him that was all. Then go home. Go home to his wife and love her.

Edward moved back. His voice was quiet. 'Watch it.'

William said nothing. He moved closer. The man was still calm. 'Tollerton'll be here soon,' he said.

Tollerton? William shook his head to clear it.

'There will be a witness. Attack on a senior officer,' said Edward.

William was shaking. 'You fucked my wife!' he screamed.

Edward was startled. He had expected outrage but not passion, not from an uptight automaton like Flynn who had never fired a shot in anger or explored the astonishing depths of his own wife. This dead bore, this homicidal lunatic who was nothing, who knew nothing about anything except gunnery, surprised him. He had expected a more rational approach. Something less gut-wrenching, less shattered, less *real* from young Flynn. What a mess.

'I love your wife,' said Edward.

Through the window William saw Leading Steward Tollerton striding up the road to work. 'I'll kill you,' he sighed. And there were other ways of destroying. He opened the door. 'Some senior officer,' said William. At the bottom of the steps he turned and spat it out, 'Groper!'

Edward closed the door.

He couldn't go home. Not yet. William turned left, ran down the hill to the still calm of Stanley Bay. It was mid-tide; a line of small waves flounced across the unwarmed sand. There was no one on the tiny cove; the launch was waiting at the old wharf. Two oyster-catchers waddled about fussing at the shoreline, then sailed into the air to fly straight and true, their cries echoing in the stillness. Kleep. Kleep.

A Grammar-school boy slipped the rope from the bollard and leaped on board, his man's work done. He slouched beside the Captain, at ease on his own private boat. The launch departed; no bells, hooters, just a gentle easing out, a widening ripple of wake breaking the mirrored clouds.

Not a soul, not a blind soul. William pulled off his shirt and trousers and raced into the water, hitting it flat with a racing dive. The cold clutched his balls, tightened his chest. The water was melted ice. He surfaced and headed for the harbour, ploughing through the water with long tormented strokes. He turned on his back gasping with pain. What the hell was he doing? He floated, shouted at the sky, gasped for breath. He was getting colder. What a dumb way to die. He dived deep, surfaced and headed for shore. There was someone on the beach. Shit.

He stood upright in the shallows. Ben, a long piece of silvered timber in one hand, lifted the other. 'Hi,' he said. 'Cold out there?'

Ben. Of all the men in all the world. Ben. William nodded. His teeth were chattering like a six-year-old's. 'Yes,' he said.

Ben draped himself around his length of wood and looked on as William struggled with dry corduroys, wet underpants and streaming legs. 'No towel, huh?'

'No.'

Ben's mouth twisted. 'Sudden mad impulse?'

William, his jaw locked to disguise hypothermia, nodded.

Ben, his face grave, nodded back. 'Nice to be home, I guess?' He was wearing a large homespun jersey. He propped his piece of wood carefully against the steps to the road, pulled the jersey off and handed it to the uni-neuronal idiot gibbering in front of him.

'No, no.'

'Take it, man. Take it.'

William took it. Warmth enfolded him, comforted and succoured him. He was alive. 'Thanks.'

Ben was still watching him. His sleepy hooded eyes saw through and out the other side. His eyelashes were too long for a man. They splayed across his bottom lids in deep sweeping arcs.

William was still shaking. 'Bit early in the morning for you, isn't it?'

'Ordinarily that would be true but I'm into lumber at the moment.' Ben patted his find. 'First up, best dressed for lumber.' He shouldered the useless dozy slab of four-by-two. 'Coming?'

There was nothing for it, not if he was ever going to be warm again. They set off up the hill.

'How's Sophie?' drawled his saviour.

'Fine. Fine.'

'And the kids?'

'Great. Great.'

The length of timber swung dangerously as the man turned to him. 'That's nice.'

'Yes.' William had thought of something. 'How's Mary?'

'Why, thank you. Mary is out for the count at the moment but I guess she'll surface, maybe two, three hours.'

'Good,' said William, misery sweeping over him once more as he thawed.

The timber on Ben's shoulder swung again. The lashes were vertical jalousies. 'Great old guy, that Arnie who's stopping with you.'

'Arnie? Oh, *Arnie.*' A twist, a twist of the knife. At the top of the hill William pulled off the jersey. No, no, he was quite warm now.

'I enjoyed yarning with him about the mutiny.'

The wet rat head turned. 'What mutiny?'

'I don't recall the name.'

The lawns needed cutting. The washing machine was thundering away as he stood at the back door. He touched the box of rotten feijoas with one foot. Couldn't she have chucked them on the compost? No time. No time even for that. He walked through to the kitchen, nodded at the old man and his son in the dining room. Kit lifted a hand. She must be in the shower. William rubbed a hand over his stubbled chin, poured lukewarm tea into a mug and picked up the photograph propped on the window sill. His jaw dropped, stayed hanging. How could she have got it? It must have been Wellbone, he would have sent it to his wife. Typical, typical, he'd known from the start the man was a scrubber, would shop every man on board if he had the chance. He stared at the black-and-white photograph, hypnotised by three-inch-by-four-inch. There were only the two of them. Missie was plastered against him, glued from knee to crotch and further. Supple as a liane and about as wide, her head flowered against his shoulder, her mouth was wide open. She was boneless, timeless, without will or support. She was his and had been all week in Hawaii.

'It fell out of a pocket,' said Sophie from the door. Her hair was wet. She was wrapped in a towel.

TEN

'I would've told you,' he said.

'Kids,' mouthed Sophie. They were fighting; vicious recriminations from the allegedly pinched and the definitely framed filled the dining room.

William put his head through the slide and roared. 'Pipe down, you lot.' They did so. Wounded and misunderstood they lapsed into the body language of hate; fingers stiffened, elbows came into play, a quick foot.

Her face was serious but unconcerned. Iced to the bone once more, he slammed the slide shut. She gave a small ridiculous start (she could see the thing bang), hugged the towel tight and headed for the bedroom.

'I would've told you,' he said again.

She turned her back on him as she dropped forwards into her bra, adjusted alignment, tugged on her pink spotted pants. The chill splintered, stuck in his heart, tightened his groin. 'I'm your *husband*,' cried William. The knowledge that it wasn't that photo-snapping prick who'd shopped him but his own carelessness increased the pain.

She turned. Again that balls-aching polite attention. 'What do you mean?'

He couldn't say it. He couldn't say, you do not have to turn your back on me while you dress. I know your breasts. I love them. I know your bush, I . . . There were tears in his eyes. He shook his head. She was dressed now, a blue jersey, a skirt made years ago. He had crawled around on his knees pinning the hem. (Stand still can't you.) He watched her. A woman parting her hair, bending forward, flinging it back, getting it straight. He picked a loose hair from her shoulder, wondered if he had ever seen her before. Ever seen her before in his whole fucken life.

'Thank you,' she said. 'You're wet.' She'd noticed. After ten hours his wife had finally noticed. 'Where've you been?'

'I went for a swim.'

Her smile was slow, almost loving. 'Oh.' She was making the bed, tugging, aligning, tucking away as if there was still some point in doing so. From habit, sheer merciless habit, William adjusted his side, smoothed the pillow, pulled up stripes and straightened them.

'What's her name?' said Sophie.

'Missie.'

Again that gentle enquiring smile. 'Missie? I suppose that was one of the hilarious photos Tricia Wellbone was going to show me.'

He had been right then. In one small, minor, unavailing point he had been correct.

'Did you sleep with her?'

'Yes.'

She looked into his eyes. Dark, swimming with tears, the eyes of her ex-husband stared back. 'Why did you never tell me you really liked me,' she said.

'Rear Admiral Tower requests,' said the invitation. 'HMS Cheetah.'

'I'm not going,' said William.

Arnie, who had been heading towards the verandah, stopped in mid-shuffle and reversed. The tapping of his stick filled the silence.

William stared after him. 'Why does he always bugger off when I say anything?'

'He thinks he's interrupting.'

'What's there to interrupt?'

She tried again. 'I thought you'd be pleased. Going on board a whatever it is.'

'Cat class cruiser,' he said automatically.

Who was the man who walked on eggshells? Edward would know, but perhaps not. The Bible was not his field. 'Why don't you want to go?'

'I wouldn't mind seeing a Cat class. But we won't see it. We'll just fart around.' Pain still clamped his forehead. 'And he'll be there. Groper.'

Sophie said nothing. It is easier to hate if you insult the enemy, call them names. It has been going on since strumpets, harlots and trollops and still is. Shock had slapped his face the other night. If it gave William comfort to be absurd about the lover she ached for, so what. He needs all the help he can get and I can't give it. 'Accommodating' old men, puddling about with plastic pottles of pudding and canisters of meat and two veg will not help William, even if it helps Mrs Rimmel who has just retired from her own cake shop where she worked six-thirty a.m to p.m. for thirty-five years and where has it got me, she asks beneath her plastic pixie hood wet or fine, eyes flashing as she takes her meal. 'I'm a miller, you know,' she says, 'I trained as a miller. I'm not just a baker. Thirty-five years day and night and where has it got me?' To broken health and near destitution, Mrs Rimmel, but think of your children and the good start you gave them after he left you for a floozie so long ago. Does this help your enlarged heart as the Mother's Day cards slip into your letterbox which is adorned with a wrought-iron Mexican asleep beneath his sombrero.

Meals on Wheels will not help William, nor the brass gleaming in the sanctuary, nor grateful lepers, nor Harvest Festival. Fluffing about with pumpkins is not enough. Charity begins at home, does it not Mrs Rimmel.

'Yes,' said Sophie, switching to robust mode. 'Edward probably will be. It's an honour for you to be asked. What are you going to do? Hide?'

'I went to see him.'

Her hand went to her mouth in a travesty of surprise. 'No.'

'Yesterday morning. The bastard pulled rank.'

'I don't believe you.'

'Ask him.' He picked up Arnie's binoculars, twiddled them, hid his eyes. 'I suppose the whole base knows.'

'I think there are rumours.' And if you look so naked, so wretched, every rumour will become fact, though this I can't say to you and anyway it already is. The facts are down.

'That's one of the reasons we must go,' she said.

Admiral Tower's day cabin was a large room with soft chairs and mushroom pink sofas. Old prints of sailing ships beating round the Horn and up the Main and elsewhere lined the walls. They all looked very similar. A female face (long nose, lobeless ears) stared unsmiling from a blue leather frame on the desk. A thin man came forward to greet them. He bent from the hip and extended a dry leaf hand. 'How nice to meet you, Mrs Flynn. I had the pleasure of meeting your husband off Tonga recently. Taut-run ship it was too. My Flag Captain and I went over by jackstay, didn't we, Jasper?' A whiskered Captain beside him laughed in happy accord with his senior officer. 'No one ditched us either. Have you met . . .'

He turned to introduce his other guests, all of whom they knew. William's Captain and his wife Brenda talked to Celia and Harold Pickett. Harold was looking hunted; he had got stuck with an olive stone. The lights were very bright. A high-ranking member of the Navy League and his wife breathed recently demolished fish balls at Sophie. A well-known criminal lawyer stood beside his dark unsmiling wife who was telling the Commodore about her childhood in Miami City, Florida. After some time she hissed at Sophie, 'Where's the john?' Celia took charge. All the women present decided the john was what they had in mind. They were directed through the Admiral's sleeping cabin which had no photographs at all nor any sign of human habitation except a narrow bed. It is a strange life.

The men were talking about the structure of Civil Defence in this country when they returned. 'Is it well organised?' asked the Admiral. 'Very,' said Harold Pickett.

'The deputies are officer types too, I presume?' said Admiral Tower.

There was a pause. New Zealanders examined the carpet; the john lady lit a cigarette. The smoke trailed from the side of her mouth, Marlene Dietrich giving herself time. She, the Admiral and the Commodore were at ease.

Edward smiled at Sophie. The john lady looked thoughtful, William distracted.

The Admiral's hectic eyebrows invited them to sit. The lights were even brighter. Place names were displayed in tiny silver holders—a rickshaw man, a fisherman beneath a large coolie hat, a fish jumping with open mouth. They come from Singapore. People buy them.

A string trio, who presumably doubled in brass in the band, assembled. Soup was served, consommé plus small floating squares of something waxy and pallid. The trio was a mistake, if not slightly nuts. They played too loudly. And shouldn't you listen. And talk. And eat. And smile.

The meal was served. You should not smile at Royal Naval stewards (William). They do not like it. It is not the custom of the country.

Celia was sitting on her host's left. 'Goodness,' she said, glancing at his plate and being forthright. 'Don't you like venison?'

Admiral Tower's smile was wistful. 'I had too much of it at prep school,' he explained. People nodded understandingly, their faces solemn. Sophie snorted. William watched her bleakly. It was part of her, that ridiculous explosion of mirth. He did not mind it.

The meat was very high. So high that no one asked its

provenance. It must have been shot on the hoof in the wild. An old shipmate, perhaps, now farming somewhere in the back country who wished to honour his friend Tommy with a well-hung haunch. The trio played on.

The port was passed. Women were allowed, in fact encouraged, to pour their own. There was a little flutter from the solicitor's wife who was unskilled in the procedure but it is quite simple if you keep your head.

At Holy Trinity Devonport before he sailed William had handed Sophie, Rebecca and Kit money for the offertory. Sophie handed hers back. She had explained to him several times in the past. 'I am a grown woman,' she had said. 'I will give my own.'

She sat there remembering, passing the open decanter to the Navy League on her left with a polite murmur and despair in her heart. Why had it taken her so long to wake up? She had been asleep, sound asleep like some bumble-footed child bride dozing her life away in rented naval castles. Edward was not responsible for her awakening. She had woken herself. She had heard the delayed-action alarm on its last whirr, its final gasp. She glanced across the table at her lover who was explaining that although he had never been lucky enough to visit Miami City, Florida, he knew the north-eastern seaboard quite well, particularly Rhode Island where he had once attended a Sea Power symposium. Did Mrs erm happen to know Rhode Island? She surely did. She had had a sophomore classmate at Cornell and had visited over several vacations at Newport and what about the cottages of the millionaire robber barons? Weren't they something? They were indeed. Sophie watched him with pride. He could talk with anyone on anything; with good sense and gravity, with playful use of his well-stocked mind, he could entertain and inform. The whole world minus God was his field: geographically, emotionally and in depth.

William was still looking at her. His hair was all over the place, his eyes dismal as a slow thaw. The Navy League lady had given him up, abandoned herself to Harold Pickett on the other side. Sophie could stand it no longer. She pushed her chair back. 'Excuse me,' she said. How many times had the phrase been murmured at her in the last fourteen years. Five thousand? Ten? 'Excuse me,' she said again and walked to the door. The Admiral, caught in mid-salmon cast, rose belatedly. William was already upright. The Commodore rose and sat quickly. Celia, her hair burnished by light, her rings resplendent, was also on her feet. 'I am not well either,' she said cheerfully. 'Perhaps it was the venison,' she explained to her host. 'Anyway, I'm going. Thank you so much.'

The three of them were escorted off the ship by the startled Captain.

They stood in silence on the empty wharf.

'What's wrong with you?' said William.

'Nothing. I just couldn't stand it another minute.'

'Nor could I,' said Celia dragging velvet around her shoulders. 'So we left. This is positively my last appearance.'

William looked at them. Defeated and sickened by his wife and every female in the world, he handed Sophie the car keys. 'I'll spend the night on board.' He strode off through the dockyard without a glance, his footsteps clanging.

'He didn't kiss you,' said Celia.

'I've told him,' said Sophie.

'Oh.' Celia shivered. 'Let's go home and have a drink.'

Sophie drove out the top gate. 'He starts his leave tomorrow.'

'Oh God.'

'Yes.'

The windscreen wipers hissed with excitement. 'Sophie, about Edward.'

'Don't say a word.'

What can you do? You can only do so much. 'Drop me off now, would you, darling?' said Celia.

Liz and Paul Kelson, their bodies close as Missie's and her protector's, were walking at speed along Calliope Road, their heads bent against the rain. Caesar ran beside them on his late-night run. Celia lifted a hand. 'Give him a toot,' she said.

Sophie did so.

'He needs it,' said Celia. 'Paul Kelson needs all the toots he can get.'

'Yes,' said Sophie.

William walked up the hill next afternoon. The change-over had taken some time and there was no point in hurrying. Small gusts of wind tossed a few old leaves about his feet. He paused near the pair of old cannons in front of the Wardroom. A fantail was teasing one of them, dancing with rump feathers fanned inches above the barrel, dipping and diving, darting upwards to flip once more. Everything was mad. Everything. He had never seen a fantail in Devonport before, let alone flirting with a war relic set in broken bricks and surrounded by a white-painted kerb. Fantails were bush birds, made to be glimpsed through slabs of green sunlight. Forerunners of joy. He couldn't understand it. The world had gone mad.

William had always played according to the rules. Had joined Cubs, Sea Cadets, given his promise and raised his right hand. And meant it, meant every word of it and still did. He knew the Commodore was a shit, everyone did, that was nothing new. But Sophie was a good woman. Too good. Lumbering him with that weird old pot, cooking her head off for the church, saving in jam jars for the lepers. His best Green Triumbles disappeared each year to tart up the sanctuary. He was happy with that. Happy to contribute, to do his bit. It was all of a piece, except now it wasn't. Now it was shattered. His eyes on the flickering bird, William made a decision. He could not go on like last night and the nights before. He was a man and would behave like one. He would bite the bullet. The fantail had disappeared.

'Where's Mum?' he said as he entered the living room.

Kit glanced at him. 'Devo.'

'And Becca?'

'She's taken Bluey next door for some cuttlefish.'

'Oh.'

Kit and the old man were sitting at the table with the Ludo board between them. 'Uckers?' said William. Again that dismissive glance. 'Yes.'

Arnie's eyes had not moved from the board. 'Blob,' he said and put a counter on top of another.

'Aw hang.'

William tried again. 'You've got an expert there, Kit.'

Kit nodded. He was concentrating on a six; arms, legs, fingers tense as he shook the dice.

William sat beside him. 'I'll give you a game later.'

'This is a match, Dad. Best of three, isn't it, Arnie?'

'Aye.'

William stood up, moved to the window.

'When did the big keeler go out, Kit?'

'I don't know.'

Sophie was at the door, her arms full of library books.

'Where've you been?'

She hefted the books slightly. 'Can't you see?'

Could he? How did he know? How did he know anything? He picked up Arnie's binoculars, inspected them. 'God in heaven,' he laughed.

Arnie's hand, dry as a lizard basking, curled around the dice shaker. 'I'll thank you to put them down.'

William held the binoculars by their cracked leather strap and swung them. He heard his voice. 'Whose house is this?'

Arnie put down the dice shaker, reached for his stick and levered himself slowly to his feet. One hand clung to the table.

'Your turn, Arnie,' said Kit.

'The Royal New Zealand Navy's,' said the old man.

'And who pays the rent?'

'You do.' He paused. 'Sir.'

'Yes. And I'll thank you,' William was breathing fast, 'I'll thank you to keep a civil tongue . . .' God in heaven. He sounded like Bligh. Charles Laughton. Someone. His wife and son were gaping at him. Pompous, idiotic, heartbroken, William veered to the right. 'I hear you were in a mutiny at one time,' he said.

Both hands clung to the long staff. The voice was a thick Geordie snarl. 'It wasn't a mutiny. It was a strike like the miners.'

'Ah, the Invergordon Mutiny. I've read a lot about that. Nineteen thirty-one wasn't it?'

'Aye.'

They stood, arms and bodies bent, hating each other. Sophie put down her books and moved forward. Kit touched his friend's hand. 'Arnie?' Not a glance.

'"Refused orders to sail." What d'you call that!'

'Passive resistance. Like Gandhi. No violence ever. There could've been but no one . . . not one.'

'One of the ringleaders then, were you?'

Arnie clung harder. He peered up at William, his eyes half-closed, his mouth a slash of hate. 'And proud to be. What would you know, you wee boy with your wee navy—four, five ships and all. What d'y'know of twenty-five per cent cuts and ruin. Ruin, man, ruin for men promised no cuts. *Promised.*'

Kit was now tugging his sleeve. He couldn't understand the thickened voice, the mad words.

'It was mutiny,' yelled William.

Arnie was fighting for breath. He lurched towards his tormentor, his warrior's taiaha held before him. Kit was sobbing. Sophie seized William's arm.

His right hand flung upwards to ward off the length of wood. The strap of the binoculars snapped. Arnie dropped his staff as they hit his chest, gave a small puff of sound and fell forward. He lay still, far too still, motionless on the haircord of the dining-cum-living room.

Kit dropped beside him howling, lay flat on his stomach as he insisted, 'Arnie, Arnie, Arnie!'

Sophie was on her knees. She seized Kit, held him to her.

William stood staring. He knelt heavily. One knee, then the other. His hand reached out. He had never seen such stillness.

'He's dead,' he said. 'I've killed him.'

Kit gave a shriek of denial.

The sound echoed from the harbour, deeper, more mournful and resigned. A tanker was sailing.

Kit hid his face against his father. 'No. No! No!'

Sophie took Arnie's non-existent pulse and stood up. 'I'll ring the doctor.' She stood hesitating at the door. How could she leave them, either of them, leave them for a second. William's face was blank above his son's hidden one. He was rocking him in his arms, back and forward, back and forward, back and forward. She touched his head. 'Don't,' she said. 'Don't,' and ran.

She stood at the door and watched them. William was no longer rocking. The doctor would come immediately.

No child should look like that. 'Kit,' she said, 'come and sit up here.' She patted the sofa beside her. Quick, efficient, Sophie was regrouping. Kit shook his head. 'Dad didn't do it.'

'Hi,' said Ben and Mary from the doorway. Mary's face changed, shifted. Ben's looked interested. 'What . . . ?'

'Dad didn't do it,' cried Kit.

William rose to his feet. 'Arnie's dead,' he said. He sat beside Sophie, picked up her hand, looked at it and put it down. Mary was on her knees beside the dead man. She put out a hand to touch him, pulled it back. Her hair flipped back. 'You've rung the man?'

'Yes, he's coming.'

They waited in silence, staring at each, separate and alone.

Kit ran for Arnie's old dressing-gown. He put it around the dead man and went to his mother to hide. Ben strolled to the window and looked around. Mary and William sat rigid. You could hear the silence. The clock ticking. The gulls.

Ben was looking for something. He glanced at the narrow bookcase at the head of the table, picked up a pottery owl and put it down on the table, moved to the slide to the kitchen and peered through it, felt with one quick hand behind the smiling family group trapped on the mantelpiece beside the clock.

William lifted his head. 'Sit down.'

Sable lashes flicked Ben's cheeks. He sat. After some time he lay back on the dining chair, scratched his groin, looked at his watch and remembered it was bust.

He could wait no longer. 'Where's the old guy's binoculars?'

Quarried from stone, William's voice answered the sod. 'Under him.'

The lashes flickered. 'How come?'

'I threw them at him.'

Mary's head jerked up. Kit was on his feet shouting.

Rebecca stood in the doorway, Bluey flapping in his cage, Nan Ogilvie's gift of cuttlefish jammed between budgie ladder and silver bell. 'What's wrong with Arnie?' she said. She had got used to him. Quite liked him in fact.

'Come here, Becca,' said Sophie.

'We came to tell you guys we're moving down the coast. Coromandel,' Ben told the silence.

The doorbell rang. William rose to answer it. The footsteps were loud.

'Good afternoon,' said Dr Pleasance. He rubbed a palm over his bald scalp, put his bag on the table beside the owl and looked around. His hands waved. 'There are too many people in here. Just the patient and me, please, and Lieutenant Commander Flynn, thank you.' He opened his bag, hung the stethoscope round his neck and dived in again. They sat staring at him. No one moved. 'Out, out,' said Dr Pleasance making shooing gestures. He had a surgery full of patients waiting as who didn't at four on a Friday and had been hoping to get out to Karekare and check on his beehives before nightfall. His bees and his bush and the hills. He sighed, looked at the man at his feet. Another one.

'I'm not going,' said Kit.

Mary took Rebecca by the hand and left. Ben went reluctantly. He glanced back at the door, opened his mouth and shut it again. He didn't like leaving them though he could always pick them up later. No one would want them. None of them had an eye for quality and he had to have them. Industrial archaeology had always interested him and they were beautifully made. He could always cut off the macramé. His hands were sweating slightly. 'I guess,' he said.

'Come on,' said Mary.

Dr Pleasance put his hand on Kit's head. 'Out, boy.'

They went out the French doors, Sophie's arm still round him. They sat on the verandah, facing south to the waves chopping the harbour in the onshore breeze. She kept talking, she talked and talked and talked to the child in her arms. Arnie had died, Arnie had loved him. They wouldn't forget Arnie. Arnie was all right now. The bullet head moved. 'Why did Dad throw them?'

'He didn't. The strap broke.'

'Then why did he die?'

'Because he was old.'

'No.'

'The strap broke,' said William.

Dr Pleasance had finished his examination. 'No need for a post mortem. History of infarct. Recent stroke. I've seen him lately.' Arnie now lay on his back in his hand-knitted cable. The doctor redraped the tartan. His foot touched the binoculars. 'Looking through them, was he? When it happened?'

Deaf. He must be deaf. William raised his voice. 'I told you. I was swinging them. The strap broke.' William's eyes closed, opened again to stare at the doctor who was restowing his kit. 'They hit him in the chest. I killed him.'

'Sit down,' said Dr Pleasance sadly. William sat down at the table, laid his head on his arms and hid. 'You didn't kill him,' said the man beside him. 'Coronary infarct killed him. His heart was worn out.' He spoke louder. 'You did not kill him.' The misery in the lifted face was excessive. Was the man a fool? A self-dramatising fool masquerading as a naval officer? Dr Pleasance had few naval patients, they have their own men, but he saw many of their wives. He sighed again. Resisted the temptation to tell the face to buck up. Flagged away Karekare for tonight and probably tomorrow. He must ring Madge and tell her. And the surgery. Bruce Pleasance, sixty years old, a smash service to reckon with and quick to the net, was a hundred and four. There was too much death. He was sick of it. He put out his hand and gripped William's shoulder. 'It's just a formality, but in view of what you tell me, I'm afraid I'll have to inform the police.'

No emotion now. The face in front of him tightened, clamped, bit on the bullet. 'Yes,' said William.

'Purely a formality. You'll find them most understanding.'

'Yes.'

'But it will probably mean a coroner's inquest and definitely a post mortem. I can't sign the death certificate, you see. Not in view of what you've told me.'

'No.'

Dr Pleasance rose, swept the back of his head with his hand once more as he nodded at the verandah.

'They'll be getting cold out there.' William sprang to his feet.

The doctor put out his hand. 'I could give your boy something. Something mild.'

'No.' The unmanageable head of hair, cross-grained with cowlicks like his son's, shook briefly. 'He's got us.' He opened the door and held out his arms. 'Come inside, gang. It's brass-monkey stuff out there. Come inside.'

The police. Well, what would you say about the police. Understanding? It depends what you mean by understanding. It's not their job to be understanding. Not what they joined for. A man lay dead at their feet. Who or what had killed him? That's what cops are for, paid for, trained for. William lay on his back, flung himself onto his right side beside Sophie. How had she gone to sleep, how the flaming hell had she gone to sleep? She hadn't for a long time. She had held him like a child. He wouldn't think about it. He couldn't do anything now, not at night. Not now. Had he killed him? The doctor didn't think so. But why had he dropped dead, puffed one groan as they hit him and dropped dead at his feet sweet

Christ. William turned again, peered at his watch, oh four double oh. Getting on. Getting there. It was only oh three something last time. He lay struggling to remember, his body rigid with concentration; oh three what? He couldn't remember; tossed again. It was starting to rain. Understanding. Why the hell should they be understanding? They weren't paid to be understanding. They had been tough. Polite, detailed and tough. They were meant to be tough. They weren't bloody hand-holders. Crime. Crime was their business. What they were trained for. What they did. He flung his arm out. 'Soph.'

She murmured in her sleep.

There was all that too. Why hadn't she fussed about Missie? Why hadn't he killed the sod? William was on his back yet again. He'd killed the wrong man. Like some B-movie plot-twister he'd blown it, blown his life and killed it dead except it was dead before. He groaned. 'Soph?' he begged again.

A sash window shook. The wind must have gone round to the north.

'Dad.'

He heaved himself on his elbows. He could scarcely see the child. 'Dad,' said Kit.

William threw back the blankets and pulled him in, held him and hugged hard, kissed the back of his neck. 'Go to sleep, boy. Go to sleep.' Hard rain drummed on the tin roof. The only soporific in the world.

Sophie arranged the funeral. There was little to do.

'Was he a believer?' said the Reverend Farrell, eyes on her face and wondering. Sophie blinked at the word. 'A believer? No. I don't think so.'

'Then I'll keep it as brief as possible. Unless you'd like to say a few words, Sophie.'

That phrase too; green shade, a row of flower pots. 'No thank you.'

'Very well, my dear. And you think St Augustine's rather than here?' The plastic hymn numbers moved in his hand as he waved a proprietary arm up the nave.

You are a good old man Mr Farrell, but I haven't heard from my lover for a week and my son needs me and also my husband yes indeed oh yes indeed.

'Yes,' said Sophie.

'You don't have to, you know. You don't have to have a church service.' Freddy Farrell's long black-robed arm waved again, indicating secular arrangements, distant crematoria, anodyne colour schemes.

'No, we must have an organ. LSBA Butterworth has offered to play. Apparently he knew Arnie. They belonged to some organisation. He wasn't very clear about it.'

Freddy Farrell nodded. 'Yes, of course.' His feet were killing him. 'St Augustine's it is then.'

They retreated to their own corners while they waited. They did not come out fighting. They waited; avoided each other's eyes, adjusted their mouth guards, kept their heads down and waited.

William refused to take sleeping pills. Kit came to their bed less often and finally not at all. He clung seldom and seemed happy, but how do you know? Children don't say.

Bluey laid an egg. There was no word from Edward. They waited.

The coroner's verdict was brief.

I hereby certify that having enquired into the time, place, causes and circumstances of how Arnold McNally, of Devonport, Auckland, retired seaman, died, I found that the deceased died of natural causes the cause of death being a myocardial infarction resulting from advanced coronary artery disease and not related to any conduct of persons present immediately prior to his death. I make no further comments or recommendations.

*

The little church smelled of warm brick, polish and something indefinable but less pleasant. 'Mice,' said Rebecca.

The four of them stood in a row in the front, hypnotised by wood and brass handles. The undertaker was pleased to have the show on the road, but careful not to rush things.

Mr Farrell stood waiting, his face grave above his freshly ironed surplice. 'I know that my Redeemer liveth,' he said.

Kit clung to his mother's hand and sobbed. Mr Farrell kept it brief. The undertaker moved forward with his trolley. Rebecca panicked, burying her head against William's dark suit in sudden despair as LSBA Butterworth swung into 'Cock of the North'. They marched out, William's numb mind tingling with indecent versions of the non-existent words. People came up to them. You have to go up to someone. Friends from the road, Nancy and John Ogilvie, Evan in his blazer. 'I'm Cora and he's Bob,' said a bright-eyed woman with a crocheted rose on her hat. 'We were neighbours. We did what we could. Didn't we, Bob?'

'Yes.' Bob shoved William a hand. 'You took him in, then?' he said.

'My wife,' said William, surrounded by desolate children and strange people.

'Ah, your wife was it?' He paused. 'And you got off all right, I hear.'

Liz was wearing the green jacket. She hugged Sophie. 'She's gone,' she said.

Sophie, bereft and bewildered, unlifted by the lively tune, glanced around. 'Who?'

Liz was smiling. Eight bells and all's well. She was beautiful once more. 'Celia. She's left Harold. He told me himself.'

Sophie turned quickly to her large and generous aunt. 'Come home, Bertha. I'm going to the, you know, but William and the children and Mary and Ben'll be there. Please, Bertha.'

'You can't go to the crème de la crème all by yourself . . . Hullo, Kit.'

'Hullo.'

'I'm going.'

'I'll come with you.'

'No.'

Liz was fussing with the strap of her shoulder bag. 'Edward's in Wellington this week, so Paul tells me.'

Wellington. Her lover was in Wellington. She must have got the week wrong.

'Poor old boy,' said Liz, her eyes on Caesar and his bars. 'I must dash.'

The mourners dispersed. Sophie followed the hearse.

Edward had made contact by the time the square cardboard box was delivered.

'Do you want to come?' Sophie asked William.

'You can't do it by yourself,' he said.

How do you imagine the leftover tags of life are knitted up when you are not present. How are the allotments juggled, the children kept safe? 'Scattering ashes,' said Sophie, 'is easy on your own.'

'Unlike adultery.'

She blinked in surprise. He would never have thought of it before, let alone said it. But then he had not needed to. William was evolving, undergoing protective coloration and imitative display. He was acquiring survival skills.

'We'll all come,' he said.

The four of them walked down the road together and rounded the side of the house. Sophie carried the box in a patchwork bag. The blackbird, presumably in full voice by now, was silent, sulking high in the pittosporum.

Sophie pulled back the green curtain. 'Neat, eh,' said Rebecca.

'Yeah.' The ashes held no qualms. They bickered over their disposal, were reprimanded, took turns shaking the box and brushed their hands against their legs. 'Good old Arnie,' said Kit.

They ran back across the ragged unmown grass, zig-zagged across the compost trench laughing and disappeared out of sight.

William glanced around him. 'What about the lawns?'

'That's the estate's business. Like the house.'

'Who gets it?'

'The Communist Party.' Sophie smiled her slow enchanted smile. 'He'd gone off the Labour Party.'

A commie. William's shoulders sagged. A bloody commie. He might've known. He should've guessed.

They stopped at the gate. Sophie broke off three granny bonnet seed heads and tied them in her handkerchief. Her hand rested on the yellow galleon. 'I liked him,' she said.

William couldn't take his eyes off her. Her bent head, her calm.

'We can't go on with this,' he said.

'No,' said Sophie. 'We're not going to.'

ELEVEN

Life went on, what else could it do, where else could they go? Sophie and William circled around each other with restraint, were gentle with the children and gave them treats. They took them to the zoo.

'You're going as a family, are you?' said Nancy over the fence.

'Yes,' said Sophie.

'You're lucky.' Nancy's head was down, her fingers busy with a drooping passionfruit tendril. 'Michael won't do anything with us now, not as a family. Not even picnics.' She rubbed her forehead, begged for an answer. 'Do you think it would help if we all took up scuba diving?'

The lions raised patrician heads and yawned. These were proud captives; they would not crack under pressure. The female's hauteur, her crossed paws, reminded Sophie of the photograph on Admiral Tower's desk.

A small padded child of indeterminate sex clutched a weeping green lollipop. 'Can those cats get out of there?'

'No,' said an older minder taking the disengaged hand.

He/she sucked long and hard. They moved on, escorted by

goose-stepping mynah birds past the Children's Zoo where Rebecca and Kit were stroking some small hand-held animal.

William leaned on the iron balustrade above the lions and turned to his wife. 'You realise I won't make Commander till he goes. Quite apart from the other business.'

Sophie's eyes were on an enormous abandoned thigh bone below. The ball joint gleamed bluish white, shiny and clear as a baby's sclerotic; the shaft was mangled and bloody. 'What?' she said vaguely.

William kicked the base of the wall, lifted his head and snapped at her.

'What sort of a two oh six would you give your lover's husband?'

Her glance was placatory. 'Two oh six?'

He wanted to throw something, to kick a lion. Married to a naval officer for fourteen years and she *still* didn't know. William's bullet was wearing thin. 'Recommendation for promotion for God's sake. My brass hat.'

'Oh.'

A shackled elephant clanked past escorted by a keeper. The trunk curled backwards, unfurled like a ponga frond and tapped its mooching attendant twice on the shoulder; a comradely gesture, generous as a heartfelt handshake. The moustached face smiled, put out a hand to the wrinkled monolith beside him.

Sophie turned back to the lions. 'Edward,' she said, 'is an honourable man.'

William slammed his clenched fist on the railing. His eyes swam with pain and rage. 'Jesus wept!'

The caged tiger was no help. Back and forth, back and forth, it rolled across the cage on oiled joints, its tail swishing, cracking from side to side as it swung around to pound once more.

The baboons were light relief.

William left Arnie's bed each morning and dug. He broke the sods, turned them over and limed them well. He refused to accept that there might be little point, that they might no longer be living in the house as a family when his unplanted beans came away. His wife was unfaithful, his near certainty of a brass hat was gone, his wife, his kids . . . He dug like a maniac. Drenched with sweat he leaned on his spade and watched the sky. There was a front coming up. Heaped black-grey cumulo-nimbus were creaming up from the south; mountains of dark clouds piled above streaks of grey. The silver disc of sun had disappeared. A line of defeated-looking herring gulls huddled head-on to the wind; three black-backs hung motionless above his ship. William reached for his jersey and stopped in mid-pull as he noticed the jack flapping in the stiff breeze. He marched to the house, kicked off his boots and made for the telephone.

A voice quacked at the other end.

'First Lieutenant here. Get that jack close up immediately. It's flapping around like a whore's drawers.'

'Aye aye, sir,' said the voice.

William went back to watch. A figure ran forward from the gangway. The jack was close up.

He dug on.

He was glad to get back on board. He had worked something else out. It was up to Them to make a move. Time was on his side, time and the children and passive resistance might save him yet. William was competitive and trained to win but he was not stupid and he loved his wife. He would wait. He could wait. He would. Each day would help. He walked down the hill to his ship each morning, did his day's work and strode home again. He was polite but distant. Emotion and trauma had almost destroyed him. He would disengage, reassemble and wait.

'What are we going to do?' said Edward. 'We have to meet.'

'Yes.'

Someone had put a red ring around the twenty-ninth. The twenty-ninth? Sophie shook her head. It meant nothing. 'We can leave letters in Bertha's box. I asked her before she went down.'

Eyes on the cave weta for August, Sophie thought of her mother. Frustration, whatever the cause, is an ache in the groin, an itch beside the bone.

'What happened in Wellington?' she said.

'I'll tell you when we meet. Soon.'

'Yes.'

He was jubilant. He loved plans of action, decisions pleased him, and it had been a long time. Rose Featherston's ex-husband now farmed north of Auckland. Captain and Mrs Featherston planned to stay in the house and keep an eye on things while he took a much-needed holiday down south. '"Much needed", that's what they said. I'll go up for the weekend and do the feeding out. There's a boy during the week but Lionel and Lettie are beyond messing around with bales of hay. So you come up.'

'But they'll be there.'

'Yes.'

'How can we talk? Anything?'

'There's a cottage. I'll work something out. I have to see you.'

'Yes.'

She rang her mother. Of course she was all right. What a fuss. And a toll call. Sophie saw the creased forehead, the anxious hands distancing themselves from wanton expenditure. 'Here's your father.'

'Hullo, Dad. How's Mum?'

'All right.'

Sophie sat on the edge of the bath watching the hand tug the cheek, the sweep of the snow-plough blade. He didn't like electric. They didn't do such a good job, not on a heavy beard.

'William?'

'Nnh?'

'Will you mind Rebecca and Kit on Saturday?'

His head ducked, a brief involuntary warding off. 'Why?'

She finished her inspection of her dressing-gown cord. 'I must see Edward.'

The clown face gaped from the mirror. 'I mind your kids while you . . .' He turned, slammed his hands at her. The razor clattered in the basin. 'What d'y'think I *am*?'

She stood up. The bath must have been wet. 'I have to talk to him.'

'Talk!'

'Work things out. You said we couldn't go on like this.'

'Mum,' screamed Kit. 'Come on, Mum.'

He picked up his watch. 'Christ!'

He refused. He flatly refused. He would not talk about it. He would not mind his wife's children while she met her lover. Passive resistance. He would not do it.

'I am going to meet Edward,' said Sophie.

'And I'm going to the navy's away match at Helensville.'

'Nancy,' said Sophie, 'will mind the children.' She smoothed the dishcloth into position on the bench, gave it a quick tweak and watched the bridge. 'I've already asked her.'

The three of them went with John Ogilvie who was going alone. Sophie made them a ham and egg pie with plenty of parsley; checked their jerseys, parkas, woolly hats. An extra thermos.

She waved them goodbye. Watched them as they walked down the drive. Kit turned at the gate. 'Bye, Mum!'

William came striding back with a pineapple in his hand.

She shook her head. 'No.'

'Take the bloody thing.' He shoved it at her. 'We don't want it.'

She put it in the car.

It was a good game. The navy backs handled better than he had expected and the forwards won plenty of ball and worked well in the loose. One of the locks forced his way through Helensville for an equaliser. 'Do it again!' screamed Kit, his face radiant, his damp nose gleaming with joy. Rebecca was jumping about. William hugged them to him. They must come with him always. His gut tightened as he inspected the thought. This is what fathers with access did. They took their kids to places: zoos, museums, football matches, places designed for access. They took their children to places for the day and then they took them home to their mothers. He had seen lonely men with children, bending over tables. They hadn't quite heard, what was that again? At school was it?

Nothing. Nothing. And yes, they wanted tomato sauce with their chips.

'Christ, it's cold,' said John Ogilvie stamping his feet, his nose purple above the trim beard.

William handed him his flask. The swig tasted tinny but John did not complain. 'Hits the spot,' he said. He could have drawn a map: heart, lungs, feet restored by firewater. He stamped more cheerfully on the frosty ground.

Why was she not singing? Joyful anticipation was absent as Sophie drove past the sad uneven trees of the Gasworks straight. This was as it should be. You do not sing songs in memorial avenues, especially torch songs. But there was little joy in Belmont and less in Takapuna. Two small wobbly boys on bikes with footie boots slung around their necks hurtled from a side street. Her foot slammed the brake. William's pineapple rolled from the front seat and bounced against her left foot. A car screeched to a stop behind her. The small boys' legs pumped harder. Rumps in the air they rode on laughing into the headwind.

The car behind roared past, an enraged face shouted, two fingers flashed at the careful lady driver. Sophie restowed the pineapple in the shelf beneath the dashboard and drove on.

It was understandable was it not, her lack of expectant delight. This lovers' meeting was not a journey's end. This meeting was a conference, a symposium, a combined exercise in damage control. A sitrep. An analysis of the situation resulting in a plan guaranteed to achieve the desired objective. The object of her desire. Her insides clenched. That was more like it. She was going to meet her lover.

'Glorious things of *Thee* are *spo-ken*, Zion, city of our God,' she yelled. She stopped at a pedestrian crossing, smiled at a crab-like old woman to indicate permission for her to exercise her legal right and cross the thing. She was rewarded by grateful joy. You never knew for certain if the buggers were going to stop. Not till they smiled.

Sophie put her foot down and sped up Forest Hill. There was now a raspberry whip house next to the chocolate mocha. She must tell Edward. He will have seen it. It will already have been noticed and we are past such exchanges by many a long chalk.

She saw Mary, aged twelve, stomping around in Erin's battered cream satin wedding shoes, broomstick arms caressing the top of the upright, stretching outwards in mock passion. 'And he'll be big and strong, / the man I lerve.'

Shut up you fool. And anyway William's bigger. Oh God.

She drove fast, glanced at the dead fish and cocktail glass motel. Remembered the white sling and drove faster.

'It couldn't be better,' Edward had told her. 'You won't have to drive past the main house, just turn left up the track by the cattle stop. The cottage is behind the macrocarpa windbreak. I'll be waiting.'

The gate was open at the bottom of the track, a farm truck parked alongside the old house. Edward stood smiling with outstretched arms, offering her his house, himself, his secret world.

The disused cottage was circa 1910: two tiny bedrooms, a living room and lean-to kitchen with a rusty coal range. There was no sign of an ablutions block. The place smelled of age and damp and decay. Bits were falling off; the doorstep was rotten, ancient water stains flowed down walls.

Edward held her to him. 'Any port in a storm, Soph.'

She kissed him. 'Sophie, and don't talk like William.'

'Sophie.'

'We have to talk,' she said afterwards. He kissed her breast, licked the nipple. 'You always want to talk. You're such a *talker*, Soph.'

'What did you tell Captain and Mrs Featherston?'

He licked the other one. 'I've forgotten.'

She took his face between her hands, studied it, searched for answers.

He rolled over, looked at his watch. 'My God!' He sprang up from William's car rug and pulled on his trousers. 'I haven't fed Clarice. The poor girl'll be starving. Come on. And bring your parka.'

He picked up the pig bucket and swung it overarm, demonstrating centrifugal force as effectively as the Wall of Death. 'From top to bottom, from bottom to top, see them ride the Wall of Death.' Not an ounce of leavings was lost. Ed Sand the farmer's son had come to play. They walked in single file around the horizontal sheep tracks to the pigsty. Snuffling, snorting through her ringed snout, Clarice gave a squeal of delight and charged the cold porridge, the apple cores, the peelings and bacon scraps mushed with bran.

They leaned side by side watching her, proprietorial and proud. Sophie scratched the pig's back. Edward snatched her hand back.

'Not while she's feeding.'

'Does she eat everything?'

He was scraping the bucket with a stick. 'She doesn't like banana skins.'

'What about bacon?'

'No obvious objection.'

'I wonder if she knows?'

Sophie watched Clarice with affection. Her solid pinkness pleased her. She radiated wellbeing, a big pink girl with both feet in the trough. 'Boots and all,' said Sophie.

He was still scraping. 'Who was it who wondered whether it was better to be a pig happy or Socrates miserable?'

'I don't know, sir, but I'll find out.'

'What?'

'William told me. Americans are trained to say it if they don't know the answer to a senior officer's question. It's designed to stop them keenly making up a wrong answer. To give them a way out. Ignorance with honour.'

'Good God.'

Large drops of rain fell. Clarice kept at it. 'We'd better get on,' he said.

The rain quickened as they ran. They snatched at each other in triumph as they reached the wooden porch, stood hiding in each other's arms. He shoved open the door. 'No,' she said. 'let's do the feeding out first. We'll take the lunch in the truck.'

'All right. They're in the top paddock.' The truck bucketed up the steep track, swung round corners, clung tight. The feeding out took time. 'I should've used the tractor,' he said, 'but I wanted to save every minute.' Black cattlebeasts ambled across from the wind break, tore at the proffered hay bales, munched with blank eyes, lifted their heads and munched again. It was strangely quiet. There was a lot of sky. Rain fell.

'Let's go back to the house.'

'No, no. Let's have lunch in the truck.'

He shrugged, reached for the string kit behind William's rug. Lunch was a modest affair. She had not made another ham and egg pie. How could she? The chicken sandwiches were adequate; he declined a hardboiled egg. They drank his wine from yellow and green plastic mugs.

Sophie reached for the rug. (All wool. Made in NZ.) Huddled like a dedicated sports fan she watched the raindrops on the window. They splattered on contact, reformed, were weighted by excess and slid downwards. Slivers of silver slid along the base of the idle windscreen wipers. They were in an enclosed world, chilly and remote. The macrocarpas behind the woodshed were too near, their branches waving too hard, thrashing about the sodden sky with flamboyant overemphasis.

It would take time she explained. She couldn't just march out on William at the moment. No woman could. He had had too much. It wasn't his fault.

He stirred beside her, put out a hand.

'Arnie's death was an appalling shock. To us all. To Kit.' Those eyes, that round-mouthed terror. 'To William.' She turned to him. 'He thought he'd killed him, you know.'

Edward was silent. Wondered whether he should move the truck further away from the lashing green of the shelter belt. Decided against it. Of course he thought he had killed him. He had hadn't he? Indirectly, by accident, without intent, young Flynn had knocked the old man off. No matter how dicky his heart, he had killed him.

'He thought it was his fault,' she explained.

He looked at her, studied her face. This, all this. She was too much for him. He breathed deeply, dragged the phrase up. 'Yes,' he said, 'I see that.' He paused, waited a suitable time, took her clenched hand and kissed each knuckle.

'What is it?' she said.

'I like you.'

'Then why look like that?'

'Your hand smells of hay. Real nut-brown maiden stuff. Ho-ro. All that.'

'Why?' she said again.

'We'd better get back. We must leave plenty of time to say *au revoir* nicely.'

'And talk.'

He started the truck, slammed it into first. 'And talk,' he said.

Cattlebeasts lifted their heads, lowered them again, swung sideways and ambled out of the way, their hip action loose as pole vaulters. A pipit scuttled from beneath the truck and kept running, its tail dipping as it darted from clod to clod. They were on top of the world, surrounded by mist, mud and silence.

The truck rattled down the steep track, leaped from rut to rut and bounced once more. Rain streamed down the windows, the wipers were useless, they couldn't keep up. Visibility was nil.

The skid was sudden, his hands clamped rigid as they careered towards the edge. 'It's all right. It's all right.'

'Yes.'

They stopped; peered out into the rain. A hawk lifted from the gorse beside him. 'It's all right,' he said once more. 'Just the right front one. It's only half over.'

Sophie jumped out. 'Is there a shovel in the back?'

'We won't need that.'

They didn't. He skidded back, revved harder. The truck roared backwards, showering Sophie with mud and slime.

He was out of the truck, loving her, kissing her mud and laughing. William would not have laughed. He had little sense of humour. She wiped her face with her woolly hat and laughed and laughed and laughed.

The corrugated iron water tanks were uncovered. A bad sign. The water from the tap smelled of death. A possum, perhaps, circling more and more slowly, claws scrabbling till death. Why do they try? What else could they do.

Sophie rubbed harder with William's rug. She was frozen stiff, stiff as a frost-bound tea-towel and as out of her element. She did not like this love nest. This willow cabin had seen better days. Its heyday was not now. She flung herself at Edward; he was warm and he loved her and was waiting. The rain drummed louder, drowning their murmured 'darlings', their 'sweetest loves'. Her 'Now, Now, Now'.

She lay in mud-splattered wool, staring at the knots in the ceiling as they talked. Everything was pine: wall, ceiling, even the floor had knots in it. They were inside an apple box. An old one, not the sweet fresh-sawn pine of the packing shed. Where had Frank and Esther operated? Even Greytown was no longer safe, if it ever had been.

The cottage creaked around them, a lump of wet soot fell in the grate, macrocarpa branches tapped windows and reared back again. They lay silent, reached for each other once more, retold their shared history. Remember the crabs? Yes. And Pickett's face? They relived their lives, became excited. I have always loved you. Always, they lied. Yes.

She sat up, heaved the rug around her. 'What happened in Wellington? Did the meeting go all right?'

He was on his feet, watching the rain flood the windows.

'Sophie,' he said.

Edward had dismissed his early doubts, his 'no wives' embargo. He loved Sophie. He had every intention of marrying Sophie. Of taking on her children. Of making an honest woman of his honest woman. He stared down at the mountain beneath the wing of the Viscount, included the snow-covered razor backs in his decision. He liked to see the mountains, especially in winter. The plane lurched and rocked. The hand of the woman beside him clenched, touched her mouth and clenched again. He hadn't noticed her before. She was small; a trembling pink and grey heap of fluff. He leaned over, smiled.

'It's all right,' he said.

She nodded, speechless.

'It's the mountains. Nothing to worry about, just a little fresh air turbulence.'

'He will look after me,' she said. 'I know that. It's just . . .'

'Sorry?'

'The Lord.'

'Ah.'

'I know him, you see.'

'Ah,' he said again. Edward shifted in his seat, stared at the disappearing mountain to distance himself from the name-dropping tea cosy beside him. He opened his briefcase and read the agenda for his meeting with the Chief of Naval and his team with exaggerated interest.

There was nothing in it he did not already know. No dramas at Naval Headquarters, Wellington, were evident from his sheet of paper. All was predictable as tomorrow; the frigate programme,

CNS would put forward his ideas on forthcoming port visits, there would be general discussion of the ANZUS and the Australian/New Zealand/Malaya (ANZAM) exercise programmes. And finally the rotation of ships in the Far East. Edward restowed the paper which he had already read and closed his eyes in self-defence. How did she know he would look after her? And if she did, why was she gibbering? Edward opened his eyes cautiously, gave a sideways glance. She was knitting something dark and hairy. Her smile was apologetic.

'Pardon me,' she murmured.

The car was waiting, the harbour glinting as they drove around. Waves slapped and chucked against the breakwater; two small sharp-angled fishing boats yawed at anchor in Evans Bay. Oriental Bay lay basking like a cat laid out in the morning sun. Three arse-up ducks bobbed in the sea.

He had always liked Wellington. He must ask her what she thought of it. They would have to live here; the job was based in Wellington. He opened his briefcase to check the enlistment figures again.

Edward enjoyed programme meetings. He was good at his job and knew it, as did others. He knew his stuff. Could present it well, was decisive and could sum up with precision and force. He also knew when to keep his mouth shut. He liked the Chief of Naval Staff. He was able, had had a good war and was due to retire shortly.

A cormorant surfaced in the bay. Edward leaned forward. 'Beautiful day, driver,' he said to the young sailor.

'Yes, sir,' said the eyes in the rear-vision mirror.

'Not a breath of wind.'

The driver laughed. He was from Matamata himself but what the hell. 'That's Wellington for you, sir,' he said.

The meeting was held in the CNS's corner office, a space curved at one side like the after-end of the great cabin in the Victory. A map of the world covered the wall beside the long table on which lay large ashtrays, carafes, papers: the gear and tackle and trim of men currently in conference.

Everything was as usual. The McIntyre of HMNZS Endeavour in Antarctic pack ice still hung beside the large desk. He must make sure it was not moved. The Old Man seemed pleased to see him.

The meeting was cordial, exchanges frank. Edward demolished Warner over port visits. Napier would have to wait. He had never liked the man: white eyelashes and an arse-licker to boot. They tidied their papers, rose for lunch. He must ring Sophie. The meeting had been put forward a week and he hadn't been able to get her before he left. And then the Club.

The Old Man was beside him, one arm offering him an easy chair. The rest of the men filed out. 'Sit down, Edward,' he said reaching for a heavy brass ashtray.

'Thank you, sir.' Edward stretched his toes in his naval issue and leaned back. A drink would be good.

'Sophie,' he said again.

Her eyes inspected him, smiled into his. 'You talk about me being a slow talker.'

'I haven't. Ever.'

Still that smile. 'It must be some other man. Some other fellow. What is it?'

He told her, he told her everything. He uncovered his heart, inspected the ice once more and told her.

Each movement of the Old Man's tough little hands came back, each glance from beneath the jutting eyebrows returned. They were not a perfect pair, one climbed higher, was more exuberant, more rampant than its mate. They became progressively excited; the voice did not alter.

'I wanted to see you face to face, Edward,' it began. 'What's this nonsense about you and some wife?'

Eyes sharp as leading lights beamed on him. CNS was on course. 'A junior wife.'

The traffic noise was loud. Brakes squealed, a sudden shout.

The Admiral made the position quite clear. Edward must stop this liaison immediately or his chances of promotion were nil. 'Nil,' he said again. 'Negative. Zero.' CNS's shoes scrubbed the new carpet. He leaned forward to inspect the fluff. Lost interest in it, turned to Edward again, slammed a hand on his knee and stood up. 'Don't be such a bloody *fool*, man,' he told the street below.

She heard him out. She knelt in front of him, thighs flat on her heels, the rug held to her neck with both hands, her eyes huge.

'No!'

He reached for her, 'Darling.'

'No.' She was on her feet, tugging on mud-stained trousers, moving faster than he had ever seen her. Every swing and twist was swift and accurate. One stab, one trouser leg; efficiency in action. 'I'm going.'

'But you must *see*.'

Snatch, grab, stow. 'I do see. I see clearly. I have faculties. You love me but you are prepared to ditch me because an old man in Wellington tells you to.'

'Sophie, it's my *job*. I'm good at it. There's no one else except that prick Warner. I couldn't let that happen.'

She stared at him in astonishment.

'Not that "loved I not honour more" stuff. Please not that.'

'It's only for two years. Less.' He insisted. Was quite definite. 'I'm not going to lose you now. It won't matter after I'm CNS.'

He saw her gaping mouth, changed tack quickly.

'What do you want? Some superannuated no-hoper? Some Duke of Windsor for Christ's sake?' He followed her around the room, picked up things, handed her socks, shoes, a floppy bag. He followed her every move, begged for sanity. While they were together, while the rain fell. For sanity and wisdom and sense. 'It's less than two years, darling. Think of the war.'

Another mistake. 'I thought you could think! I thought you could reason, understand.' She was shouting with rage. 'I don't think I'm lying. I don't think so. I could wait. Asunder. Apart.

That's what it means. But I won't be dumped till I'm no longer flammable and picked up when I'm safe.' She gasped, shook her head. 'When the firemen have gone home to bed.'

You cannot love if you have not known hate. She had never believed it. She still did not believe it, refused totally and absolutely to believe anything so insane.

'Keep your job,' said Sophie.

She was packed now. Booted and spurred. Ready to leave. He had no intention of letting her. Not Sophie.

He grabbed her arms. 'And another thing,' she said, swinging away to attack once more. 'Why didn't you tell me at once? Why didn't you tell me the minute I arrived! Why did you fuck me first? Fuck me,' she said again, her mouth wide with loathing. She shut her eyes, clenched them tight. 'Why did you *use* me?' yelled Sophie.

She ran for it.

The car was pointing downhill. She threw in her bags, started the engine. He was banging on the window. 'No! No!'

He ran to the gate to slam it shut as the Holden started down the track. He leaped in front of her, shouting. As she lifted her foot to brake, the pineapple rolled from beneath the dashboard. Her foot jerked back, slammed hard on the wrong pedal. Edward screamed, his body lifted into the air, arced onto the bonnet and slid sideways. She found the brake.

He was in great pain. 'My legs. Sweet Christ, my legs,' he whispered.

TWELVE

She wrapped the rug around him, tucked it into the mud beneath him. She could hardly breathe. Not even his name. 'I . . .'

He took her hand, turned his head.

'The house is up the other drive?'

His head moved again.

'Ambulance. I won't be long. I won't be . . .' No breath. None.

She flung the pineapple into the mud and slammed the car through the gateway. Terror flattened her belly, clutched her throat. You've half-killed him, now save him. She drove too fast, braked too hard; gravel spewed sideways onto the rosebed.

Another ship's bell. She could hear it jangling down passageways. She banged with both fists on the locked door, importunate, insistent as a child screaming. Now. Now. Now.

Captain Featherston opened the door. He held it back with one hand and peered out. It was getting dark. He couldn't see a damn thing.

She nearly knocked him over. 'It's me, Sophie Flynn.'

'Who?'

'There's been an accident. Edward Sand. I must get an ambulance.'

The voice sharpened. 'Edward?'

She shoved past him, ran to the telephone in the hall and prayed to the God she had given up on.

Captain Featherston's shuffle had gone. He was rooted to the spot; both hands clutched the carved handle of his walking stick. 'Not Edward. Not Edward.'

She was giving directions, accurate and explicit directions, telling St John's all they needed to know. It would take them some time to get there.

'How long?'

'It depends if there's a unit back at base,' said the voice. 'It's Saturday. Rugby injuries.'

'He's badly hurt.'

'Keep him as warm as possible.'

She turned to the old man, her face blank with shock. 'You're Sophie,' he said, 'Edward's friend.'

'Yes.'

He put out a shaking hand. 'What happened?'

'I ran over him.'

Mrs Featherston appeared, touching her way down the dim hall. 'Ran over whom?'

'Edward. At the cottage. His legs are broken. I need some blankets.'

Mrs Featherston leaned against the wall for a moment. She did not believe it. The woman was lying. She heaved herself upright. 'We'll come and get him.'

Sophie barred her way. 'No! Just the blankets.' She picked up the telephone, put it down, turned to the old woman. Just this once, just this once. 'Please would you ring my husband.' She scribbled the number on the pad by the potted pink chrysanthemum. 'I must get back,' she told the seascape beyond Mrs Featherston's right ear.

The old woman put up a hand to ward off evil. The rheumy excess of age filled her eyes. 'No I will not. But I'll get some blankets.'

The Captain touched Sophie's shoulder. 'I will, child. I will.'

Sophie gave a shuddering gasp, seized the blankets from Mrs Featherston's arms and ran.

The rain had stopped.

They took a long time to get there. There were two of them. The driver turned at the gate, backed the ambulance up the track beside Edward and left the headlights on. The men leaped out, sucked their teeth and worked out how they would play it. They agreed it wouldn't be easy, not at this angle and both of them broken, and the mud didn't help. The lights were dazzling against the darkness. There was no world, nothing beyond the blazing circle of light. Blades of black grass framed the tableau: the rain-drenched 'Death of Nelson' at the bottom of the track. Macrocarpas lashed and sighed above them.

They agreed he would need a tetanus shot immediately he arrived. It was a pity they couldn't give him morphine but they were not allowed.

'Shut up and get on with it,' he muttered.

They did so. The radio telephone crackled. They were being nagged from base. There was a pile-up on the main north highway. How long will you be on this one, Geoff?

More lights. Lionel and Lettie sat blinking, two small owls in a Wolseley. They had come to help. Sophie got rid of them. She thanked them; she knew how they felt, she told them to go. They could be no use here. She would ring them from the hospital. He was going to be all right. Just two broken legs. Tears slid down Lettie's face. 'Two,' she whispered.

They would give him oxygen on the way in. It helped, they said. She held his hand. His eyes opened. 'Sophie,' he murmured, 'did you mean to?'

'No.'

He smiled. 'That's all right then.' He opened them wider. 'Eighteen months, no more.'

She could not go in the ambulance with him. There was the Holden.

*

There are no thunderbolts. Sophie and the children moved into the flat vacated by Mary and Ben who were now in the Coromandel. Sophie had asked Bertha. It had not been easy, but the tension was crackling at the end of William's well-trimmed drive. Sparks snapped in the dining-cum-living, ignited in the blue-and-white-striped bedroom where they retreated each evening to fight. Perched on the bed, surrounded by small cushions in tones to suit, they hissed at each other. She had made them, the cushions; chosen her remnants with care and frilled them in blue to pull the colour scheme together. She had piled them at the head of the bed each morning and removed them 'before retiring' so she could pile them again next morning. Scatter cushions they were called. Mad. Quite mad. And never again. Sophie had abandoned decor, had scattered interior design to the four winds of hell. William shut the door. She hugged glazed polka dots to her chest as his voice rose.

It was the first time he had asked, 'How did you *do* it?'

'It was the pineapple.'

Details. He must have details. How had it rolled, whereabouts had it landed, how could a pineapple rolling at her foot result in such a débâcle? She tried to explain, became entangled in technicalities and feet and gave up.

His face was more shocked than ever. 'You don't mean to say you used your left foot?'

'I don't know!'

He took no pleasure in Edward's pain. But the situation appalled him. The mess, the sheer ludicrous muck-up of their lives, left him reeling. The flickering grass fire of rumour had become an inferno, the buzz had roared to scandal. Groper had been warned off Flynn's wife, Flynn's wife had tried to kill him. You couldn't pick up a paper. 'Com Auck breaks legs' (*Star*). 'Com Auck in freak accident' (*Herald*). The *Advertiser* gave a resumé of Commodore Sand's brilliant career—so far.

Kit had a fight behind the boys' toilets and refused further comment. 'I hit him,' he said.

Nancy slipped through the hedge, took Sophie's hand and

pressed it. 'I just came to say I don't believe a word of it,' she said.

'Well, you'd better start,' said Sophie, snatching back the hand from her friend to peg socks on the whirlygig.

'What did she want?' said William.

'She doesn't believe a word of it.'

'I always knew she was nuts.'

Large, dark and fighting for his life, William was forced to reappraise the situation again. Forces beyond his control were causing their craft to founder. Action must be taken. They were destroying each other and their offspring. They could not go on like this. He must take charge, lower the boats, abandon ship temporarily. They would return later when the storm had passed. Salvage would be achieved, the ship would be saved eventually. William knew this.

Bertha's reaction was a surprise. Sophie had expected to be welcomed with joy and no questions asked. For the three of them to be enveloped in Bertha's voluminous kindness and given space to rent for which Sophie would pay as soon as possible. To be given the key to her safe house with love.

'I think you should stay,' said Bertha. 'The children need you both. Especially now with all this nonsense.' She waved a hand, dismissing sex, slander and career scuttlebutt with a flick of a still graceful wrist. 'In my book,' she said, 'William does not deserve this.'

'We're destroying each other. He hates me.'

'No.'

'Bertha, I know what it's like growing up in an atmosphere like that.'

'You don't know what it's like growing up without a father.' They both thought of Keith. Their thoughts differed. Bertha remembered bumbling incompetence, Sophie gentleness, rope-like brown arms lifting her up so she could see.

But that was different.

'William'll be there, just along the road. He doesn't want me.'

'So you say.' Bertha was slapping herself again: a gesture as individual, as characteristic as her damp kisses. 'Where are my smokes?'

Sophie handed them to her.

'And what about the other man?'

'My fancy man?' said Sophie, her eyes pricking with grief for her good, her true friend Arnie and his lonely cantankerous love.

The archaic phrase stopped the match in mid-air; the cigarette sagged in the corner of the mouth.

'That's all over,' said Sophie. 'And you're going to light the cork tip.'

Bertha gave a quick practised spin of her fingers. 'You don't love him any more?'

'No.'

'That's that then.' Bertha paused, started a smoke ring and decided against it. The spiralling wisp of smoke held her gaze for some time.

'I wish I believed you,' she said.

They moved in. William hired a truck and moved his bewildered children and estranged wife ten houses down the road; same side, worse view, semi-furnished To Let. Evan and Lou watched hand in hand across the road. Lou had nearly finished the bedcover she told Sophie last Friday and didn't she miss Mrs Pickett now she'd gone back to the UK. 'Yes,' said Sophie. 'Yes, I do.' And Mary. And Arnie who is dead and Edward whom I used to love.

William did not reduce the allotment. He was concerned for his family's comfort, insisted they take this, that, the other thing. The Valor, why not, and all the stuff from the sitting room. He wouldn't be using it. He packed and sorted, took things down, put things up, did what he could. He had cauterised the stump, sealed it with pitch. 'Why don't you stay here?' he said suddenly as they loaded the last carton. 'I'll live on board. This is mad.'

'No,' said Sophie. 'No!'

Bluey's egg was infertile. What would you expect? Sophie suggested a change of name. Bluette, perhaps. 'No,' said Rebecca, 'and why are we down here when Dad's up there? Why, Mum?'

'We both love you,' she said, demonstrating yet again. 'You know that, but Dad doesn't love me as much as he used to. That's why.'

'Because you're the Commodore's girl?' asked Kit from the senile leather pouf abandoned by Ben.

'I am *not* the Commodore's girl.'

'Good. Boy, you should've seen his nose. Talk about blood. And where're Arnie's binoculars?'

Their father could field this one. Law is men's part of ship.

'Run along and ask Dad,' said Sophie, trying it out, getting the words right. 'He'll be home now.'

'Coming Becca?'

They had come to see him. His children had been in the flat for a couple of hours and they had come back to see him. He welcomed them, showed Kit a new card trick. No, he wouldn't tell him how it was done. He would have to work it out. 'But Dad.'

'What did the reprieved murderer say?' he asked Rebecca, loving her white teeth, her smile.

'I don't know.'

'You remember: "No noose is good noose."' He laughed to show her how funny it was.

'But they don't kill people now. Mum said.'

'They used to,' he said, hiding his flicker of disappointment at the flop. He told them that he'd get some Coke and chippies. That he would have to stock up. 'And next time we'll have saveloys and pink eggs, why not?'

'Neat,' they said staring at the depleted house, the empty spaces.

'Dad,' said Kit, 'where's Arnie's binoculars? He said I could have them and I need them down there because there aren't any.'

*

Dr Pleasance had not moved the binoculars. They lay beside the tartan-covered body, the slippered feet. 'The police might want them,' he said. 'Don't let anyone touch them.'

'No,' said William.

'Well, I'll be going. And keep people out of this room.'

'Yes.'

The thin cop interrupted him. 'Where *are* the binoculars?' The fat cop took notes. They were not meant to be fat. Steel, wire and whipcord. Fit. That was cops.

William felt his mouth drop, a caricature of shock and idiocy. His foot pointed. 'They were there, right there.'

'And where are they now?'

'I don't know. No. Hang on.' Images, wheels turning, cogs slipping into place. 'I'll bet I do,' said William.

Ben had taken them. That fucken irresponsible shit had sneaked in and taken them. William would put money on it. He had admired them, dropped hints, sought them out every time he appeared. Where else could they possibly be? William did not rush it. His voice was slow. 'I think I know where they might be . . .'

'But why would Mr Underwood, was it, Underwood? Why would he take them?'

'He wanted them.'

The cops glanced at each other. They would call in on the way back.

'I'll come too. Show you the place.'

'No,' said the thin one. 'That won't be necessary.'

'The thing is, Kit,' said William holding the skinny body between his knees. 'They are not ours, you see. They belong to the estate.'

'What's estate?'

William explained.

'But he gave them to me. They were mine. He said they were mine, didn't he, Becca?'

Rebecca was miserable. It was half-empty here, and it was no good down there and all the kids kept asking her why. She looked at Kit's face and tried harder. 'Yes,' she said. 'I heard him.'

'Well.' William clapped his hands together. Sophie would have recognised the gesture. It showed up in photographs. William leaving the ship kitted out for rugby. William on a run ashore, cheerful, laughing, at ease with his world. 'That's all right,' he said. 'You should've mentioned it before, Kit. I'll,' he paused, 'I'll write to the beneficiaries involved and request that they consider Christopher Flynn's statement that the deceased, that Arnie, had said he wanted the said Christopher Flynn to have his binoculars.' All it would involve was for the man who threw them to write a cringing letter to the Commies asking for his ball back. William's knees hugged his son, held him tight. 'That's all,' he said.

Kit's lips brushed his forehead. 'Thanks Dad. Beat you home Becca.'

Sophie flung herself at the dirty flat like a lemming bent on leaping. Life would be clean, it would shine, it would be splendid. She tried it out. 'Glorious things of Thee are spoken.' Later perhaps. She scrubbed harder.

The stove was a challenge, the bath took some time. The Crown of Thorns in the bedroom had gone leaving a white patch on the wall in remembrance. Ben had not had room in the van for his three-dimensional art work but he would come up for it as soon as possible. Sophie must take good care of it. He was missing it like crazy, its absence gnawed him, his hands were twitching to get at it. He rang several times to check. She hadn't touched it had she? No? Well don't honey, don't, and for God's sake watch the kids. Sophie watched the art work. She gave it the benefit of the doubt but it had little to say to her. She lay on the bed at night reading *The Woodlanders* while the children slept, glimpsed its textured layers from the corner of her eye as she read about Giles who was a good man and did good things and smelled of apples and died for love.

*

They snapped her up at Eventide. Sophie was not surprised. She was competent and partly trained. She could cope, keep calm in a crisis as demonstrated, and, as Matron said, she obviously had a nice nature or she wouldn't have applied in the first place. 'You can always tell,' she said, head nodding behind a leftover arrangement of gypsophila and lilies delivered by the recently bereaved after a funeral. 'Frankly,' said Matron, 'flowers are not always the blessing people think they are but the hospital won't take them, just being Emergency and that. They're very stretched. But then again,' she sighed, her eyes on a woman submerged by greenery, delphiniums and gerberas who was heading up the path, 'aren't we all, and flowers take a lot of time and sometimes I wonder whether the residents even notice them. People think just because they're old they're going to fall about when it's flowers. Well, a few maybe, but why should they? It's like peggy squares. Why would you suddenly want to knit peggy squares just because you're eighty-five and your fingers are arthritic. We're all different aren't we? It doesn't follow.'

A woman of empathy who leaves room for difference. A woman who does not automatically trip little accidents, peggy squares, floral tributes and confusion through the same slot of the grader labelled Old. I like this woman.

'And Monday will suit you, Mrs Flynn? Lovely. And what about school holidays?'

'I will have to make suitable arrangements,' said Sophie.

Matron was pleased. A brand-new, semi-trained permanent with plenty of savvy and pleasant to boot. 'Well, you've got till August to arrange things, dear,' she said.

'Yes,' said Sophie as the doorbell rang.

Edward spent several weeks in the Naval Hospital in Calliope Road. Both tibias were fractured. The alignment in the left one was not good enough. There would be gross deformity and trouble later if it was not reset. Nancy Ogilvie, up to her welts in sawdust, lips damp with drama, just thought Sophie would like to know. And then of course there would be months of physio. And what about Liz!

'What?'

She and Paul had gone to Hawaii for a week. A second honeymoon on the Outer Islands. Imagine. Nancy restowed her chops in her carrier bag. They had been too close to the Rinso. 'Bye,' she said. 'Bye.'

Sophie wrote to him.

Dear Edward,

I can't come and see you. You would not want me to. Otherwise, I would be there. The pineapple slipped and I got my feet wrong. I know you know this. I am sorry beyond thought for your pain.

Sophie.

She walked down the road to post it in Devonport. *Old Yeller* was on at one of the cinemas. She would suggest it to William. How about taking the children on Saturday she would say. After rugby, or Friday even. They could sleep in, being Saturday.

She crossed over to the sunny side of the street and felt the sun on her back. George Orwell had watched a man being marched to his execution. Watched him as he stepped over a puddle rather than through it. It was instinctive, irrelevant as his non-existent tomorrow.

She posted her letter.

As a child the face in the mirror had not reassured her. Its dreamy absent-mindedness had given her reason to fear she might be the one found hiding under the bed in a crisis, while others (Mary?) dealt with the situation. Giving up her place in a lifeboat she could understand; manning the pumps, parachuting into enemy territory, taking control in moments of stress, she had thought was beyond her.

Not so. The meek are not stuck with it, apologies can cease. A sitting duck, even the vaguest, has wings on her back to soar.

Her heart had gone underground, curled up and shrivelled to a corm. It was not dead. The throb of action, the one-step two-step beat of life was still thumping. She loved her children, would make them happy. Two jobs was nothing. The work at Eventide pleased her, tired her satisfactorily and paid the rent as well.

'Why no letter?' said Mary's postcard of Hot Water Beach. 'Come and stay in the spring. Plenty of room for the tent. Ben is sculpting Ches. All love, M.'

Edward went home escorted by LSBA Butterworth who had been seconded from the Naval Hospital until the Commodore was on his feet again. 'I suppose they've painted his stripes on his plasters,' said William, who had come to pick up the children for *Old Yeller*. He watched her face above the cat mug.

You have razed his world. His dogged decency is harrowing. He is allowed words.

'Bye,' she said later. 'Have fun. Goodbye.'

She walked along the road, past St Augustine's locked and barred in safe-keeping from felons. Past a house which used to have a different pepper-pot tower till maintenance became too much and it was lopped off. She walked quickly, arms swinging, eyes focused straight ahead in pursuit of her mission.

Mrs Featherston opened the door and shut it quickly. Sophie, exigent as a door-to-door survivor, slammed her foot in it. She had business here.

Mrs Featherston was shaking. 'He won't see you. He won't.'

She shouldn't do it. Not to an old woman. Sophie pushed past, flattening the backs of frail knees against a four-and-a-half-inch brass shell case filled with walking sticks. She knew her way around.

Edward sat in a wheelchair with his back to the view and the light. One fully plastered leg was supported horizontally in front of him, the other plaster finished at the knee. She recognised his shorts; the old faded Bombay bloomers had travelled north with them. His socks were striped above leather slippers. The gesture was the same, palms upward, expectant, welcoming. The voice was different. 'You shouldn't have come here.'

Letitia Featherston was still shaking. Distressed, enfeebled, she could not keep still. Her hands waved, fingers clutched. 'I told her, I told her. I said.'

He put out his hand, touched his friend briefly. 'Don't worry, Lettie. It's all right. Sit down, Sophie.'

She sat. Letitia stood. Edward smiled at the old woman. Gently, lovingly, the filial piety of a surrogate son embraced her. 'Perhaps, Lettie?' he murmured.

Letitia left. She turned at the door, drew herself upright. 'Haven't you,' she said, 'done enough damage already?'

He was silent, watched her go.

'What do you want, Sophie?'

'To talk to you.'

'God in heaven.'

'Your legs. Are they painful?'

He moved his head, a quick backwards chuck of dismissal. He wasn't going to tell her. He loved her and he wanted her to shut up and go away and leave him with his pain and his plaster and his misery and his pair of skittering old jailers nodding and becking at him all over his house. He hadn't wanted them to come. Had begged them not to. Butterworth was very efficient he said and Tollerton came every day. No necessity. Please. He meant it.

They came. It was hell. They could not cope and neither could he. They were too old and too pathetic and loved him too much. Fussing and nit-picking, they laid waste his days. Beef tea, that was what he needed. Couldn't Tollerton even make beef tea? Lettie had forgotten how but she would look it up. Surely there must be some more recipe books. Just these? She would have to go to the library. Lionel was completely disoriented. He couldn't work the radio let alone the record player and didn't Edward have any Gilbert and Sullivan at all? He hated the morning and evening rush of the dockyard traffic along the road. The hooting road hogs wouldn't even let the Wolseley out the gate. He hid in his cabin-like room and read *King Solomon's Mines* yet again. 'To whom it may concern,' said the sign.

Sophie sat on a pink Larnach Linen chair and stared into the light. She was thinner, her hair longer, the eyes the same. Edward moved in his wheelchair again. 'I love you,' he said. 'You know that.'

'Yes.'

'But my life is who I am.'

'You said.'

He tried again. 'The job comes with me.'

She shook her head. Her hair was curlier too. He wanted to snatch it, grab handfuls, make her *listen.* 'No,' she said, 'you come with the job. I would be the stripe on your arm. Nothing more.' She smiled. 'Nothing less.'

'Stop hiding behind clichés. No job can swamp a woman. Not a real woman.'

Two arms, two legs, a nose. 'I am.' She stopped, startled by truth. 'But I won't accept the two-year ban, the decontamination period before the shelved product can be picked up again . . .' She spat the phrase out, got rid of it, '. . . with impunity.'

That face was saying these things. Those eyes. Her hands hated him. 'It's not the time. That's nothing. But no woman would love on these terms.' Her mouth mocked him again. 'Not a real woman.'

His leg was throbbing. Frustration at her idiocy, his inability to *move,* to knock sense into the woman he longed for, was killing him. He was cast, impotent, beached. A dumped castaway. He couldn't sit gaping for ever. He had to say something.

He could hardly get it out. 'So that's it?'

'Yes.'

She was still there. Still watching. Still twisting bones, sinews, gut.

His head was framed in light. 'What are you going to do about young Flynn?'

'He doesn't want me. I've got a job at Eventide,' she said above the hooting ferry.

He gave it all his rage, his passion, for the fool who wouldn't see.

'Cleaning up after old women!'

'And men.'

To leap up, to hold her, to make her stay. He could make her stay, he knew he could. He moved the leg too quickly, jarred it; the muscle went into spasm. He almost screamed. 'You've only got one life, woman!'

'I know,' said Sophie.

She leaped up, knocked a stool over, ran for the hall. The wheelchair charged after her. The door slammed a yard from his outstretched leg.

She ran down to Stanley Bay. No one would see her like this. No one. She dived into the ladies' changing shed, hid in a lavatory cubicle and composed herself. Composed. He composes. She composes. They are composed. She sobbed a gulping grabbing gasp of air and sat. Deeply, breathe deeply.

It is better is it not to have loved and lost than never have loved at all. Who says? Who knows? And anyway she hadn't lost. She had ditched her lover, the light of her life. Services no longer required. She burst into tears.

Mopped up.

And what about William? Is it better to have loved and not known till it's too late and you've lost? Hell's fangs what a mess. There were puddles of water. The sour smell of wet concrete filled the air. The top of the wooden seat (pine) had a rough patch. Sophie stood and automatically pulled the chain. Instinctive, ridiculous, understandable. Calm down woman. You've done it. It's said and done. Calm down. In, out. In, out. She examined the graffiti to give herself time, wiped her nose again. They were uninspired. Rude urchin words, raucous obscenities, a crude diagram or two. The one on the back of the door was different. 'Schoolgirl to whip man,' she read. 'Ph. whatever. Genuine.' Well, he would say that wouldn't he? But what about the schoolgirl? She must get some paint from the shed. Composed and seething, Sophie strode up the hill inventing graffiti. 'Heart to remotor. Send photo.' 'Heart to restick. Send pics.' Answered them. 'Strong-willed ex no-hoper seeks no one.' She sniffed. 'Yet.' Incandescent with rage, she walked on.

LSBA Butterworth had finished for the day. He walked out of the Commodore's gate, his Pusser's grip in his hand. He had a loping walk; he sprang from his toes.

'Hullo, Mrs Flynn.'

She had been staring straight ahead. She turned, looked at him blankly for a second. 'Oh, hullo, Mr Butterworth.' She paused. 'It was so good you could play at Arnie's funeral. It made all the difference.'

'He was an old friend.'

'A fine man.'

LSBA Butterworth considered, his head on one side, his bright eyes thinking. A stroppy jack, yes, get the boot in, yes, but yes, a fine man. Butterworth watched her. He liked her, quite apart from Arnie. She was looking peaky.

'Excuse me, ma'am?'

She looked at him warily. Junior wives weren't ma'am. 'Yes?'

The words came in a rush. It was just that he liked her. The loyal, fully paid-up member of the party thought the poor little thing had had a rough deal.

'You mustn't worry, Mrs Flynn. Accidents do happen. He's a fit man, the Commodore. Healing well. I've seen the X-rays. New bone beginning to form. New bone,' said LSBA Butterworth, 'is good bone.'

'Like no noose is good noose?'

'Pardon?'

'It's a joke. My husband's.'

'Oh.' He lifted a hand to a large petty officer overflowing a passing motor scooter. 'Oh,' he said again.

'Do you live this side, Mr Butterworth?'

'Yes, ma'am. Takapuna. We've moved in from the Bays to be near Mum. She's at Eventide. Her mind's gone but she's happy there.'

You would think he'd given her a present. 'Eventide? I work there. What's her name?'

'Well, ah, Butterworth.'

She gave a strangled snort of mirth, wiped the corner of an eye with one finger. 'Of course. I'll look out for her.'

'That'd be nice, ma'am.' There was something else he had to tell her. He swung his bag, walked faster. 'He's a good officer, the Commodore. Very pleasant. Always a bright "Good Morning, Butterworth". Likes a chat. You appreciate that sort of thing.'

Sophie lifted her face. Cloudy sky. No wind. Anti-cyclonic gloom (William).

'Yes,' said Sophie. 'He can talk.'

They walked on. One foot after the other they walked up the road in silence, past the oleanders, the letterbox and the concrete strips to the flats with the tower and North Head beyond.

'I'll be off then,' said LSBA Butterworth changing his grip to the other hand. 'Goodbye, Mrs Flynn.'

'Goodbye. And thank you for the lively tune.' The corners of her mouth twitched. 'And for the chat,' said Sophie.